IRONHAND

CHARLIE FLETCHER

DISNEP • HYPERION BOOKS

New York

First Disney•Hyperion paperback edition, 2009

Printed in the United States of America

1 3 5 7 9 10 8 6 4 2

Library of Congress Cataloging-in-Publication Data on file.

ISBN 978-1-4231-0178-9

Visit www.hyperionbooksforchildren.com

*With all my love and thanks
to Domenica, without whom
none of this would be possible
or nearly as much fun*

TABLE OF CONTENTS

Wounds are for the desperate, blows are for the strong.
Balm and oil for weary hearts all cut and bruised
*   with wrong.*
I forgive thy treason—I redeem thy fall—
For Iron—Cold Iron—must be master of men all!

"Cold Iron"
—Rudyard Kipling

IRONHAND

THE STORY SO FAR . . .

On a school trip, George breaks a fragment from a carving of a dragon on the front of the Natural History Museum. This wakes an ancient force imprisoned in the Stone—a rough block hidden deep in the City of London. As an immediate result, a vengeful carving of a pterodactyl peels off the side of the building and begins chasing him. Just when all seems lost, the Gunner, a statue of a World War I soldier, steps off a war memorial and saves him.

So begins George's ordeal, trapped in a layer of London, an unLondon in which the mutually hostile tribes of statues in the city, the human-based spits and the inhuman taints, walk and talk and live in an uneasy truce, a truce that George's action has thrown into jeopardy.

The thing that makes his ordeal all the harder to endure is that no one else in London can see what is happening to him. Except Edie Laemmel. Edie's a glint. Glints are women or girls who have a gift that enables them to touch stone and metal and experience past events that have imprinted themselves in them. But nobody's ever explained Edie's gift to her, so she just sees it as a curse and thinks she's crazy. She's also on the run.

George, Edie, and the Gunner set off on a journey to make amends; but unknown to them, the Stone has alerted the Walker, one of its servants, who stalks them through the streets with the help of his minion, the Raven.

On this journey, George discovers that he has special powers, which make him a target for the enraged taints. One of the dragon statues that guards the City of London slashes a scar onto George's hand. Another statue, the smiling but sinister Black Friar, tells him it is a maker's mark, which identifies George as a maker, someone with a special gift for sculpting things from stone or metal. The Friar also tells them to find the Stone Heart and put the broken dragon carving back, to make amends for the damage George has done. Helped by benign spits and threatened by violent taints, George, Edie, and the Gunner eventually find themselves at the Stone Heart of London, the London Stone.

But once there, the Gunner sacrifices himself to try to save Edie, and ultimately falls into the clutches of the Walker. It is left to George to use his newfound gifts as a maker to rescue him.

And now the story continues. . . .

CHAPTER ONE

Darkness Falls

The Walker and the Gunner fell into the dark, pitched into a deep abyssal blackness beyond the memory of light. But though there was no possibility of seeing anything, the Gunner sensed they were plummeting through a succession of layers, as black flashed black in an unpleasant negative strobing, which he felt rather than saw.

And then the horrible movement through the void stopped abruptly as they hit something solid.

The Gunner's knees crunched down into wet gravel, and his free hand instinctively palmed out to halt his fall, sending a jarring shock up his arm as it smacked into an unseen stone wall in front of him. He hung there, head low, angled between the wall and the ground, panting for breath. He felt wrong, more wrong than he'd ever felt, more wrong than he'd known it was possible to feel. He felt it in ways he couldn't begin to list or explain; it was as if an invisible hand had reached into his core and wrenched everything off-true and left it hanging there, twisted and broken.

He heard the birl of gravel beside him as the Walker moved his feet. Using the last of his strength, he swiped a hand into the darkness, but his fingers only caught air and blackness.

He opened his mouth in an "oof" of pain at the effort, instantly clenching it shut and cutting off the giveaway sound. Whatever was happening to him, he was damned if he was going to give the Walker the pleasure of knowing how much it hurt.

And then the lights came on.

The first thing he saw was the upturned bowl of his tin helmet lying on the stones in front of his thick hobnailed army boots. Then he saw the protective legging cinched on to his right calf with three buckled straps like the residue of an ancient piece of armor. On a real soldier the legging would have been leather; but in this case, since he was, of course, a statue, it was made from bronze, like the rest of him. His left calf was unarmored, tightly wound with bandagelike puttees instead. Above that he saw his hands, strong blunt fingers splayed on the knees of his army britches, as he took a breath.

He scooped up the helmet, smoothed the front of his uniform tunic, and adjusted the cape around his shoulders. It wasn't a real cape. It was a canvas groundsheet from a one-man tent, to keep the weather off, tied in place with a piece of string through two grommet holes. He put on the helmet and stood up straight, every inch the battle-worn World War I veteran that he'd been sculpted to be.

And then his mouth, despite his best intentions, fell open again as his jaw dropped in shock.

They were in a large and ancient underground water tank. His feet stood on a small shelf of pea gravel that sloped against one wall. This tiny beach took a bite out of a rough square of black water, about ten yards on each side. The irregular blocks of stone lining the walls of the tank were greasily mottled with age and tumored with sickly blooms of damp fungus, which hung around them at what looked like a high-water mark. Drips from the stone roof of the chamber plopped concentric circles into the dark surface below.

But it wasn't the claustrophobic dimensions of this doorless chamber, with its dark water floor and half-moon gravel beach that made the Gunner gasp in surprise.

It was the lights.

Each wall had an outline of light blazing from it, a shape about the height of a man and perhaps a third as wide. The shapes were made from irregularly placed pieces of broken glass, and all had the same distinctive outline of a squat turret, the kind of thing a child might draw when trying to represent a castle. The light blasting forth from each of the four tower shapes intersected at the center of the water tank, where a silvered disk about the size of a plate spun lazily on the end of a piece of chain, reflecting the light randomly around the room.

"What is this?"

The question croaked from the Gunner's throat before he could stop it. He heard a sniff of contempt and focused on the gaunt figure, up to its knees in the water at the edge of the gravel bar. The Walker wore a long green tweed overcoat with a hooded sweatshirt underneath. He swept the hood back and ran his fingers through long rat-tailed hair brindled with gray. He had a skullcap on the back of his head, and a jutting goatee framing a mouth twisted into a permanent half-open sneer. His hands held two small circular mirrors, which he clipped together and stowed in his coat pocket. He bent and lifted a long dagger from the edge of the beach. He unpeeled a thin sour smile as he gestured around the water tank with the gleaming blade.

"This is a dream of four castles," he replied, indicating the turret shapes on the walls around them. "It is a vision that came to me in a dream, long ago, when I was a free man. It is a vision that I have made real. It is nothing that you could begin to understand."

He shifted the blade in his hand and sliced angled reflections of light around the room, revealing more edges of the subterranean tank.

"It was a void, and darkness was all it contained until I came across it. Now it is a place of power. My power."

The Gunner felt squeezed by the great pressure of earth above him. He felt as lost as if he had been spirited into the bowels of the earth and pinned beneath a mountain. But he was damned if he was going to let the Walker enjoy his discomfort.

"Where are we? Where is this?"

The Walker spun slowly in a full circle, sending the reflected beams of light around the dank edges of the chamber.

"We are under London. A city you will only ever see again in your memories."

The Gunner would have swung a fist at the Walker, but the wrongness inside him seemed to have sapped his normal strength and had left him needing all his energy just to stay on his feet. And besides, he had to know what was going on. He was nowhere he'd ever been, feeling like nothing he'd ever felt, and he could always try to flatten the Walker later, when he came within easier reach. Although, he had a suspicion that escaping or even surviving whatever was happening to him was going to require more than swinging fists.

"Talk plainer."

"This is where you stay. Forever, perhaps. Enjoy the light. When I leave, it goes too."

The Walker looked at the Gunner with something like pleasure. "You feel it, don't you; inside, the emptiness, the rising horror, the loss of strength, the sense that you're not master of yourself?"

The Gunner made himself stand straighter. "Don't you worry about me, chum. I'm right as a trivet."

"Oh, I'm afraid you're not. You broke an oath sworn to me by the maker. You have to do what I say."

"Not happening," the Gunner snorted tersely.

"Oh, but it is. You're a proud man. I won't offend you by treating you like a lackey. After all, all I require of you is that you die. And all I have to do to effect that happy outcome is to forbid you to dig your way up out of here. And I do. I order you not to try to dig up toward the light and the clean air. Simple, isn't it? One instruction and you're doomed. Midnight will come, your plinth will be empty, whatever animates you will die, and you will be just so much scrap for the smelter."

The Walker's eyes burned bright with banked-up malice.

"Do you still feel master of yourself?"

The Gunner tried to lift his hands, determined to wrench one of the ceiling slabs down into the water to show the Walker he was wrong. But his arms wouldn't move. He shook his head in frustration. "I think I'm gonna grab you and shove your mirrors where the monkey put his nuts, that's what I think."

He lurched toward the Walker, but he was much too slow, and the Walker danced out of his reach. The Gunner stumbled against the wall, horrified by how weak he'd become. As he reached back to stop himself from falling, he dislodged one of the bright pieces of glass.

It fell at his feet. He stared at it, at the opaque surface, the rounded, sea-tumbled edges. And as he stared, his memory fired on reflex, and he saw a similar piece of tumbled glass in Edie's hand. Then it fired again, and he remembered the first time he'd seen her smile, like sunlight breaking cleanly across her face. He relived the surprise he'd felt when he'd realized that all it had taken to kindle that blaze was to smile at her and call her by her real name; and he remembered strongly how that realization had made him feel suddenly protective of this strange and outwardly flinty girl. It was that surge of paternal protectiveness that collided with the dreadful realization spreading slowly across his mind like a dark stain that made something shift uncomfortably inside him.

He bent and picked the sea-glass up between thumb and forefinger.

"These are heart stones."

He heard a dry humorless chuckle and looked up into the sour slash of the Walker's smile.

Then he heard the horror in his own voice as the question gritted out of his mouth, unbidden.

"What have you done, Walker?"

The gaunt figure above him just kept smiling, like a wolf airing its teeth.

"The glints, Walker. What the hell have you been doing to them?"

CHAPTER TWO

Sticks and Stones

Edie and George hurried away from Cannon Street, happy to leave the London Stone behind them. They were both shocked and footsore, and because both kept their eyes on the hard road in front of them, neither noticed the leaden cloudscape darkening the sky above, or indeed anything that was happening overhead.

Which was a shame. Because what was above was definitely noticing them.

The stone gargoyle on the roof didn't have to look up to see the storm clouds. It felt the rain even before it started to fall as a kind of itchy premonition right in the middle of its back, high between the spiked shoulder blades, in a place it couldn't have scratched even if it had had normal arms instead of the talon and wing arrangement its sculptor had given it. Feeling rain coming was part of what it was. When rain came, it normally had a job to do, spouting water on the roof of St. Pancras

Station, a mile or so to the north. This was not that roof. On this roof it was hiding and watching.

It was hiding because it was in the grip of a new and dangerous sensation: it was feeling curiosity. It bared its savagely curved fangs and stretched its head over the gutter to scan the street beneath. For the first time in its existence, it knew that it had something more important to do than respond to the raindrops now inbound at twenty miles per hour from the clouds above.

The gargoyle was far more interested in the boy and girl walking along on the pavement below. And as they moved west along the street, it stalked the parapet, keeping down, batlike wings folded behind it, stony tendons quivering in anticipation—ready to pounce.

At first glance, George and Edie looked like any tired kids after a day at school, heading back to secure, reasonably normal homes where hot teas waited and a long day would come to a happy ending.

But at a second, closer look, it was clear that these children belonged to quite a different story.

Look deeper and you could see the marks of that story all over them.

George seemed about thirteen, shoulders starting to fill out, bones beginning to lengthen into early maturity, muscles stretching to keep up with the growth spurt. His hair was unkempt and just long enough for him to have to keep sweeping it untidily behind his ears. His school blazer was torn at the shoulder and all scuffed up, as if he'd been rolling on a very dirty floor. His knee flashed white through a tear in his dark trousers as he walked, and a smudge of dirt smeared along the upper curve of his left cheekbone. The disheveled look was, however, at odds with the steady and determined set to his eyes.

The look in Edie's eyes was different. She was walking with her head bent down, a long swath of dark hair keeping them in shadow. But in the glimpses of them that George was occasionally getting, he could see that they were troubled, and he could also see that whatever her eyes were seeing wasn't only what was actually in front of her. Her normally pale skin was even whiter, as if all the blood had drained from it, stretched taut with exhaustion. She tripped on a curb, and only his hand whipping out to catch her stopped her from hitting the ground.

"Edie!" he said, "Watch where you're going!"

He saw himself swimming into focus in her eyes as she returned from wherever she had been.

"You ever think you're cursed, George?" she asked abruptly.

George took a second to absorb what she was saying, and why. "You think you're cursed?"

She shook her head in irritation, as if he weren't keeping up. "Not like by a witch or something, not like turned into a frog, but you know, like you done something bad once, so bad that bad stuff happens to you because of it?"

George rolled his eyes. "Um. What, like break a statue by mistake and end up being chased through London for a day and a half by gargoyles and minotaurs and all that? Er . . . yes."

She shook her head again. "No, I don't mean that either; I mean before that. Your whole life, like something bigger, something that made you break the statue in the first place, something that screwed up your luck forever, that sort of thing. . . ."

George had a brutal flash of memory: he was shouting something vile at his dad. He was shouting so loud that snot and tears were flying from his face. He saw the answering tears start in his father's eyes. He saw the door he had slammed on his father. And he saw that same door opening later that night, revealing the policeman and woman who had come to tell his mother that there had been a car accident, that his father would never walk through that door, any door, ever again.

"No," he said.

The tough spark in her eyes kindled a little as she cocked her head at him. "Been that peachy and perfect, your life, has it?"

It was his turn to shake his head. "Edie. We don't have time for this. We need to come up with a plan. We have to rescue the Gunner. If we don't find him and get him back on his plinth by turn o'day, by midnight—"

"I know. He's a dead statue. He'll never move again. I know, George. I'm not stupid."

"I didn't say you w—"

"I want him back as much as you, you know. I mean, it's not just because he saved us and we owe him—"

"We do owe him," George cut in emphatically.

"I know. But it's more than that." Edie took a deep breath. "The Gunner made me feel safe."

"Me too."

The first few fat drops of rain flecked the pavement, followed by a lot more right behind them. In no time, rain was falling so hard that it bounced back upward off the slick paving stones beneath them. George instinctively stepped sideways under the cover of a café front, pulling Edie in after him. They had the wall at their back and the meager protection of a thin awning overhead.

Seven floors above them, the gargoyle on the roof snarled and leaned out, trying to keep them in sight; but all it could see was the pigeon-splattered plastic canopy above their heads. It hissed in frustration and scuttled back, trying for another angle. It stopped when it could see Edie's feet. It was pleased they hadn't gone inside the building. That would have been complicated, and it had enough novelty in its head right now.

"What are we doing?" Edie asked

"I need to think. We might as well stay dry while I do."

"Okay. But you're right. Time's ticking away. It's getting dark already. Think fast."

They stood there watching the deluge. George tried to come up with a plan. The problem was that first he had to conquer the sick fear that was telling him that finding the Gunner, who had been spirited into thin air and could now be anywhere in the vast city, or indeed outside it, was just too big a task for him. He knew he really didn't know enough to make a plan. His mind just kept spinning and returning to Edie's question about whether he felt cursed.

A young dad walked past with his toddler in a backpack. The backpack had a clear plastic rain hood on it, and the toddler was reaching out from its protection and tapping his father on the head with a series of gurgling laughs, as the dad reached back and squeezed his thigh, tickling him. They didn't seem to mind the rain.

George watched them walk past until he became aware of Edie watching him watching them.

"Do you remember when you were a kid and it all seemed safe because your dad was there?" he said.

It was her turn to shake her head. "Not really."

He took a slow breath. The only way to rid himself of her question was going to be to answer it honestly. Maybe then he could stop his mind sliding about on the how-to-rescue-the-Gunner problem.

"Okay. I do. Before he . . ."

He realized this was probably going to be hard to say.

"Before he died?" Edie asked.

"No. Before I messed it all up. Between him and me. I said stuff."

"Everybody says stuff."

He took a deep breath. "Yeah, but not everybody has their dad die before they get a chance to say they didn't mean it."

He was surprised. Saying it wasn't as hard as he'd feared. Time passed. More rain fell.

Then Edie spoiled the moment by snorting derisively. "That's the *sooo* terrible thing you did? That's why you think you're cursed?"

He didn't like her tone much. "What?"

"So you said something nasty. That's nothing."

He didn't like her tone at all. "Yeah well, it doesn't feel like nothing."

"*Yeah well*," she mimicked, "it's peanuts."

He hated her tone. Maybe it was the way she spat the P in peanuts. When you expose a private part of yourself, you really don't want people to snort in derision. He pulled his dignity back around himself like a protective cloak.

"Oh, and I suppose you've got a deeper darker secret, right?"

"Yeah."

"Great."

There was no way he was going to give her the satisfaction of asking what it was. She always had to have the last word. There was no way he was going to ask.

Then she said, "Sticks and stones."

And because it made no sense, he almost said,

"What?" but then he remembered he wasn't going to give her the satisfaction, not after she'd snorted at him and made as if her big secret was *sooo* much darker and more important than his. So he didn't.

She looked at him with eyes as shiny and tough as the rain-slicked street behind her. "It wasn't just words with me and my dad."

George suddenly knew she was telling him about why she felt cursed, and although he also knew the answer was going to be bad, he knew she needed to say it. So he asked.

"What does that mean?"

And she said:

"I killed him."

CHAPTER THREE

Black Bird

Something was wrong. The Raven felt it in its bones and feathers as it flew over the green space of Regent's Park. It looked down and caught sight of its shape, doubled in the reflection of a pond below.

For a moment it was distracted from the feeling of wrongness as it saw itself as others must see it. It made, it noted with grim satisfaction, an ominous sight—an elemental winged silhouette starkly outlined against the bruised cloud base above. In the past, it knew people would have looked up from their campfires or plow handles and shuddered at the black bird-shaped hole it cut across the sky, casting a baleful shadow over their lives. They would have seen it and thought it was an omen, and not a good one at that. Not that the Raven put much store in what people thought. Against the scale of time that it had to measure things against, most people were scarcely here before they died and were forgotten.

It flew on and returned to the wrong feeling, which was this: it didn't know where the Walker was. Most of the time the Walker's presence exerted a magnetic pull on the ancient bird, which had spent the last four centuries or so in his control.

It circled over the sharp-edged hump of the British Museum, slowing its flight as it came in to hover over the front courtyard, where the white-and-pink brick grid design on the ground was broken by a perfectly circular sunken area. It was here that the Raven felt it had the best chance of finding the Walker. But the circle was empty.

It needed to find the Walker, and it needed to find the children the Walker had sent it to hunt. And because the Raven had an infinitely retentive brain, but only one pair of eyes, it decided it needed help looking. And with that in mind, it flew south into the tree-crammed space of Tavistock Square. At the center of the square was a statue of an emaciated man, half naked and cross-legged, sitting on top of a plinth that had a small arched shrine cut into it. The shrine held a couple of crumpled beer cans and a jam jar full of bright marigolds. The cross-legged statue had his lap filled with cut flowers in varying stages between fresh-cut and compost. Opposite him, on one of the park benches, sat a tramp with plastic bags over his shoes and a hank of dreadlock hair hanging off the back of his head like a dead badger. He leaned back to upend a beer can, blue alcohol-washed eyes staring at the sky.

As he satisfied himself that he'd shaken the last drop from the can, he belched and adjusted himself more comfortably on the bench, deep within a parka so greasy it looked as if it'd been dipped in engine oil at some time in the distant past.

The Raven dropped onto the back of the bench where the tramp sat, and waited as the dreadlocks were racked by a complicated spasm of coughing that resulted in a small green gob of phlegm splatting onto the ground between the shopping-bagged feet.

The Raven hopped onto the tramp's shoulder and gripped hard. The tramp stiffened but showed no surprise. His voice slurred and rumbled in a deep, partially gargled bass.

"What would you be wanting, bird? What would you be wanting with the Tallyman?"

The bird ducked in closer to the side of his head and began a disjointed clacking. The tramp started to judder imperceptibly. His eyes closed and his lower lip disappeared under his upper teeth as he bit down, like a child concentrating. He nodded slowly.

"We'll see what we can see."

The tramp opened his eyes and stood up abruptly, tossing the empty beer can to join its mates in the shallow arch beneath the statue of the cross-legged man.

The Raven hopped into the air and hung there, watching. The tramp still juddered, but his eyes had changed. Where once they had been pale and booze-bleached, they were now black, black eyes with no whites, as black and sharp as the eyes of the Raven itself.

Which was exactly what they'd become.

And all over London, under bridges and on park benches, in back alleyways and in hostels that smelled of old soup and new disinfectant, eyes that had been rheumy and bloodshot, blurred with drink or just simple hopelessness, suddenly changed. Men who had closed normal eyes as they went to sleep in the shelter of vacant shop doors woke up with Raven eyes and walked out into the street, scanning the roadway. Lonely women shuffling flat-footed under the weight of a life boiled down to what could be carried in old carrier bags stopped avoiding people's eyes and straightened their necks, scouring the streetscape.

The Raven had spoken, and all over the city, the eyes of the Tallyman had opened.

CHAPTER FOUR

Smiler with a Knife

Edie was staring at the downpour beyond the awning, face unreadable as she hugged herself against the cold. George was still absorbing what she'd just told him.

"You killed your dad?"

"Well, yeah; no, not as such."

He looked at her in outrage. "Edie! That's not funny—"

"No. I mean, he wasn't really my dad. My real dad. He was a stepdad sort of thing."

George deflated a little. "Oh."

"No, don't worry. I killed him all right."

George nodded slowly. Keeping up with Edie was sometimes exhausting, and this was not only exhausting but also distinctly confusing.

"Right."

"No. It was all wrong."

A stream of water changed direction in the breeze and splattered them. The awning wasn't much help. In fact, it seemed to be doing a better job of channeling water onto them than actually offering protection. Edie pulled her clothes tight around her and ducked into the alleyway beside them. George was still trying to get used to the fact that she had just claimed to be a killer, so a couple of seconds passed before he realized she had gone, and he hurried after her into the rain.

The alley was empty.

"Edie!" he shouted, suddenly panicked. There was nothing in the alley but a dead end and a dented Japanese car by a Dumpster.

"EDIE!"

He ran into the narrow space, checking the car as he went, looking for a hidden way out. He couldn't believe it was starting again.

"It shouldn't have happened," said a small voice from knee level. "I just belted him."

He looked down. Edie was squatted in the dry area provided by the angled lip of the skip and its overhanging tarpaulin, looking up at him. She shuffled sideways, making a space.

He exhaled in relief and ducked out of the rain next to her. Once more he couldn't make eye contact because she seemed to be looking at something beyond the wet traffic hissing past at the end of the alley.

"Don't do that again."

She might as well not have heard him for all the reaction she had to his words. She just carried on with her train of thought.

"I just hit him. Didn't know how else to stop him. See, he kept coming after me. With a knife. It was on a beach. I just hit him. I didn't mean to kill him. I just hit him."

"You killed him by just hitting him?"

"Well, I had a big rock in my hand. He . . ."

She pulled her legs up to her chin and rested it on top of them. George waited for her to go on.

She chinned herself hard on the knees, as if punishing herself for the momentary catch in her voice.

". . . He was a boozer, drunk all the time. When the pubs were closed, he'd go fishing. That's what he called it, but he just went to his beach hut and drank more; that's what my mum said. And then later, when my mum went, when she was taken away and never came back, and it was just me and him, he took me down to the beach. It was the first time I'd seen his hut. It wasn't much. It was one of a half dozen, sort of set into the cliff next to each other. I'd always thought it'd be wooden, a cool shack on the beach kind of thing, but it was more like concrete bunkers set into the rock, and when he unlocked his, I saw something and I knew I was in the wrong place, and . . ."

She ground her chin harder into the tops of her knees, jamming her mouth shut to help keep something inside.

"What did you see, Edie?"

She shook her head and exhaled. "Doesn't matter. It wasn't something that was really there anyway. It was something that had been there. Once upon a time. When I touched the wall, I saw it, and I knew I should never ever go in that hut, and I ran."

He thought of her gift for touching stone and metal and experiencing the memories of highly charged past events recorded in them.

"You glinted it? You saw the past?"

"Yeah."

She wasn't going to tell him what she'd seen. She'd made a deal with herself that what she'd glinted in the beach hut was one of the things she just wouldn't ever talk about.

So instead she turned and looked at George and told him the rest of it, the other stuff: she explained how she had just run, and when her stepfather had tried to grab her and ask what was wrong, she'd hit him in the middle of his smile and sprinted off along the pebble beach.

She told him of how tired she had got, running on pebbles, and how calmly he'd followed her, climbing over the wooden dividers on the deserted beach, the smile on his face wholly at odds with the open knife he held in his hand.

She told George how she'd run up a final steep hill of pebbles and found her way blocked by a deep chasm between her and the new wooden wall being built to contain the pebbles in high storms.

And then she explained the worst bit: how he had caught up with her on the lip of this man-made ravine. She didn't tell him what he'd said, or how unnaturally bright his smile had been. She did tell him about the knife, and how she had felt the smooth flint stone under her hand, and how when he had lunged, she had hit him with it.

He had gone down like a tree, tumbling into the dark pit at the bottom of the chasm, dislodging an avalanche of stones that landslid down in his wake. When things stopped moving he was more than half hidden by pebbles. She hadn't known what to do. She had looked at the heavy stone in her hand, and when she saw something wet glistening on it, she'd tossed it in after him.

And then she'd walked back into town and got on a train and come to London.

George nodded slowly, trying to make sense of what she was telling him.

"So it was an accident?" he said slowly.

"No," she said flatly.

George saw the doors closing in her eyes, locking whatever heavy burden she was carrying back inside.

"Look, Edie—" he began.

"Have you thought where we're going?" She dropped the question in front of him like a roadblock.

It took him a moment to slam on the brakes and change mental gears.

"I thought that's why we stopped," she continued. "So you could think."

He was aware that she was staring at the side of his face. When he turned, she turned away faster, as if she hadn't been staring. But he knew she had. Her jaw worked.

"So what's the plan?" she asked.

"Stay alive. Rescue the Gunner."

"How?"

"No idea. Start by asking for help seems like a good first step."

Edie thought of the things that had helped them before, things and people who hadn't really given them straight answers, only riddles and obscure clues. Still, he was right. They had helped, after a fashion. But there was a problem.

"We can't go to the Sphinxes or Dictionary, because of the City dragons. We're on the wrong side of the boundary, aren't we? They'll still be guarding it, on the lookout for you."

"We could go to the Black Friar."

She stared at him. "The Black Friar? Are you mad? You said you didn't trust him!"

"I don't. Not entirely. Not as such. But he did show us the way to the Stone, didn't he? I mean, he dressed it up and made it all flowery, but the information was good. He just—"

"He just smiled too much and seemed too eager to

get his hands on that broken dragon's head of yours, right?"

George felt the now-familiar heft of the dragon's head in his pocket.

Edie went on. "—and the Walker, he was awfully keen to get his hands on it, too."

He nodded slowly and then shook his head. She was right but she was wrong, too. She had to be wrong, otherwise they really didn't have a place to start.

"I think he might be dodgy, but I don't think he's evil. Not like the Walker. I think he's just out for himself a bit more than the Gunner or Dictionary, you know? I think he'd be open for a deal."

"A deal? What have we got to deal?"

He pulled out the broken dragon's head and looked at it. He realized that though he'd been sure it was a dragon's head, when he looked closer it was beakier. More like a gryphon kind of dragon—

"This. I didn't give it to him because I wanted to make amends by putting it on the Stone; but I decided not to, didn't I? So maybe we can give it to him in exchange for help. Yeah?"

In the absence of a plan, and in the presence of fear and danger, sometimes all one needs to feel better is forward movement. Edie couldn't argue with George's thinking. So she nodded.

"The Black Friar it is."

He saw she was still shivering. He took off his jacket

and handed it to her. "Go on. I'm warm enough."

"I'm okay." She tried to push it back toward him.

"Edie. You're shaking. Put the coat on and let's get moving. We're not going to save the Gunner just sitting here shivering."

After a long beat, she gave in and draped the coat over her shoulders.

And then she stopped and pointed.

"George. Your hand."

"It's fine."

His eyes followed her look. He suddenly felt sick.

"Okay," he swallowed. "It's not."

CHAPTER FIVE

Death of Glints

Something was very, very wrong. The Gunner could feel it like a kind of cold heat filling the whole underground space.

"The glints, Walker? What the hell have you been doing to them?"

His voice echoed around the watery chamber. In the beat of silence that followed, the only sound was gravel crunching under the Walker's feet as he paced the half circumference of the small beach. His tufted beard split lopsidedly to reveal a cruel smirk.

"Oh, I have done much; more than you could begin to understand. And when I have the boy in my power, I shall do more still."

"I'm not talking about the boy," grunted the Gunner, putting the thought of George away for later. Right now the blazing pieces of glass on the walls were what had his attention.

"The glints. The wise women, the sharp girls. You've been hunting them. All these centuries. The reason we all thought they were dying out as a breed; it wasn't dying out, it was you. Picking them off. It was you. . . ."

The enormity of it robbed him of words for a moment. It was as if a great puzzle had been revealed to be the simplest of things, as if a fool should have seen it. The horror of it made his voice raw.

"Wasn't it? How else could you get these heart stones?"

The Gunner held up the glass in his hand like an accusation. The threadbare shoulders of the Walker's coat rose and fell in an irritable shrug.

"Heart stones? Pah! Baubles. When a man is doomed to walk the world beyond the natural span of his days, he needs a . . . hobby. Mine has been to collect a few dainties and eye-brighteners that give me pleasure."

It was the pause as the Walker chose the word to describe his actions that confirmed the Gunner's fears and triggered an explosion of outrage.

"You been killing them and stealing their warning stones for a bloody *hobby!*"

The Walker waved a bored hand at him. "You exaggerate. I don't kill them. Killing them is superfluous. I may kill some, but it's far from a habit and entirely not the point. After all, without their heart stones they're lost and spinning in the wind. Their minds unspool and they're fit for little but chattering and mowing like senseless apes, squatting in their own filth and dribbling into a cup."

The Gunner shook his head. "Why, Walker? Why've you been doing this? Why would the Stone want it?"

The Walker almost spat his reply. "The Stone? The Stone wants none of it. This is *my* doing. The Stone has me cursed and in thrall to it, so I must do all its bidding; but not all I do is at its beck and call. I was a great man, centuries before you were anything—when you were just ore at the bottom of a mine that hadn't even yet been dug—and I will be a man of power again!"

Spittle flecked his beard as his voice rose, and the light blazing out from the sea-glass mosaics reflected wildly from his eyes.

The Gunner overrode the rising wave of despair in his gut and twisted his face into a dismissive grin.

"Man of power, my Aunt Fanny. I seen blokes with gibbering shell shock make more sense than you. . . . Only reason you're still around is you got on the wrong side of the Stone, and now you're one of its servants."

The Walker's eyes blazed angrily at him. "And what are you, I pray? A lump of bronze in man shape who has broken his word and is himself now doomed to die alone and in the dark? These warning glasses light up when I'm here because that's what they do when a Stone Servant or a taint is near. When I'm gone"—he waved his hand like a magician—"abracadabra, out go the lights."

"Wait," said the Gunner, appalled at the desperation he heard cracking through his words. "Those kids . . . don't . . ."

"Oh, the children? The boy who thwarted me? Don't worry about the boy. I shall turn him to my will."

"I doubt it. You saw how he chose the Hard Way. He's got grit, more grit than I gave him credit for."

The Walker snorted in irritation. "He's willful, Gunner, that's all. He's shot through with the stupid impetuosity of youth."

"It's grit," insisted the Gunner. "He may not have known exactly what 'e was signing up for, but 'e knew it'd be rough. And he did it for the girl. He wouldn't leave her in the lurch, and good on him I say."

Dark humor danced in the Walker's eyes. "Yes, *good on him*, as you say. Good on him for protecting the girl, good on him for caring, good on him most of all for show-ing me what he cares about, because if you find out what a man cares about, then you can take it and threaten it, and then you have a lever. And with a lever and the right place to put it, you can move the world. And I shall move the world. I shall change everything."

"Leave the kids be, Walker. Don't mess with them."

"Sorry. Can't oblige. I have a job for the boy if he is the maker he seems. Once, many years ago, I had two black stone mirrors, darker than the blackness you will be left to die in when I leave."

He reached into his pocket, unsnapped two small cir-cular silver mirrors from each other, and held one in each hand.

"Compared to the stone mirrors, these little pieces of

glass in my hand are like a baby's toy. A thief and a cheat took one of my black mirrors from me, afraid of the power they would give when used together. One stone mirror made of the right stone is a thing of some power, but two together . . . ?" His eyes blazed with an intensity that matched the heart stones on the walls. ". . . Two together can open portals, portals into worlds where there are vast powers that make even the might of the Stone pale into insignificance. And it is that power I shall harness and then free myself. The boy will make it for me, the girl will choose the stone he should shape—"

"No, Walker, the boy and the glint are j—"

The Walker cut across him with a dismissive wave of his hand. "The boy, the unmade maker and the plucky little glint? The poor dears. Poor, poor dears . . . Strange word 'dear.' Say it one way it's something you love, spell it another way and it conjures up stags and antlers and the thrill of the chase. I love the chase, but you know what, Gunner? You know what part of it I really enjoy?" His smile widened, red and wet.

"The killing," said the Gunner hollowly.

"Not just the kill." The Walker grinned. "It's the moment just before, when you know you can either kill or choose not to, and the prey knows it too. That's the best part. When life or death are in your gift. That's where the real power is. . . ."

He lifted his foot, and with an eye-twisting pop, gently and impossibly stepped into one of the mirrors he was holding, and then he was gone. The lights on the walls faded, and in their afterglow, before the blackness descended, the two mirrors hung in the air, facing each other; and the last sound the Gunner heard was the Walker's voice, diminishing and very far off. It sounded like he was saying: "'Whoso list to hunt, I know where there is an hind. . . .'"

Because the Gunner knew that *hind* was another word for a female deer, he knew exactly who the Walker was talking about, and he was filled with another surge of unbearably helpless fear for her.

CHAPTER SIX

The Flawed Hand

Edie stared at George's hand, eyes wide in shock at what was happening to it. She tore her eyes away and saw that George had gone very pale as he examined the changes. He was staring so intently that he had completely stopped blinking.

"What's happening?" she asked quietly.

He had no idea, but it was something. From the scar that the dragon had slashed on it, three distinct lines had begun to emerge, dark lines coloring the pale skin of his hand as they spiraled down and around to his wrist like tendrils on a briar.

"Is it blood poisoning?" Edie asked tentatively.

He examined the three lines closely, although everything inside him made him want to pull his eyes away.

"No," he said, mouth drying up. "It's something worse."

Each twisting vein was a different color and texture from the others. All three were slightly indented into his skin, like flaws in a rock.

"George. We should get you to a hospital or something."

He shook his head, fighting the waves of nausea rising inside him. "I don't think this is something a hospital's going to help with."

She bent in to examine the triple skein of veins more closely. "They're all different."

"Yeah . . . and they're not me. I mean, they're not made of me." He couldn't keep the revulsion out of his voice.

"Can I?" She reached a hand hesitantly forward.

He turned his head away, not wanting to see.

"This one's smooth. Like metal."

He decided he couldn't duck this. He swallowed hard and turned back. "It is metal. I think it's bronze or brass."

He moved her hand out of the way and made himself trace the mottled bluey-green channel twisting next to it. It was cool to the touch. "This one's not so smooth. It's like marble."

That left the last pale corded flaw twining down to his wrist. He rubbed it, feeling the rough shaley texture of limestone. As his thumb skated along the channel, tracing its course, he could feel a piece of grit detach from the surface and stick to it.

"Okay," he said, clenching his teeth before managing to cloak them in a grin, "this *is* scaryish."

"Does it hurt?"

He flexed his arm. The veins of bronze and stone seemed to flex with it. He shook his head. "No. But you know when they say something makes your flesh crawl?"

Edie nodded.

George pointed to his arm.

"It's crawling. It's like I've got something inside my arm that isn't me. I mean, if I think about it, it's definitely going to creep me out."

"So what are we going to do?" She stared into his tight smile.

Seeing the concern in her eyes somehow triggered the opposite reaction in George; he found himself once more determined to erase that look by making sure she was okay. It wasn't necessarily a rational impulse, but it was one thing in their almost entirely ungraspable predicament that he could hold on to and work with.

"Not think about it," he decided.

He stood up. The rain was easing. He reached down and pulled her to her feet. He didn't really know what to say, so he dragged up things he'd heard other people say on TV and in films.

"Edie. We're going to be okay. We're going to do this together. I'll be right there with you. Anything, anyone trying to get you, they're going to have to get past me first."

As he said it, he was pretty sure he wasn't as convincing as the actors he was trying to copy had been. Maybe you had to be an adult to sound macho.

Edie swept the hair out of her eyes and gave him a long, appraising look. "What? All ninety-eight pounds of you?"

He grinned back at her. At least she hadn't laughed. Not outright. He curled his lip and mugged at her, making a caricature of a tough guy.

"Yeah. All ninety-eight pounds of me. Until we get out of this, I've got your back. Look around anytime, I'm there."

He waited for her to join in the joke. Instead she nodded slowly.

"That's"—she struggled for the word, then leveled her eyes right into his—"that's good."

And because the earnestness of her belief in him was so unexpected and so sharp, George immediately felt as if he wanted to escape the moment.

"Come on, then. Let's go see the Friar."

And because she felt buoyed by his confidence, and strangely comfortable that he had her back, she straightened, walked ahead of him into the dwindling rain shower, and pointed down the road. "Blackfriars is down this way."

Because she was ahead of him, she didn't see the stone gargoyle take a headfirst leap off the gutter along the top edge of the alley, falling like the half ton of rock that it was, before its batlike wings snapped open. It swooped upward, one foot-talon neatly hitting George between his shoulder blades while the other closed around his ankle like a gin trap.

And because a half ton of wet sandstone packs quite a punch, Edie didn't hear George yell. He couldn't yell. All the air had been knocked out of him as the gargoyle carried him, looping up and away into the darkening sky.

Instead Edie turned around to see what was taking George so long, and saw nothing. No George where an instant before there had been, and no friendly face in the stream of wet pedestrians hurrying along the pavement. No one watching her back. It was as if someone had thrown a switch and George had simply been turned off.

Edie was alone.

CHAPTER SEVEN

The Icarus

There was a pop, and unseen by anyone hurrying through the rain-spattered fastness of Old Change Court, the Walker stepped out of his portable mirror and looked around. There were only a few young office workers chattering and laughing their way to the pub near the bus stop. He slotted in behind and followed them across the square.

Their talk withered as he trailed them, becoming less cheery and more gloomy—and then dying off into an uncomfortable silence. He stopped and let them carry on into the street, plans for a convivial beer before going home having become significantly less appealing, but for no reason that any of them could have put a finger on.

He stopped by a pinch-waisted bronze plinth, on the top of which stood a grotesquely distorted winged figure. From the back he was naked, attached to chopped-off wings by a torturous harness that looked more like an instrument of punishment than a means of flight. His head was jammed uncomfortably backward, and his torso was bound inside an openwork breastplate device that curved around the front, hiding his face and trapping his arms within.

It was a monument to agony, not flight.

It whimpered as the Walker came around to the front, where the only human pieces visible were the legs, buckling under the weight of the painful apparatus.

"Icarus, I thought you might like to know. Your brother is dead."

The Icarus flinched and started to twitch. After a moment, low stifled moans began to emerge from the brutal constriction of the cage hiding the face and torso.

"Yes. Your brother, the Minotaur. The Minotaur that was sculpted by the same maker as yours. Your brother is dead."

The Icarus screamed, a deep man's scream, horrifying and raw, though muffled, as though the mouth hidden inside the apparatus was sewn shut.

"Yes. He died badly. I could do nothing to stop it."

The scream changed tempo and was punctuated by rhythmic panting sobs as the man, or the creature within, absorbed the news.

"I thought you might like to help me find the people who did it. Two children. I have a use for them, but if you bring them to me, I will give them to you when I am done. You have my word."

The Icarus screamed more deeply, as if some of the stitches in his lips had been ripped out with the force of his previous cries. He hopped grotesquely, awkwardly, off the plinth and landed in a kind of hunched squat, his chopped-off wing tips clapping together above his head in furious eagerness.

CHAPTER EIGHT

Airborne

Everybody wants to fly. At some stage in their lives, everyone looks up in the sky and sees the seeming effortlessness of a bird in the gulf of air overhead and thinks: I wish, just one time, that could be me.

Nobody wants to fly like George was flying. He was upside down, back arched, staring at the ground below, winded by the sledgehammer blow between his shoulder blades, gagging soundlessly for a breath that just wouldn't come.

All he could do was reach a despairing hand back toward the rapidly diminishing figure of Edie as she spun the wrong way on the crowded pavement, trying to see where he'd gone. She was turning like a leaf caught in the whirlpool of a fast-moving stream, looking everywhere but the right way, which was up.

And then, just as his vision started to spot and dim through lack of oxygen, he found a breath and took a

deep whooping lungful of air, then another, and yelled—
at the very moment the gargoyle crested a building, and
Edie was lost to his sight.

"Edie!"

He shouted his throat raw in one ragged word that
tore out of him like the death of hope, but his yell was
lost in the greater noise of the city below.

Above him he heard the gargoyle hiss in disapproval,
and felt its grip on his leg tighten. In a couple of thunderous wing flaps, they had cleared the next block of buildings and were flying across the Thames.

George looked at the water below, then he looked up
just in time to see the stone creature taking a quick
glance down at him. In the microsecond that they were
face-to-face, he recognized the snarling cat head. He
gaped in disbelief.

"Spout?!"

There was no doubt in his mind. This was the gargoyle he'd called Spout, the gargoyle who had tried to kill
him at the Monument—the gargoyle he had seen shot to
smithereens by the Gunner. The taint that was definitely
dead.

"But you're dead!"

The gargoyle hissed, and George turned and saw the
brick face of the industrial chimney above the Tate
Modern building coming closer and closer. Though he
was sure that Spout meant to dash him against it, he just
stared, without even the energy to put out a futile hand

to ward off the inevitable. But at the last instant, Spout twisted in the air and jerked the talon at the end of one wing over the lip of the chimney and brought them to a sudden halt.

George hung there, nose to the brickwork, head throbbing with blood, just filling his lungs and wondering whether his heart was going to actually pound its way out of his chest, as it was trying to.

CHAPTER NINE

Red Queen

The Black Friar walked purposefully east, past the end of Westminster Bridge, through the thin flow of pedestrians, none of whom, of course, could see him; or if they could, had strong rational brains that wouldn't believe the evidence of those irrational and untrustworthy eyes.

The Thames was to his right, and the great tower of Big Ben soared overhead, the illuminated clock face shining out into the gathering dark.

His eyes flicked sideways as he passed an impressive double equestrian statue. A regal woman in a simple shift dress, flowing cloak, and a small spiky crown stood in a chariot, her right hand holding a businesslike spear and the other hand languidly urging her two surging chargers forward.

She was flanked by her two daughters, crouched for balance over the brutally curved blades sticking out from the center of the chariot's wheels. The whole group seemed on the very point of careering off the plinth and into Westminster Square.

The Friar nodded as he walked past. When it was clear he had no intention of stopping, the Queen spoke.

"Friar."

He paused, waited a beat, then turned, not entirely hiding the fact he didn't want to do so by the polite smile he erected on his face.

"Queen."

"You do not bow."

His smile deepened.

"Indeed."

"You never bow."

He spread his arms wide, the gesture of a man with nothing to hide, nor a care in the world. "I am friend of all men, equal to all, subject to none. I mean no offense by it."

Irritation ticked across the royal brow. "And yet you give it."

"Not by intent. It is my way, the way of my calling."

"Priests bow to kings."

He exhaled in the long drawn-out way that people do when they wish to make it clear how long-suffering they are. "Not *good* priests, dear lady. Not ones *I* should value, at any rate. But I was not talking about my calling. I was talking about my profession. As a publican. Why, as a host and a tavern-keeper, all men are equal in my sight."

"And women," she interjected sharply.

A shadow of a smile passed over his face, gone as soon

as it appeared. "Women, in my experience, are perfectly equal as long as they keep to the lounge side of the bar."

She bristled and gripped her spear tightly. Behind her, the two daughters exchanged a look. "You find this amusing? This is how you preach, fat man?"

The Friar raised an eyebrow at her. He smoothed the cassock over his belly. "You crave a sermon, lady? Why, upon my word, I thought war was more your pleasure. . . . But certainly, I'm sure I can conjure an improving text for you to consider. Let me see. Yes, it goes like this: 'When Adam delved and Eve span, who was then the gentleman?'"

She glared at him as if trying hard to work out both where and how deep the insult hidden in the words was. Eventually she waved it off as too much trouble. "Blowhard words beyond my understanding. Perhaps they make more sense in an alehouse."

He smiled his unimpeachable smile. "Well, I can see they wouldn't make sense in a palace, where queens imagine themselves better than ordinary people."

The spear shook in her hand as she spoke, the huskiness of anger building within. "You are purposely insolent!"

His face broke into a perfect grin of good humor, like a great round cheese splitting. He chuckled apologetically. "No, ma'am, I beg your pardon. It is a childish pleasure in me to tease a fine fiery redheaded woman such as yourself; for as the woodsman knows, no tinder is quicker to kindle than the red-barked."

The daughters gasped and immediately looked away. "You take me for a redhead, priest?"

"Certainly. Why else would they call you the Red Queen?"

She finally exploded, eyes flashing, jerking the sharp end of the spear at him as she did. "Not for my hair, fat man, not for my hair! They call me red because I swept down on this city in vengeance for the wrong to my daughters, and when I and my army turned our backs on the smoking ruins and hied us homeward, my arms were red to the elbows with the blood of London and its insolent—"

"Mother," said the daughter on her left, taking her arm, trying to slow her down.

The other one took her right arm and attempted to stop the tirade by redirecting her attention. "Mother. The glint . . ."

The Queen controlled herself with visible effort.

The Friar's eyes were all innocent good humor, much too innocent—enjoying the fallout of the detonation he had provoked.

She spoke as calmly as she could. "Yes. Of course. The glint. A glint, Friar. Last night we saw a glint run past us. With a boy."

His eyebrows rose skyward in a show of surprise belied by the entirely uninterested face below them. "Oh. And you're sure it was a glint?"

"You know as well as I that we sense them as strongly as they sense what is in stone. She was young. She was strong. And she was brave. But she ran. We wish to know what has happened to her."

"And why is that, pardon my impertinence, but what business of yours are glints?"

The Queen gripped her spear and banged the haft on the floor of her chariot. "They are strong girls and they live at a peril beyond bearing. We have not seen one in years."

"Perhaps you are mistaken." The Friar shrugged.

"Not about that, Friar. Any woman in peril is my charge and care."

"And why is that, pray?"

She slammed the spear down even harder, making her daughters jump. "Because I will it so. I have ALWAYS willed it so!"

Fire seemed to blaze from her eyes. The Friar had been right about how quick she was to kindle. "Why do you ask me this, madam?"

"Because she was running along the river, and sooner or later, the bank passes your door."

He ran a hand over his face and wiped off all mirth. He inclined his head again, but not far enough for the gesture to be considered a bow of any kind. "The river passes many doors. I saw no one. Good night, ladies." And with a nod of his head, he strode off eastward.

The Queen watched him go. She took several deep breaths, then turned to the daughter on her right.

"He lied. There is a glint abroad. We must ride. If this feeling I have in my bowels is true, there is a girl in peril."

CHAPTER TEN

Edie Alone

One minute he was there. Then he was gone. It was that simple, that horrible, that brutal. Edie stepped into the street from the alley, looked right and left, turned to say she thought they might as well run if he was up for it—and he just wasn't there anymore. It was so sudden and so shocking that her mind wouldn't let her see the truth of it. Her first reaction was to be annoyed that George was playing games with her. She was tired, bone tired, and trying as hard as she knew not to let him see how close to the end of her rope she was feeling; and now here he was, playing hide-and-seek or something.

"Come on, George," she said tightly. "I'm not in the mood—"

Then a nasty thought hit her: maybe he was hiding because he'd seen a taint or the Walker coming for them. She spun and checked the view behind her again. There was nothing.

An old homeless woman pushing a rattling shopping cart full of plastic bags and newspapers passed on the other side of the street. She was too far away for Edie to notice that her eyes were entirely black—and looking straight at her. And whatever she was mumbling to herself was drowned in the sound of the passing traffic.

Edie, seeing nothing threatening, let a half grunt of relief escape, then stepped back into the alley, looking for him.

"George!"

He wasn't there. She checked the Dumpster and beside the car. There was no mistake. He was gone as cleanly and brutally as if he'd never been there in the first place. Panic swelled in her gut and swirled up into her chest, tightening around it, making her heart beat faster. Again she whirled around, looking for the hiding place she must have missed, fist already bunching so she could punch him when he jumped out and laughed at her. But she hadn't missed a hiding place. George was not there.

All there was was the city and the street and the people hurrying past in the rain. And then just for a treacherous instant she was sure she heard George calling her name, impossibly far off and desperate; but when she spun in the direction she thought it had come from, there was nothing to see, and she knew her mind had betrayed her, making her hear things that weren't there, just because she wanted them to be.

And as she spun slowly on the edge of the street, she felt her connection to it, and to everything around her, slowly begin to unravel; her mind finally allowed her to start believing that George had just vanished from her world. The hard fist at the end of her arm unknotted itself, the bony bunch of white knuckles and taut sinew slackening into an open hand whose limp fingers trailed in the air, making a lifeless circle around her as she turned, beginning to wonder if she were going mad. . . .

Then her foot stumbled over something, and she looked down. Her knees bent and straightened as the limp fingers flexed and came back to life and scooped up the thing that had caused her to stumble.

A shoe. George's shoe.

It was wet and scuffed, but when she put her hand inside it, it was still warm. Then a piece of normality reasserted itself, and she realized she had voluntarily reached inside the shoe of a boy who had spent the last twenty-four hours or so doing little else except running, and she quickly pulled her hand back out of the clammy interior. Her nose wrinkled in momentary disgust that flattened out into a tight little smile as her hand clenched around the shoe, drawing life from the concrete proof it gave that George had been there, was real, and she was not going mad.

Holding the shoe made her stop spinning around, and she knew that was good, too, because she was suddenly aware that she had temporarily lost her grip and had been slowly unspooling herself.

She was done with that.

She banished the weasel voice back into the shadows by thwacking the heel of George's shoe on the palm of her other hand, insistently beating toughness back into herself. The shoe, with its trailing laces, reminded her of the Gunner's tightly cinched army boots and the reassuring clatter of hobnails when he walked or ran. Thinking of the Gunner seemed to help. She knew what he would have said if he had been there, if he'd been able to be inside her mind, listening to that sing-song chorus in her head.

He'd have dismissed the doubts and sent them away. She knew exactly what he'd have done, and so she did it.

"Right. Enough of that. Job to do. Get going," she gritted. "Go mad later."

And because she had thought of him and drawn strength from that thought, in a way the Gunner was with her, riding inside her head. And maybe that was the thing that put the iron back into her eyes and made her stride off with her back straight, heading for the river.

Chapter Eleven

Hung at the Tate

All the blood in George's body was obeying the call of gravity as he hung upside down, nose to the brickwork of a high chimney. He could feel his heart slamming as it fought a losing battle, trying to pump blood out of his head and circulate it normally, back up around his body. His ears pounded with a percussive swoosh and thud that got louder and louder until he was sure his head was going to burst with the pressure. He hadn't been held upside down since he was a toddler. He had a sharp memory of his laughing mother stopping his father from dangling him over a pile of leaves, and he remembered the relief as his dad had turned him the right way around, and how they'd all tumbled into the pile and had a leaf fight. He must have been about six, and those were the happy days, when his mother's laughter was just that, not a means of hiding something. The thought of her seemed to come from another life. He wondered if she was back in the country yet, if she knew he was missing. She must. Somewhere out there, she must be looking for him. She had to be.

He tried to think what he should do, and then just at the point where he was beginning to see little dancing spots of black unconsciousness whirling in from the edge of his vision, the gargoyle's other leg talon closed around his neck—not hard—and he found himself being turned the right way up and brought face-to-face with the great feral cat head.

Spout's stone eyes seemed to bore into him as the pressure that had built up in his head drained away and the black flecks whirled out of sight. His heart was still jackhammering in his chest, but the noise in his ears quieted to a background bass thump.

One feline eyebrow rose higher than the other, signaling a question. The stone mouth worked, trying to get a word out from behind the great teeth, with the awkwardness of someone trying to dislodge a fish bone without using his hands.

"Gack?" he said, and paused as if waiting for a reply. When none came, he grimaced and appeared to try again. *"Gowk?"*

Somehow the strangest thing, stranger than hanging off the top of the tall industrial chimney in the grip of a flying gargoyle, was the fact that the gargoyle appeared to be trying to talk to him.

George knew there was something wrong with this. He knew it in his guts.

"Why aren't you dead?" he asked, his voice as raw as the wind whipping around the top of the stack. He realized he also wanted to know why *he* wasn't dead, why the thing hadn't ripped him limb from limb or dropped him to shatter on the stone below.

Spout looked at him, and though he said nothing, George was shocked to see that he shrugged. When something with a twenty-foot wingspan shrugs, it's about as big as a shrug can get.

By all the rules about spits and taints that George had learned since he had fallen into this layer of unLondon, where statues walked and talked and flew and fought, Spout should have been dead, back on his perch, never to move again. George had seen the Gunner smithereen him with some of the last bullets from his gun. He was a taint. That meant he was dead. When taints were damaged like that, they were finished. On the other hand, spits—like the Gunner—had a stronger animating spirit holding them together. Even if they were badly damaged, as long as they could find their way back to their plinth by midnight, the time the Gunner had called "turn o'day," they were revived. Taints didn't have the same strong animating spirit to hold them together. They had a void at their core. Instead of a personality, they had malice and envy.

Spout was a taint, and Spout had been blasted to

shards in front of his eyes. That meant he should never walk the city or swoop over its rooftops again. That meant he should no longer be a threat. That meant he was just an ornament.

Except he had swooped. He had swooped and grabbed him. And he was looking at him expectantly. And George had no idea why. Unless . . .

With a jolt, he suddenly thought he knew what Spout wanted. It wasn't complicated. Spout wanted what the Walker had wanted. He wanted the broken dragon's head in his pocket.

The jolt he felt was elation: a moment ago, George had had no hope and a strong conviction that there was no way out other than a long drop or a short (he hoped), nasty encounter with Spout's ripping talons. Now he had something to exchange for his life. He didn't mind giving up the broken piece of statuary, not if it bought him his life, not if it bought him the time to rescue the Gunner and find Edie.

"Look!" he blurted. "Look, I know what you want. Here. I've got it. Put me down and you can have it—Oh."

Until his scrabbling hand found nothing where his coat pocket should be, and his mouth hit the "Oh," his plan had been almost instant and great.

He'd bargain with Spout by threatening to toss the broken dragon's head into the deep river below, unless the thing put him on the ground in one piece. Only, what his hand had discovered, an instant before his mind remembered, was the now presumably lethal fact that he had given his coat to Edie when the rain had set in. The coat in whose pocket he'd put the dragon's head.

"Oh," he repeated. "Bugger."

"Gugger?" echoed Spout nastily, head still cocked.

"Exactly." George's voice sounded as defeated as he felt.

"Gackly?"

"Yes," said George. "Gackly."

He was getting hysterical. He must be. There was a big sound rising like a tide inside him, and it wasn't a scream or a yell. It was laughter, and there was nothing funny about any of this.

And then he couldn't stop the laughter, not even as Spout adjusted his grip on George and launched himself off the top of the chimney into the great gulf of air below. Tears of mirth streamed into George's eyes as he flew through the air, so he saw the white metal blade of the Millennium footbridge below him through a blur, as the gargoyle swooped low over the river, heading north.

"Gackly," he choked, as the first chunk of laughter burst out of his nose in a convulsive snort. The great white dome of St. Paul's loomed straight ahead.

"I'm guggered. . . ."

CHAPTER TWELVE

The Killing Bull

The Walker emerged with a pop from the small glass mirrors in his hands and looked up at the classical front portico of Tate Britain and then turned around. There was no one around except for people waiting for a bus on the other side of the road.

He approached the gray steps and hurried up the left-hand side of the wide stairway. He kept his hood pulled over the right side of his face in a gesture that seemed to have an unaccustomed air of furtiveness for a being who was, by the very nature of his curse, so good at not being seen.

The truth is that he had come to visit one new statue, but was very keen to not see or be seen by another one.

The statue he sought was around the left-hand side of the entrance, on a little adjunct balcony space beside the double-columned edge of the portico. The one he particularly didn't want to see was on the other side.

As soon as he was around the corner, he relaxed and resumed his normal arrogant strut.

He looked at the group of statues he had come to see. It was a hybrid, because not all statues are either spits or taints. This was both, or rather, the human statues were spits, two muscular men like Greek wrestlers struggling with a taint, a huge and murderous bull on whose back had been tied a naked woman.

It was not a happy group. It was a monument to the fact that the ancient Greeks had had much too much fun thinking up ways to execute people.

The Walker cleared his throat. "I want to talk to the Bull."

No one moved. The frozen moment of struggle remained paralyzed in midair.

The Walker sighed. "It's the Minotaur."

The Bull's eye swiveled and looked at him.

"He has been killed," the Walker flatly informed the Bull.

The Bull convulsed and threw the two men into the corner of the balcony. The woman tied to its back screamed.

"Yes," said the Walker, unmoved. "Yes. It's distressing."

The Bull stood there, snorting angrily through its nostrils as the woman struggled to free herself.

"I wondered if you'd like to help me punish the ones responsible."

The woman screamed louder as the bull tossed its

head and horns back and then drowned her noise in the primal bellowing it blasted up into the night sky.

The Walker looked up and smiled, as a darker shape dropped out of the night and landed gently on his shoulder.

"Ah. There you are."

The Raven clacked its beak in his ear.

The Walker nodded.

"Good. If they are to be found, the Tallyman will do it quicker than anyone else. Now come. We must go east.

Chapter Thirteen

The Tallyman

Edie was stuck at the curb, waiting for the crossing light to change from red to green. She was on the edge of a knot of pedestrians, all of them impatient for the traffic to stop so they could continue their way on toward Blackfriars station. Everyone was in their own worlds, listening to music on their earphones, talking into mobiles, or just staring vacantly ahead, lost in their own London. No one paid her any attention.

"One glint. Topper Puddleduck."

Her ear caught the words right on the edge of her hearing. The voice was a man's, lumpy with phlegm, flat and uninflected as a machine talking. She turned, half sure that she'd misheard, half certain that she was getting jumpy and starting to imagine things. Nobody was looking at her. She must have imagined it. The words didn't make sense anyway. "Topper Puddleduck" was just gibberish. She'd obviously just caught a snatch of conversation that she couldn't really hear properly, and her mind had filled in gaps in the sentence with sounds that made semicoherent nonsense out of them.

"Puddleduck" was a word from her childhood, not this London. She had a flash of memory, real memory, not a glint's vision, of pale little drawings of a white duck in a pink shawl and a blue bonnet, the exact blue of the frosted glass earrings her mother had always worn, and her mother's fingers tracing the words around the picture and conjuring a story out of them. The memory was a happy one, and therefore treacherous and not to be kept in the mind too long, in case it started to hurt too much.

The light changed, the obstruction cleared, and the tight little bolus of humanity that had been blocked at the curb started moving again, thinning out as people walked on at different speeds.

Edie angled down toward the river, and as she did so she caught sight of the street name bolted to the building on the corner, clearly outlined in black and white. She was walking down Puddle Dock. And just as she was turning Puddle Dock into Puddleduck and back again, she heard the phlegmy voice once more, very clearly.

"One glint. Top of Puddle Dock. Walking down to the river."

This time when she turned, she saw him, and for a stomach-jolting instant she knew it was the Walker, and then an equally strong wash of relief hit her as she realized it wasn't. It was just a tramp wearing a long coat that gave him a silhouette like the Walker's, and instead of the Walker's hood, he had a cowl of matted hair framing his head in dreadlocks. He was squinting, eyes slitted, jaw hanging slack as he mouth-breathed at her in lumpy gurgles through gappy black-and-orange teeth. He stared back as if waiting for her to do something. Then a tiny shudder twitched through him, and he shrugged.

"One glint. Top of Puddle Dock. Standing still in the middle of the road . . ."

His voice was still uninvolved, almost disembodied. He had the look of a man who had zombified himself beneath relentless waves of alcohol. She decided he was deeply drunk.

The other pedestrians had moved on. The two of them faced each other in the middle of the road.

Edie should have run, she later decided, but he was a street-crazy, and street-crazies and drunks were things that didn't frighten her. First, because she felt somewhere deep inside that she was a street-crazy herself, and secondly, she knew all about drunks and the different levels of zombification into which they fell. It wasn't just because she was not frightened by the tramp—she was intrigued by what he seemed to be saying. So, keeping out of the reach of any sudden lunge that he might make, she took a couple of steps toward him.

"What did you say?"

"One glint. Top of Puddle Dock. Standing still in the middle of the road . . ." His voice repeated itself, a flat and exact replica of the previous sentence he'd uttered.

"Why d'you call me a glint?" she asked, mouth drying as she tried to anticipate the answer.

"Because you are a glint," he said, without taking his squinting eyes from her. The lack of interest in his voice was somehow more disturbing than the fact that he seemed to see what she was. She jutted her chin forward, determined not to betray the unease and the intimidation beginning to rise around her.

"Who are you?"

His tongue roiled wetly in the stump-scattered ruin of his mouth.

"We are the Tallyman."

"You're the what?"

"We are the Tallyman."

Again the inflection was identical to the first time he'd said it: flat, uninterested, lifeless. Like a recording. Like a computer speaking.

"We?" she said, looking around. She was relieved to see he was alone. The drivers in the cars now passing them on both sides weren't relieved. They were irritated, and a couple of them used their horns to communicate the fact.

"You're a 'we,' are you? Royal, like the Queen, are you?"

"We are the Tallyman," he said, echoing himself, uninterested, immovable eyes locked on her.

This flat repetition was annoying as well as unnerving.

"What are you doing?" she asked as a truck rumbled past her right shoulder.

"Counting you."

"Counting me?"

"Counting you. One glint. Top of Puddle Dock. Standing still in the middle of the road . . ."

"Why?" she asked, confused. "Why are you counting me?"

As a high-sided lorry paused in the traffic behind Edie, it threw the Tallyman into shadow, and he stopped squinting.

"We are the Tallyman."

Again his flat answer came back as if he were explaining the obvious. It wasn't his tone that made her feet suddenly feel as if they were being glued to the tarmac. It was his eyes, no longer squinting. Because they weren't a man's eyes, not the bloodshot whites she would have imagined; they were entirely black eyes, eyes with no whites at all—they were dark and beady and inhuman, like the Raven's eyes. Edie was filled with the sudden and horrible conviction that more than just a tramp was staring at her out of them. She wrenched her feet into motion and darted between a car and a shrieking taxi driver and sprinted toward the river.

The Tallyman didn't run after her. He just spoke calmly as he waited for a hole in the traffic.

"One glint. Running down Puddle Dock. Toward the river."

CHAPTER FOURTEEN

Gunner in the Dark

"'Whoso list to hunt, I know where there is an hind. . . .'"

The Walker's words seemed to hang in the dank air long after he had left the Gunner alone in the darkness, reminding him that the Walker had left to hunt Edie. The Gunner was sick with the certainty that the Walker would get her. There were just too many heart stones belonging to other glints arranged on the four walls of the underground water tank, like grisly trophies, to leave any room for doubt. The Walker clearly knew what he was doing. Each of those worn pieces of sea-glass had been the precious possession of a woman or girl, the kind of possession none of them would have given up without a fierce fight. The Gunner wondered how many of the heart stones had been pried from cold, dead fingers.

He felt weak at the thought.

"Right," he said to himself. "Smoke break."

He felt for the wall behind him and slid down to a sitting position, hunched against the damp stone at his back. He reached under the tarpaulin cape he wore around his shoulders and fumbled something out of a pocket. There was a scrape and then a match flared into light, and the red end of a cigarette was ignited.

He held the match out at the end of his arm, not wanting to waste a moment of its illumination as he sucked hungrily at the cigarette between his lips. He used the fleeting light to orient himself in the space: he saw the castle-shaped outlines of the sea-glass fragments, and he noted the disk hanging in the center of the room, reflecting the tiny flame in his hand. Then it guttered out and he was in the dark again.

The only sound was his breathing, interspersed with his inhaling and exhaling the tobacco smoke. Each time he inhaled, the red dot at the end of the cigarette glowed brighter, like a tiny heart pulsing.

He took an inventory of how he felt, and what his options were. He felt wrong inside, still twisted and hanging by a thread, which he realized was the result of having broken his oath in order to try to save Edie. He imagined this wrongness was going to get worse. It certainly made him weak, and it seemed to be making it hard for him to think as straight as he normally did. The thing he was most worried about, after what was going to happen to Edie and then George without him there to help them, was what was going to happen at midnight.

Midnight, or turn o'day, was the time when the statues based on real people, the spits, had to be on their
plinths. It wasn't optional, it was part of what they were
and how they were. An empty plinth at turn o'day meant
the death of a spit. When it returned or was returned to
its plinth after turn o'day, it never walked again, and
became no more than a human-shaped lump of metal or
stone. Since he was now paying the penalty for breaking
an oath sworn by the Stone and the hand that made him,
he imagined that midnight might mean, if not the end of
him, the start of an eternity of wandering, like the
Walker, in thrall to the dark powers pent in the Stone.

He didn't seem to have much chance of leaving this
subterranean cell before midnight unless the Walker got
him out the way they'd come in; and there just didn't
seem much likelihood of that. Even if he'd had his normal strength, he didn't know how deep underground he
was, and he certainly didn't think he could claw his way
to the surface, given the fact that the last time he had
tried to lift his arms to do so, he had failed so badly. The
Walker's power over him seemed to be working. He wondered if the Walker would be back before turn o'day,
before midnight came and brought his death.

He wasn't looking forward to the Walker's return, if
only because his sneering boastfulness was hard to bear,
on top of all the bad things that were happening to the
Gunner. And then he thought of a way to stop having to
see the Walker's face at least, and that gave him a plan.

"Come on, you dozy beggar," he said to himself as he grunted and heaved himself back onto his feet.

If the glint's glasses blazed into life because of their power to warn when a taint or a Stone Servant like the Walker came near, and that was the perverse way the Walker provided light for himself in his subterranean lair, there was something the Gunner could do. The fact that it involved disassembling the Walker's carefully made castle shapes only increased his desire to do it.

He unhooked his tarpaulin cape and felt for the mural on the wall behind him.

By sucking hard on his cigarette, he caught a pale reflection in some pieces of glass on the wall. He carefully laid his cape on the gravel beneath the castle outline, and reached high and wide, using both hands to brush a glass piece off the wall and onto the tarpaulin.

"Abracadabra to you too, mate," he muttered in grim satisfaction.

Once he'd convinced himself that he'd cleared that wall of heart stones, he bundled up the tarpaulin and turned one hundred eighty degrees to the wall and walked in a straight line off the gravel spit and into the water. As he passed the center point of the space, he stopped and cast around with his hands in the air until they clattered into the spinning disk on the chain. He tugged hard, and there was a percussive *spang* noise as the chain parted and the disk came free. He reached into his pocket and pulled out his matches. He lit one and stood there, hip deep in the water, looking at the disk in the light of the small flame.

It was an old pewter plate: on it, someone had scratched a series of concentric circles with turreted castles around the edge, as if marking the points of the compass. Roads led from the arches in the base of each castle. They made a cross where they met in the center of the plate, joined by another series of circles like the central boss of a shield. There was writing all over the design, but all the Gunner had time to read was "The King and his princes . . ." and "Occidens" before the match guttered out. He carefully stowed the plate inside his jacket and headed for the glass castle on the wall.

"King, my eye," he snorted. "You won't need all this malarkey, because when you pop back in here with the lights out, I'll bloody crown you for nothing."

And though there was no one to see it, he grinned as he reached for the first piece of sea-glass on the wall ahead of him.

CHAPTER FIFTEEN

Paternoster

At the same time Edie was running south toward the river, George had just recrossed it heading north. Spout held him firmly around the chest as he flapped toward the great dome of St. Paul's Cathedral. It was a jerky passage through the air as the gargoyle grunted and flexed his muscles on each downbeat, swaying so precariously from stroke to stroke that flying was more a matter of will than aerodynamics for the bulky stone creature. There was a strong sense that he might plummet to the ground at any moment. One improvement on things was that he wasn't carrying George upside down anymore, so his head no longer pounded with blood.

The flash of a camera caught his eyes as they overflew a gaggle of tourists taking pictures in front of the cathedral. He shouted, "Help!" more for the form of it than from any real hope, trying to throw a verbal grappling hook back into a safer reality that he barely remembered.

Just as he'd expected, not one single tourist looked up. They couldn't see him in his layer of London. The unconscious, instinctive part of their brains stepped in and erased him, protecting their consciousness from the shock of seeing the impossible: a boy being flown through the city beneath a gargoyle, like a mouse being taken by an owl. The last day had been so full of terror and running and people not seeing or helping him that he'd gotten used to it.

Because he had given up expecting anyone to notice him, he missed the wiry old broken-toothed man in the mismatched grimy suit sitting on the ground in a doorway. He didn't see him put down the cider bottle and squint into the sky at George. He didn't see the unwashed hair or the broken veins crimsoning the man's face in a drinker's blush. And he neither saw the jet-black eyes nor heard the lifeless voice saying:

"One boy inna sky. Carried by a gargoyle. Flying around St. Paul's, heading nor' nor'east."

Spout suddenly stood on one wing and turned an ungainly right angle in the sky, diving low around the side of the dome across the radiating white sunburst design inlaid on the surface of Paternoster Square.

Now that it was clear that the gargoyle wasn't going to kill him immediately, there was room on top of the fear for anger, too: George desperately needed to rescue the Gunner, but he could do nothing about it because he'd been grabbed and was being taken wherever the gargoyle felt like going. He thought of the Gunner and how relieved he'd been when he'd reappeared as if back from the dead at the Monument. In the pit of his stomach, George nursed the conviction that you really only got to come back from the dead once, if you were lucky. And the Gunner had done something fatal to his luck by sacrificing himself for Edie. George knew that if they didn't get the Gunner free and back on his pedestal by midnight, he'd have no need of luck at all, because he'd just be finished.

He caught a smeared vision of a strangely familiar arched gatehouse, its Georgian elegance at odds with the modern piazza beyond, and then unaccountably he heard a noise so out of place that he looked wildly around for the source of it: it was the sound of sheep, bleating plaintively in the middle of this windblown stone piazza.

It was a peaceful sound, of grass and hills and summertime, and for all its alienness, it flowed into his overheated brain like cool water after a long dry spell. For some unaccountable reason, the sound of innocent animals in the midst of all this turmoil just made him lighten inside.

Then, as if he really had become less heavy, he and Spout suddenly lifted higher and climbed up and over an office building, too quickly to be certain, but just slowly enough for George to be almost convinced that he heard a voice amid the sheep shout after him:

"Hold on, my son!"

He twisted and wriggled in Spout's clasp, desperately trying to see the sheep or the man whose voice he was sure—heartbreakingly sure—he recognized. But the gargoyle flew on, over the rooftops, and the square was lost to his view.

It had only been a snatch of sound, but it had gone through George like a burst of adrenaline. He felt invigorated, as if he'd just had a night's sleep. He didn't feel any less scared or confused by what was happening to him— he just suddenly felt a lot more able to cope with it. The zigzag scar on his hand twinged sharply, but it wasn't an unbearable pain, and it didn't stop the unaccountable surge of well-being he felt coursing through him. He snatched a look at the three lines twining down to his wrist. Unless he was mistaken, they'd traveled farther, one of them actually crossing his wrist and starting a curving fissure onto his forearm. Somehow, looking at these flaws that seemed to be spiraling through his flesh made him feel more nauseous than all the swerving through the sky.

"*Gaven,*" Spout croaked suddenly. There was another swooping heave, and the world tilted alarmingly.

If you can trip in the sky, three hundred feet above any possible obstruction, that's what it felt like. George concentrated on keeping whatever was in his stomach on the inside; and then once he'd gulped it back into place, he looked upward to see what was troubling the gargoyle, and saw that Spout's neck was craned backward.

The world bucked and roller-coastered once more, and George's stomach popped up to say hello to his tonsils again, and he realized that Spout was taking evasive action, diving down between two skyscrapers to get below roof level—as if trying to put them between him and something else in the night sky. George craned around and followed the direction of the gargoyle's eyes, but saw nothing but the city as the lights came on and the colors drained from the day. The sky was empty, apart from a large crow, or some such bird, flapping slowly north in the distance. There was nothing obviously threatening. George couldn't see why Spout was acting so frightened.

"Gaven!" panted the gargoyle, this time more intently.

The early night sky disappeared, and they swooped over the rooftop of a large older building that seemed to take up an entire city block. George caught a glimpse of the pillared frontage of the Royal Exchange building to the right, and realized they must be flying directly over the Bank of England on Threadneedle Street.

He looked down and saw the dark hollow made by the central courtyard of the building, and then he heard someone singing.

It was only a snatch of song, but it cut through the rumbling snarl of the city and came to his ears as cleanly as the sound of the sheep had in Paternoster Square. It was a girl's clear voice, and it had a lightness and clarity that spoke of sunshine and light spring breezes. It was the happy sound of someone singing purely for her own enjoyment, drawing out the trilling rhyme at the end of each line with a joyfulness that had something unmistakably pure and elemental to it.

"'Where the bee sucks there suck I:

In a cowslips bell I li-i-i-ie;

There I couch when owls do cry.

On the bat's back I do fl-y-y-y . . .'"

The singing was coming from the top of a small domed cupola at a sharp angle of the building to the north. The singer was a bright splash of gold against the gray of the building and the darker shadows of the narrow street beyond. She was balanced like a ballet dancer on the toes of one slender foot, while her other leg stuck out behind in the beginnings of a dainty arabesque. Golden drapery shimmered around her legs and torso, as if blown by an invisible breeze that ruffled her gilded hair as she sang, her throat arched back in joyful abandon, singing to the sky and the moon that had just started to rise.

For an instant she was a vision of poise and grace and happiness—and then, just as George saw her, she saw him; and though her mouth stayed open, she stopped singing and stared at him in unfeigned surprise as Spout flapped past.

It seemed to George that her face shone, more than just because it was gold. It shone because her eyes were bright and full of hope and something that made him uncomfortable—though not in a necessarily bad way.

"A boy?" she said in a voice running clean as a mountain stream. "Hello, boy."

As Spout flew away from her, her smile changed to a small sad pout, and she traced a half-wave with her hand. "Good-bye, boy."

"Help?" he shouted awkwardly.

Spout hissed in disapproval. George twisted to see her getting smaller in their wake.

"No, really!" he shouted with more conviction. "HELP!"

And then she was lost to sight behind the angle of the next building they flew over. Spout was looking back, too, and something he saw didn't please him at all, because he suddenly hissed even louder, dropped a shoulder, and curved in and down behind a tall office building with the sudden jerking swoosh of a skier abruptly swerving to a halt.

His talon reached out and grabbed a parapet, and he neatly pinwheeled himself to a stop and flattened against a sloping roof of greasy greenish-gray tiles. His wings were spread out like a partial umbrella, and George was stuck between them and the angle of the roof.

For a long minute they stayed there, unmoving. The only sound was Spout panting and George's heart hammering. He looked down and saw that his feet were braced on a slippery gutter above a lethal drop to the street below. He noticed that he had only one shoe on, because his sock immediately became soaked. Then Spout did something terrifying.

He let go of George.

George scrabbled with his hands and then realized the only way not to fall was to flatten himself on the sheer angle of the roof and hope the gutter didn't give way.

He stopped scrabbling and pressed forward. Spout kept his eyes on him and nodded slowly. He pointed one claw warningly at George. And then he reached above himself and slowly began to crawl to the edge of the roof above. His ears were flattened back on his head, like some great hunting cat. George could see the spines that ran up his backbone quivering, like the hair on a dog's back when it's alarmed. He wondered what it was that was frightening the gargoyle. It gave him a treacherous spark of hope: perhaps there was someone out there looking for him. Perhaps the Gunner had got free and was coming to his rescue, perhaps having enlisted some flying . . .

And here the hope dwindled a bit as he realized the only statues he could think of that could fly were taints instead of spits. He saw Spout cat-crawl to the roof ridge and slowly slide halfway over. Spout paused in that position, only one leg and the edge of a wing still visible to George, ready to duck back into hiding if his search of the sky revealed anything alarming.

George concentrated on keeping a grip on the distressingly sheer slope of the roof. He thought he'd be okay if he didn't make any sudden movements. He was pretty sure he could be still, especially since the consequences of not being still were going to be moving very quickly downward and then being still forever. He concentrated on sticking to the roof. He could do this.

He felt his hands splayed against the slates. He saw the greenish flecks on the gray surface in front of his nose. He felt the stone under his fingertips. Maybe because he was concentrating so hard on staying stuck to it, he somehow felt that he could feel the structure of the stone itself, the tight grain, the compressed layers running parallel with the face, the layers that made it possible to split it into the thin roof tiles. He even felt a magneting tingling, as if those green flecks were not stone but little flecks of iron embedded in the slate.

He was so taken by the immediacy and intensity of what he was feeling beneath his hand that he forgot to be scared.

Then something tapped him on the ankle.

He jerked away on reflex and nearly tumbled onto the street. He flattened against the tiles, trying to become part of the roof, hoping that every extra bit of him that he could press against the surface would help him stick there. Even his face was squidged against the cold slate.

"Are you perchance trying to hold on with your nose?" said a tiny whisper behind him. He looked down and saw the golden girl looking back up at him, both elbows perched on the gutter, chin cupped in her hands, as nonchalant as if leaning on a bar—despite the fact that there was nothing but a lethal gulf of air beneath her feet.

His eyes automatically flicked upward, to see if Spout had heard her. All he could see was the one talon on the ridge and the bit of wing. Spout was still on lookout.

The girl pushed herself off from the gutter and held on with her hands, arms at full stretch, still looking up at him.

"Come," she said simply, and held out one hand.

"Who are you?" George whispered, trying to put off the moment when he might have to reach away from the comfort of the wet tiles and find out if her ability to hang in the air included being able to carry him, too.

"I am minister of your fate," she said with a heart-breaking smile. He returned the smile. It seemed the polite thing to do, even though he hadn't a clue what she was talking about.

And then she tugged his ankle off the gutter.

He didn't even have time to yell or grab a handhold. He just fell, snatching handfuls of air . . .

—And then she caught him.

"Wha—?"

"Shhh," she whispered, mouth pressed close to his ear, breath warm on the back of his neck. One finger pointed at Spout's back on the ridgeline above them. He shushed and nodded.

"Hold on, boy," she breathed. His hands locked on to her arm, which wasn't hard and metallic, but as warm and soft as her breath.

"What do we do now?" he asked very quietly, eyes locked on Spout's back view.

He could hear the smile in her voice as she answered, "I fly."

She let go of the building edge and fell slowly backward with the clean grace of an Olympic high diver, pivoting on her toes as her head described a perfect one hundred eighty–degree arc, and George went along with her as upright changed to upside down, and they were suddenly diving face-first for the paving stones beneath.

He opened his mouth to shout, but her free hand clapped over it and stifled the yell, and all he could see racing toward his bulging eyes was granite oblivion.

Chapter Sixteen

Careless Talk Costs Lives

Edie hit the pavement at the end of the pedestrian crossing and trotted downhill, turning right and heading under the dark railway overpass at the bottom of the slope. She saw the white triangular shape of the Black Friar pub beyond, jutting toward the Thames like the prow of a landlocked ship.

She stopped as a taxi slowed and turned past her, heading up the hill. When it had passed, she didn't continue crossing the road. She just stood there, staring at the pub facade; not at what was on it, but rather at what wasn't. The clock below was stuck at five to seven, but above it, where the statue of the Black Friar normally stood like a figurehead, was a blank plinth.

The Friar was gone, and the empty space stared back at Edie like a threat.

She'd been running all the questions she wanted to ask him through her head, trying so hard to imagine what he'd say, how he might help, how she might have to cajole him into doing so, so that the one scenario she hadn't catered for was that he might not be there to ask in the first place. She also hadn't thought how she might get into the pub if he wasn't there to let her in, with his jovial laugh and jangling keys. Another car turned in front of her and splashed the curbside puddle across her ankles, jolting her out of her frozen state.

"Right," she said, smacking her palm with heel of George's shoe. "Right."

She jogged across the road and under a railway bridge as a train rumbled ominously overhead. She rounded the point of the building and slowed, suddenly wary.

The door to the pub stood open, but the lights were off. As she approached it she saw two builders carry out a stack of planks and load them into the back of a white van double-parked near the curb. Edie flattened herself against the side of the building and went very still, concentrating on not being seen. Not being seen was a skill she'd realized she had very early on in her life. Sometimes she'd thought people were just ignoring her, but she'd later decided that they just found it hard to see her a lot of the time, and this was because she could, when she concentrated, be very still and unnoticeable. Once she'd noticed this was something she could do, she did it more and more, really putting a lot of mental effort into making herself invisible. She knew she wasn't actually invisible, but she also knew that she had something that made people's eyes slide off her as if she were covered in non-stick coating.

She waited for the men to go back inside the pub, then slid quickly up to the open door and pressed her back against the outside wall. She slipped the frosted circle of sea-glass out of her pocket and checked it. It was dull and unthreatening, no inner fire kindling within to warn of the closeness of danger. Edie slipped it back into her coat, and as she did so, she felt the heavy lump of the dragon's head in the pocket of George's coat bump against her thigh. She knew whatever had happened to make him disappear was bad, because he'd said that he would stay with her, and his word was good—and even if it wasn't, he'd never have run off and left her wearing a coat that contained such a precious object.

Before she could think more about this, the builders came back out, knees buckling under the weight of a second, bigger stack of planks. They walked it right past her as she stood there, not breathing. As soon as the second man had passed her, she pivoted neatly and slipped inside the door, into the gloom.

The interior was much the same as it had been the last time she'd been there, still shrouded with drop cloths and littered with builder's jumble. She heard the rear door of the van slam and feet heading back toward her. She lifted the edge of a drop cloth and bent double beneath a low pub table, flicking the cloth back into place to hide her. She held her breath again and listened as one man walked into the room. He picked up something that clanked like a toolbox, switched off the lights, and walked out again. She heard the door shut with the finality of a church door slamming, and keys turning in the lock. As she relaxed a fraction and breathed in quiet shallow breaths, she heard the hollow thump of the van's side door closing and the noise as it drove off into the traffic on the main road beyond.

She still didn't move for about five minutes, just crouched there in the darkening room behind the grubby canvas of the drop cloth, listening for noises made by anyone or anything locked in with her. When the complete absence of sound or movement from anywhere had told its incontrovertible story of emptiness and abandonment, she rolled out from under the table and walked purposefully toward the bar. The room smelled rank and overheated. It smelled of workmen and wet plaster.

She shrugged out of George's jacket and put it on the countertop. She boosted herself up onto it, swiveled her legs over, and dropped onto the barman's side in one decisive movement. She bent down and examined the cardboard boxes stacked neatly along the foot of the bar. She plunged her hand into the torn hole in the side of the one with pink writing on it and fished out a pair of prawn-cocktail crisp packets.

She was so hungry that she'd torn the first one open and was munching a mouthful of tangy potato shards into starchy shrapnel by the time she stood up again.

She closed her eyes and allowed herself the momentary pleasure of enjoying the taste and feel of eating. Then she got down to business.

"Okay," she lisped through a full mouth, "come down here. We need to talk. . . ."

Nothing but silence answered her.

She opened her eyes and tipped the other half of the packet straight into her mouth. She chomped happily for a moment, clearing a passageway for her next words.

"Seriously. Don't make me come in there after you. . . ."

Silence. She reached under the bar and came out with a bottle of ginger beer. She stuck it in the opener screwed to the inner wall of the counter and popped the cap without looking. She chugged a couple of mouthfuls and swilled the impacted potato wodge from the spaces between her teeth. Then she burped and smacked the heavy glass bottle onto the bar top.

"Oi. Tragedy. I need some straight answers."

She made a point of not looking into the dark alcove beyond the three low arches to her right. To the trained ear it was entirely clear that this was where all the silence was coming from.

"I know you're there."

Silence. And then, just as she was opening her mouth to speak, another voice dodged quietly out from under the arches.

"No I ain't."

It was a cockney voice. Edie hid a smile by popping the second bag of crisps and pouring some of them into her mouth.

"Where's the Friar?" she asked.

Now that it had leaked a voice, the silence seemed much more eloquent. It spoke of someone trying to find a way to avoid a straight answer, she thought.

A small throat cleared itself. "'E's not here an' all."

"You're both not here?"

"No. Yes. Er. Yes . . . only 'e's more not 'ere than what I am. See?"

A tousled head of bronze hair poked into view at the top of one of the arches, hanging upside down; then a face dropped into view, the impish face of a street cherub carrying a mask, which a sculptor had carved into the distinctive features of Tragedy. His face was grinning and mischievous.

"I do now," Edie said drily.

"You're in a pickle."

"Am I?"

"Biggest pickle in the barrel is wot I heard."

"Heard from who?"

"Dunno." He dropped to the ground and looked at her. He looked at the mask he held in his hand. He put it in front of his face and then took it away, grimace giving way to smile.

"You get all sorts in a pub. Keep your ears open, you pick up a lot of stuff."

"What kind of stuff?"

He hid behind the mask again, and then half took it off, winking with the one visible eye. "'Careless talk costs lives.'"

She had no idea what he was talking about. "What do you mean?"

"'Careless talk costs lives.' You know."

"No. I wouldn't ask if I knew."

"It's what they say. What they used to say."

"Who?"

"I dunno, do I? Them. Everyone. There was posters. We had one over there."

"When?"

"In the war. You know. When they was dropping bombs and all that. In the wossname. The Blitz. You remember."

She realized he was talking about the Second World War.

"The Blitz?"

He looked pleased. His little chest swelled in front of her, and he nodded enthusiastically. "There you go. You remember. We had the poster over there. You liked it."

"I wasn't alive during the war. Not that war."

His eyes flicked left and right and then centered on her beneath a newly wrinkled brow. "Wasn't you?"

She shook her head. "My mum wasn't alive in that war."

"I thought you . . ."

"I'm twelve."

"Well, that don't mean nothing. That's older than me. I think. I mean, I think I'm not twelve. Not yet."

He began to look confused.

"You look about ten. But then you'll always be ten, won't you?"

"Will I?"

"You will. Statues don't get old. You'll have been ten in the war like you're ten now. But I wasn't born, my mum wasn't born. I don't even think her mum was born. . . ."

The furrows on his brow curved and deepened. "But you liked the poster. I'm sure I remember."

She shook her head. "I never saw any poster."

He held her gaze for a couple of beats longer. "I thought you did. I—"

"I didn't." She cut him off hard. She didn't have time to waste.

He looked offended and suddenly deflated. He twirled the mask in his hands and examined his feet. "Okay."

His toe traced a pattern in the carpet. "It's just that I seen so many things for so long that I get it all in a ball, you know? Like knots. It all gets tangled. Like, I think I remember stuff I ain't supposed to have seen, and I seen things I ain't supposed to remember. And that's not even counting the stuff I definitely ain't seen, don't remember, and can't forget. You know what I mean?"

"No."

"I got so much stuff in my head, I can't keep it all apart. It gets jumbled. It's one of the things makes me feel like I'm made wrong, you know?"

There was a small gust of wind from behind her. It rustled a newspaper on a stool beside him. He reached out and caught the top sheet as it lifted off the pile. He held it as if surprised to find it there. Then he scowled intently at it and crumpled it into a ball. He kept it bunched tight in his hand and smiled hopefully at her.

The last time Edie had met Little Tragedy, he had been keen that she use her power, her ability to glint, to suck the past from rock and metal to touch him and see if she could sense if there was something wrong with him. She hadn't touched him, but she could see there was something not right. She didn't know if he had been made wrong, or made to be wrong, but his eagerness to be glinted, when every other statue shied away from the pain and distress caused when she touched them, had been one of the things that she and George had mistrusted about the whole setup of the pub and its threateningly cheery landlord. She thought Little Tragedy was a spit. The suspicion was creeping up on her that he might have a dual nature like the half-human, half-fantastical Sphinxes. Maybe he was taintish when he had the mask on, spit-like when he didn't. So she didn't answer his question directly. Instead she changed the subject, back to the reason she'd come back to the pub.

"Look. I haven't got time to talk. I need to find the

Gunner. And I need to find George. I don't even know where to start, except with this one thing: what's in the mirrors?"

He looked perplexed again. "What mirrors?"

She pointed to the two mirrors on either side of the arch he was standing in. They faced each other on the inside pilasters of the arch, and standing between them and looking sideways gave the impression that the reflections in the mirrors not only framed each other, but repeated themselves into infinity.

"Those mirrors. I need to know about the mirrors."

Little Tragedy scratched the back of his head with the hand that still held the balled-up newspaper and shifted his weight from one foot to the other, avoiding her eyes. "Nothing. They're just mirrors, yeah?"

Edie stepped toward him. He raised his eyes and smiled brightly, as if seeing her for the first time. Whatever look she had parked on her face clearly wasn't returning fire on the smile, because his faded fast, dimming to a grin before curdling into a grimace and an awkward rise and fall of his shoulders.

"Just mirrors. Straight up, no messing. That's all they are . . ."

Edie cleared her throat. The question she was about to ask was going to be so outlandish that she didn't want to give it the chance of catching on something before it even got out of her mouth.

"Are they the kind of mirrors you can step into?"

"Do what?"

His head suddenly tilted and bobbed from one side to the other as he squinted up at her like a raccoon eyeing up a particularly complex trash can.

"There are mirrors you can step into, aren't there? You said there were other places, other 'heres.' You said you could show me how to get to them."

"Oooh, I never, what a whopper!"

Edie turned on him, hand clenched into a fierce and knobby fist. "The only whopper you're going to get is when I lay one on you if you don't straighten up and start telling me the truth. I want to know about the mirrors, because I think it's to do with them, isn't it? When we left here, I looked in, and it was all like this, hundreds of reflections of the same thing snaking off into the distance, all copies of each other, except for one thing."

Her finger stabbed at the mirror. Little Tragedy flinched as her hand passed his shoulder, but his eyes followed the direction she was indicating.

"It's not there now. I hoped it might be, but it isn't. But it was. There was one slice that was different from all the others, and you know why?" asked Edie.

"No. I don't want to know an' all . . ."

He was backing into the shadows again. She could hear him nervously crumpling the newspaper ball in his fist. Her voice cracked like a whip, and he stopped dead.

"Tragedy! Stay there."

She followed him into the gloomy nook.

"The rest of the slices were identical to each other, just getting smaller; but there was this one slice with a bowl and a knife lying on the ground. Only, that's what I thought they were. Until I saw them again, later."

Little Tragedy's Adam's apple bobbled up and down twice. His eyes slid around the room, looking for an exit. Or help.

"You saw them later? This bowl and knife whatsit?"

His Adam's apple came up for the third time, as if it were drowning.

Edie nodded grimly. She knew from the unmissable awkwardness of his body language that she was on the threshold of something new, something powerful.

"I saw them again just after this evil bloke called the Walker pulled two little round mirrors out of his pocket and stepped into one of them. I saw them just after he disappeared into the mirror, taking our friend with him. Only, it wasn't a bowl and a knife. It was the Walker's dagger and the Gunner's tin helmet. And they lay there on the ground, and these two little mirrors hung there in the air on either side of them for a moment, like a magic trick, with no one holding them. Then there was a little pop, and the mirrors and the hat and the dagger just sort of disappeared. So what I want to know, what I need to know is: are these the kind of mirrors you can step into? And if they are, how come I saw the hat and dagger lying there before it happened?"

"Er," said Little Tragedy. "Well. Ah." His eyes were

sliding all over the room. "You should ask himself. He's got the words. I only see stuff, really. Ask Old Black."

"I'm asking you."

"Ask him."

"He's not here."

Tragedy looked at the newspaper crumpled in his hand. Then he placed it delicately on a tabletop. Edie flashed the memory of him catching the paper as it lifted off the pile in the gust of wind from the door, and only then remembered that the door was shut. Had been shut. Locked. Tight enough to keep drafts out.

Little Tragedy grimaced again, as if knowing what she was belatedly realizing.

"Er."

The hairs on the back of her neck went up. Her hand reached instinctively for the warning glass in her pocket. The deep booming voice behind her froze her hand.

"The little imp is trying to say, 'Yes he is.'"

She turned, knowing what she was going to see. She was nose to belly with the Friar himself, towering over her like a dark cliff face. And as her eyes traveled upward, she couldn't help but notice that the previously jolly face was as cheery and welcoming as a black thundercloud in a cold dark sky.

CHAPTER SEVENTEEN

Ariel Rising

George plummeted toward the ground, held in the tight embrace of the golden girl. He knew he was dead. In one short second his head would pile-drive into the pavement. And the Gunner would be dead, and Edie would never know he hadn't deserted her by choice, and his mother, his mother would never know how much he—

He threw his hands out reflexively, and two things happened at once: the girl batted them down with the arm that wasn't wrapped around his chest and clamped them tightly to his side.

And she swooped.

There was no other word for it. At the very last moment she defied all the laws of aerodynamics and flattened out her dive, acrobatically swooping left in a ninety-degree barrel roll, so that instead of splatting into the stone sidewalk, she flew along it at an altitude of about one foot.

"Keep your arms in or you'll hurt yourself," she said calmly. George just stared at the paving stones whipping past his nose and got used to being alive again. He nodded and then made the mistake of looking ahead.

Not only were they running out of pavement, the intersection ahead was busy and in motion. Buses and lorries sped through in opposite directions, and the girl seemed to be leaving the sidewalk too late, suddenly much, much too late if she hoped to gain altitude and fly over the vehicles powering across their path at right angles.

A big high-sided lorry hurtled in from the left on a certain collision course, much too close to miss or avoid; and once more he knew he was dead, and once more he refused to close his eyes—and then he wished he had, because instead of hitting the lorry, she dinked even lower and underflew it, between the moving wheels.

He heard her laughter gurgle in his ear, and she banked left and up; and where George had been terrified, he realized that his mouth wasn't shrieking but smiling.

The reason was this: she flew.

Just as she had said she did.

And when she flew, she *really* flew.

Spout, by comparison, had not really flown. Spout, by comparison, had dragged himself painfully through the sky by grabbing great untidy chunks of air and forcing them under his wings as he desperately snatched for the next one. Spout had propelled himself through the sky in a constant battle against the air and pull of gravity. The girl didn't fight the air. She flew in it, as if she were a part of it.

He realized that this was why she laughed. She loved the simple freedom and exhilaration of flying.

As if she had read his thoughts, she slalomed between three lampposts and then down into a tunnel under a modern building, which quickly opened up into a small square in front of an ancient stone church. She cut a wide arc around the right-hand side of the building at gargoyle height, close enough for George to see with relief that the only gargoyles on this church were grotesque medieval heads pulling ugly faces.

She tightened the radius of the arc and circled down to the pavement at the foot of a bulging gherkin-shaped skyscraper that was as modern as the church at its base was old.

She daintily released George and stepped back, running her fingers through her hair to restore some order to the windblown golden locks. She and George were both panting and took a moment to get their breath back. As they did, George could see her eyes were bright with exhilaration.

"I guarantee we lost him," she said.

He looked upward and was pleased to see no sign of Spout. He nodded. "Thank you."

"It was nothing more than a pleasure, boy." She smiled.

"My name's George," he said. And he held his hand

out because he didn't know what to do, and shaking hands always seemed to be part of a good introduction. She looked at him oddly, and then took his hand. But instead of shaking it, she turned it over and examined it. He saw she was looking at the scar, the dragon's wound, his maker's mark.

"Oh," he said, "that's a—"

"I know what it is, boy." She laughed. "Being one of the 'made,' how would I not?" She gave him his hand back.

"Who are you?" he asked.

"I am Ariel."

George kept a wary eye on the sky, in case any spouts suddenly appeared out of it.

"I'll hear him coming," she said. "He punches great holes in the sky as he drags his ungainly bulk through it. I will catch the vibrations. I am, after all, a spirit of the air."

And George remembered who Ariel was, because his class had been to see a play in the park two summers ago.

"Er, no offense, but I thought Ariel was a boy."

Her head came up and she looked at him with an expression that was half-hurt, half-outraged pride.

He swallowed and hurried on, before the insult could take root. "No, I mean, when we saw it in school. The play. That's when I thought Ariel was a boy. In the play, right?"

He was burbling. He knew he was burbling. He definitely wasn't making it better.

"Do I look like a boy to you, boy?"

It was a disconcerting question, and she had a

disconcerting way of asking it. It wasn't just her voice, which, for all its disapproval, was rather low and quite velvety. It wasn't the sense that she was always on the point of laughing at him either, although that was quite irritating. It was that there was something unnerving about her clothes. It wasn't that they were golden or filmy, or even that they were covering—barely—a body that the sculptor had made disconcertingly lithe and curvy. It was that they were, he realized, not really clothes at all. They were floaty bits of material that seemed to be held on by nothing more than a light breeze.

"No. You look very . . . not like a boy."

She held his look for a long and predictably disconcerting moment. A smile twitched at the edge of her mouth. Somehow, somewhere—actually in the pit of his stomach—he found that hint of a smile the most disconcerting thing of all.

"I am very *not* like a boy, boy. No boy could do this."

She reached out and took his hand again and leaped into the air. His stomach flipped and his arm was half wrenched out of his socket. She hoisted him higher and put an arm under his armpit and held him, his back tightly clenched to her as she soared up, spiraling around the curved skyscraper.

He saw the office floors, layer after layer as they rose and circled toward the swelling middle of the building. He saw empty desks and winking computer screens. He saw a conference room with men and women sitting around a long table. He saw a man in a suit standing on his head against a wall as a couple of business-suited women laughed and applauded. And he saw entire empty floors with a lone cleaner pushing her cart through the anonymous maze of booths and dividers. And then the building ceased to belly outward and started to taper, and Ariel twisted in midflight, laughing as she gave them a widening panorama of the whole city below.

He saw the sparkle of the river and the closer high-rises, and then the distant skyscrapers at Canary Wharf to the east, and he began feeling as giddy as her laughing sounded, as the circuits around the building got narrower and narrower as they neared the apex.

The whirling panorama really did start to blur with the velocity at which she was circling, and then they reached the rounded point at the top of the building, and the circling became a pirouette that got faster and faster until George felt like one of those ice-skaters spinning on one skate, so fast that he ceased to be a recognizable person and just became a high-velocity whirling smear.

"Please," he choked, half laughing, half panicking. "Please. Ariel. I'm going to hurl. . . ."

Her spinning slowed and eased, then ceased. Once she had stopped, it took a while for his brain to settle back on its gimbals and stop its own sympathetic whirligig.

Ariel stepped gently down to the rim of the building's cap and lowered him onto it. He grabbed a bar set into a recessed hole and clung on tight.

"No, don't—" he began, but she did.

She let go of him, and there he was, sitting on top of the world, a shiny glass-and-metal world that arced away from him on all sides, curving so radically that there was nothing to see but drop-off whichever way he looked.

Ariel stepped in front of him, spun on one toe, and curtsied, as if she had just completed a virtuoso performance. She looked expectantly at him, a prima ballerina waiting for applause.

"There's no way I'm letting go of this bar in order to clap. It's just not going to happen," he explained, deciding that given his precarious position, anything other than complete frankness would be suicidal. "But you're right. No boy could fly like that. That was amazing."

"Amazing?"

A single golden eyebrow curved higher than its mate. Obviously, amazing wasn't doing it.

"Brilliant. Crazy. Superb."

Her eyebrows regained their symmetry.

"Yes," she said. "It was superb."

"Yes." He nodded, really hoping that she would take the compliment and put him back on the ground. He had a sudden horror-struck premonition of being left there, perched on the sharp end of this fantastically elongated egg shape as the night drew in and darkness covered the city. He knew if that happened, he would eventually fall asleep and slide off the curving edge and into death.

He saw with huge relief that she was smiling

triumphantly. She looked off into the west and pointed.

"There is a boy who lives over there, a babyish boy in a babyish park who thinks he too can fly. Should you ever see him, I would be eternally in your debt if you could repeat what you have just so kindly said. Especially the 'superb' bit. He is an odious crowing coxcomb of a boy. And he flies with all the grace of a thrown turnip."

"Thrown turnip. Gotcha," he said, clenching on his handhold like a very determined limpet. "Could we please go down now?"

"You want to go down so soon?" She stretched languidly, her hands back to back, fingers intertwining, reaching for the sky, her toes straining on point. "But you can see everything from here."

"I know," he said. "Except, I can't see Edie, and I can't see the Gunner, and frankly"—all the frustration of being snatched up and put down and snatched up again and flown all over the city boiled over and choked him—"frankly, I'm fed up with this all. I've got friends in trouble, and they need help and I need help to help them, because they're my responsibility, yeah? And all that happens is I seem to be being carried farther and farther away from any place I might find them. So please. Ariel. I have to do what has to be done, or I don't know, burst trying or something, but I have to do it. So the flying is tip-top, okay, but what I really need to know is: can you help me or not?"

He ran out of words and stared at her. She watched her fingers make a butterfly as they descended to her sides, and then she smiled at him.

"Of course," she said. "To help do what has to be done. That's why I came for you."

He didn't know what she meant.

"I'm sorry?"

"I'm not. I told you what I was." She flashed a grin.

"A spirit of the air?" he guessed.

"A minister of fate," she said with a gasp of exasperation. She tugged his ankle, and he lost his grip, and the whole falling thing happened again, only this time he was ready for her to catch him, which thankfully she did.

"There's an easier way to do this," he choked as they angled groundward in a shallow dive.

"Ah, but you don't get the easy way, do you, boy?" She laughed as they flew down and cut north up the street known as St. Mary Axe.

"You get the Hard Way."

The way she said it, the way she knew it suddenly, made his stomach drop faster than any of the flying had done, and then he heard a sound that made everything much worse.

Ahead of them, somewhere in the darkness ahead, he heard a single bell tolling as if for a funeral, deep and low and solemn. And he knew with absolute certainty that it was a warning bell, and that the warning was for him.

Chapter Eighteen

The Icarus Alone

The Icarus flapped its rigid wings and gave a series of short muted shrieks of agony as it flew over the office buildings that made up the Broadgate development.

It was screaming because it hated people, and the more of them it saw in one place, the worse it felt. It preferred the safety of its plinth, where it could stay hunched inside the contraption that attached it to its wings, and close its ears to the noise the people made as they walked past.

The reason it was shrieking was partly because it had accustomed itself to the habit and partly because the flying harness was so ungainly and heavy that being attached to it was like being permanently jammed in its own personalized torture chamber.

It found it hard to fly effectively because the wings it had been given were more like ragged and sawn-off windmill sails than anything designed for graceful passage through the air. This meant it could fly only short distances without exhaustion, and never got higher than about twenty feet off the ground. Whenever it had to overfly anything taller than that, it had to do it in a series of hops, using sinewy man's feet that had become accustomed to a new life as talons.

It was shrieking particularly intensely because the space it had tried to fly over was too ambitious, and it was going to have to land in the middle of the crowd of people leaving the office buildings; and its hatred of people was so intense that it had convinced itself, somewhere in the back of its mad mind, that the closer they came to him, the more it hurt.

It landed in front of the only group of unmoving office workers amid the flow—six black figures, frozen in time, tired and work-weary men and women who would never make it home, because they were cast from bronze.

The taint stood in front of them, protected by their tight immobile grouping from the other, real, office workers flowing past.

Six unmoving pairs of bronze eyes watched the taint panting and sobbing as it flinched from any contact with the people passing by.

The real reason the Icarus was mad was because it didn't know who or what it was—man, machine, animal, or bird. That's why it couldn't fly very well. That's why it walked like a bull on its hind legs. That's why it lived its life in a scream.

The only other creature who had ever been able to understand or soothe it was the Minotaur, because the Minotaur had been made by the same maker, and had the same mad split at its core.

The boy and the glint had killed the Minotaur. The Icarus would hunt them down, no matter how much the hunting hurt.

It took a great ragged breath and launched itself into the sky.

It would find them.

CHAPTER NINETEEN

Digging In

The Gunner's wrongness seemed to be getting worse. He felt tired beyond normal exhaustion, and his hands and limbs were beginning to not do what he wanted them to, as if the instructions coming down from his brain were subject to a game of Chinese Whispers and losing a lot of the detail in translation.

His hands had begun to feel as if their normally strong, agile fingers were wrapped in stiff new boxing gloves. His back ached, and he was fighting the overwhelming desire to find a piece of ground and just sit down for a bit. He knew this was a fatal impulse, because once he sat, he was pretty sure he wouldn't want to get up again. So he wiped his now-clumsy hands across the rough stone of the wall and confirmed to his satisfaction that there were no more heart stones left on it.

He grinned and hefted the oilskin bag that his groundsheet cape had become. It clinked satisfactorily.

He had two choices, he thought: he could drop the bag underwater, which would leave the Walker floundering around in the dark, trying to find the heart stones. The only trouble was that the tank floor was barely two meters below water at its deepest points, and a lot shallower over most of its area. Floundering around would eventually lead the Walker to trip over the package, and then when he opened it, he would have all the light he could want.

"Bury it," he grunted. "Smart arse didn't say I couldn't dig *downward*, did he?"

He stumbled up onto the gravel, moving by touch alone. He found the back wall and dropped to his knees. He put the bag of heart stones on the ground next to him and allowed himself the luxury of a cigarette.

The match scraped, and he ignited the end and sucked in the smoke. He pulled the pewter plate out of his jacket and looked at it in the light of the match as it burned down to his fingers.

"Dream of four castles, my Aunt Fanny—know what you are, my beauty?" he asked it as the match died and darkness swept back in from the edges of the tank.

"You are a bloody short-handled shovel."

He rolled the cigarette to one side of his mouth and chunked the plate into the pea gravel at his knees. He hoisted a plateful of stone to one side and dug in again, pleased to see that the injunction forbidding him to dig up was not preventing him digging in the opposite direction.

And as is often the way of it, once he was working he felt less tired. It was as if the physical labor took some of the worry out of him, and the rhythmic shoveling left less space for him to worry about the wrongness of things at his core.

He knew he had plenty to worry about, not least of which was the fact that he was running out of time. Turn o'day must be approaching up on the surface. And if his plinth was empty at midnight, he knew he was a goner. He didn't know how being a goner would work with the fact that he seemed to be under a curse. Perhaps it meant he'd be a walking dead statue, a sort of pair of dead hands, the same way taints were, only ever moving from the plinth to do the Walker or the Stone's bidding. The thought of becoming a taint in spit's clothing turned his gut, and he took it out on the gravel by digging faster and harder. Whatever happened, even if he kicked the bucket at midnight, he was going to bury the Walker's profane booty as deep as he could. He dug so hard that the pewter plate buckled in his hand. He put it aside and started digging with his hands alone.

And for the longest time in the darkness, the only sounds were the chunk and hiss of gravel being scooped out of a hole and tossed aside onto more gravel, and the quiet pop of a man working with both hands, a cigarette parked in the side of his face.

He wondered what George was doing right now.

CHAPTER TWENTY

Friar's Deal

"Where's the boy?"

The Black Friar glowered down at Edie.

"Gone."

"Gone? Gone how? Gone where?"

Something in the accusing way he asked gave the strong impression that whatever had happened was going to turn out to be Edie's fault.

"Just gone. Don't know how, don't know where." Her chin jutted forward as she refused to look away from his eyes.

"You don't know how, you don't know where. And now . . . you're here."

"Yep."

He exhaled, a long and noisy out breath whistled out of his nose like a safety valve taking the pressure off a steaming boiler.

IRONHAND

"Well. That's fine and dandy, no doubt. Capital, even. And I suppose you—"

"I thought you might know why."

He didn't look like someone who was used to people interrupting him so bluntly. He cleared his throat.

"You thought I might know why you're here?"

"Why George has gone."

The safety valve blew as the Friar detonated in a spluttering explosion.

"Why he's gone? You think I know why the boy has gone? Sunder me from my bones, girl! I assure you it's nothing to do with me! Why the very thought of—"

"I thought you might know if it's to do with the Hard Way."

The explosion stopped. The Friar ran his hand over his bald head and down to his chin. It was as if he were wiping off the look of shocked indignation and replacing it with one of genuine puzzlement.

"The Hard Way?"

"You said if he didn't put the dragon's head on the Stone, he'd be guaranteed the Hard Way. I wanted to know if suddenly disappearing was part of that."

The Friar stepped back. Looked less ominous. Scratched his head.

"You're saying he didn't put the head on the stone?"

"Yeah."

"Because he ran out of time? You surprise me, indeed you do. I saw the mark he bore, I sensed the power within,

I felt he would succeed." The monk looked genuinely puzzled. "Well, devil me kidneys . . . I'd have wagered on him finding the Stone Heart, indeed I would. I thought more of the boy."

Edie had a sudden flashback to George, his face set and determined as he held the pistol steady, aimed right into the Minotaur's eye. She remembered how he hadn't flinched, not even at the thunderous detonation when he'd pulled the trigger.

"He didn't run out of time. He found the Stone Heart. It was the London Stone. He worked it out. He followed the map of words you gave him. He did other stuff, too. He was a bit amazing. He just chose not to put the dragon's head on the Stone. He chose the Hard Way. And I want to know if that's why he disappeared."

"He chose the Hard Way? You're telling me he actually *chose* the Hard Way? Trophies and trumpetings, why would he do that? Unless . . ."

The Friar looked at Little Tragedy. Then at Edie. And then slowly took three steps back to the bar. He reached back over it and grabbed a Coke bottle. He popped the metal cap thoughtfully between his teeth and held the bottle out to her.

"Have a drink, in as much as this hellish soda water can be called a drink, then tell me everything, leave nothing out. We'll see what we can see and mayhap do what can be done."

Edie took the bottle and sat down on a stool and,

suddenly very conscious that the broken dragon's head was in the pocket of George's coat, only an inch from the Friar's elbow, started to talk.

She told him of everything that had happened since they'd left this room the night before, and ended on the Gunner being spirited into the mirrors by the Walker.

"And that's why I want to know about the mirrors. And that's why I want to know about the Hard Way. I have to find George, and we have to help the Gunner."

"And why is that?"

"Because it's the right thing to do," she answered, without thinking. And when she heard herself say it, she realized that that was exactly why, for her, it had to be done. Take a life, save a life.

Only then did she drink from the untouched bottle of Coke. The bubbles rose inside her; she burped thunderously and looked defiantly at the mountainous spit.

"And you have told me everything that happened?" he asked.

"Yes," she said, crossing fingers in her mind. "I've told you everything I saw."

Which was strictly true. They had left last time pretending that they had to go to fetch the broken dragon's head, not telling the Friar that it was with them, in George's coat pocket. And that brought her eye back to the same coat and the same heavy pocket lying on the bar top by the Friar's elbow. She looked away and hoped he hadn't noticed the weight inside it as he'd pushed it aside to reach over for her Coke.

"I didn't ask you if that was all you saw. I asked you if that was all that happened."

For a being made of bronze, his eye was disconcertingly steely.

"That was what happened."

"Still not quite what I was asking, but close enough for a glint, perhaps."

She heard Little Tragedy try to stifle a small snort of derision. He didn't do a very good job, and the sound irritated her more than she would have expected. Her head came up, eyes bright and defiant.

"I've got nothing to hide."

The Friar peered at her for a moment, and then his shoulders started to twitch, and the twitch turned into a quake, and the quake rumbled into a laugh, and soon the whole room was reverberating to the deep rolling mirth of the mountainous figure at the bar. He reached for a beer towel and dabbed at the tears streaming out of his eyes as he chuckled and chortled and generally did a very poor job of trying to control himself.

Being laughed at unexpectedly is never a very pleasant experience. Being laughed at by a ton and a half of bronze alloy in a cassock is even more annoying.

"Hoi," she said, trying to stem the tide. "What's so funny?"

"Sorry," gasped the Friar. "Intolerable rudeness, eternal

shame, gross lapse of hospi . . . hospitality. But a glint. Having nothing to hide? Why the thought of it. A glint is nothing but a veritable warehouse stuffed to the gunwales with hidden things. The hidden and the hiding are two sides of the same coin, as you know in the core of your young being, whether you acknowledge it or no. A glint absorbs the hidden in the world and must hide to survive in that world. Why if it were not so nearly a symmetry, it might be a paradox."

And he erupted into a fresh spasm of laughter, shoulders heaving and chins wobbling at the sheer hilarity of it all.

She had no idea what the avalanche of words meant. It felt as if he were using his booming voice to bludgeon her. She did understand what a paradox was, and it was a paradox that this smiling figure, who seemed all hospitality and good cheer, was in fact particularly frightening. It was as if he'd found a way to use all that bonhomie as a weapon. He was a million miles away from the smiler with the knife who'd pursued her on a distant beach in what seemed a different life, but there was something about all the mirth that seemed to suggest, if not a hidden knife, then a hidden agenda that might be just as fatal to her as a blade.

All the laughter and the good cheer had the effect of making it hard to think, and thinking was how Edie stayed ahead of things.

"Hey," she said. He kept on laughing.

Without thinking why she was doing it, she picked the bottle cap off the table in front of her, held it between thumb and forefinger, and flicked it at the Friar. Metal hit metal as the cap hit him square on the forehead with a distinct *tink* that chopped off the laughter like an ax. The bottle cap bounced up and off the sloping head, glinting in the headlights of a car passing outside the window, and the Friar's left hand snapped out and opened and closed in one astonishingly fast reaction from a man who was so mountainous and fat. He caught the cap and crushed it in one movement. Then the hand opened and gently dropped the mangled disk on the table in front of her.

"Oh-oh," said Little Tragedy behind her.

"Silence, You Imp!" boomed the Friar. He lunged forward, hoisted the knees of his cassock, and sat on the stool in front of Edie. The crushed bottle cap was still rocking on the small circular tabletop between them. Edie decided to be intimidated later. Right now she needed answers.

"The mirrors," she said. "I told you all that happened. Now you tell me about the mirrors, and then tell me about the Hard Way."

The Friar rubbed his chin with one hand, while the other drubbed out an irritated tattoo on the table. He stopped the finger tapping and looked off to one side at the mirrors.

"I'll make you a deal," he said shortly.

"A deal?"

"A deal. Something for you, something for me."

"What kind of something?" she asked, trying hard not to look at the coat on the bar top with its suspiciously bulging pocket.

"I want your word. I want your word that if the boy lives and you find him that you will bring him to me."

"You want George?"

"I want to talk to him. I want him to talk to me."

"And that's all?"

"And that's all."

She didn't need to think.

"Deal."

The Friar peered at her, peered so intently that she felt he was in fact peering into her, and then spat in his hand and held it out. She was unsure what to do. Little Tragedy cleared his throat from the shadows.

"Spit in your 'and, and shake 'is."

Her mouth, now she thought about it, was too dry to muster any extra spit. She worked it, trying to generate some moisture.

"It's more for the look of it than the actual spittle, my dear," said the monk.

So she dry-spat into her hand and let the big bronze hand close around it. She was surprised by how soft and warm the smooth metal was.

The Friar sat back with a smile.

And for an instant she wondered if she had just unwittingly betrayed George in some way.

Chapter Twenty-one

The Last Knight

George heard the bell tolling ahead of them, deep, regular, and doom-laden. They flew straight, as if locked on to the source of the noise like a homing beacon, shooting like a missile through the sheets of rain that were now gusting down with a vengeance.

Ahead of them, black metal railings and a spiked gate loomed between two worn stone gatehouses, barely larger than sentry boxes. Ariel flew over them and between two old colonnaded brick buildings that led into an inner courtyard complex beyond. The back end of the courtyards were modern glass-fronted office buildings, and as they flew in, George saw groups of umbrellas hurrying through the rain as workers headed through the downpour. There was so much water on the ground that George could see the rain-pocked reflection of Ariel, gold and bright against the lowering night sky beyond.

She swerved and landed so delicately that it wasn't

clear where flying ended and walking resumed, but it was clear that they'd arrived. The tolling of the bell was very loud against the white noise of rain. She pointed up to the side of one of the renovated warehouse buildings.

There was something red and boxy high on the wall above them, but because the rain was falling directly into his upturned eyes, it took George a couple of seconds to realize that it was the bell and its mounting. It must have been a fire bell at one time. Now it rang its relentless funeral note and sat there in the rain, red and slick as new blood.

He knew he wasn't going to like the answer to his next question, but he asked it anyway.

"What's that about? Why are we here?"

Ariel smiled brightly at him, spun on a toe in a single pirouette, and came back around without a hint of the smile or laughter in her eyes. "Send not to know for whom the bell tolls, boy, it tolls for thee."

"Okay," he said, very deliberately. He wasn't surprised, because he'd known the bell was for him from the first clang he'd heard, but he wasn't any clearer, either. "Why is it for me?"

She stretched a long arm out with a theatrical flourish and pointed over his shoulder. "It is a summoning bell. It is summoning you to meet the Last Knight."

He turned slowly. Forty feet away, on a raised patch of grass surrounded by a low box hedge was a full-size knight in armor sitting on a fierce-looking mount, carrying a long lance at the ready. The knight's helmet covered his face, except for a narrow slit in his visor. The horse wore a surcoat made of interlinked plates of metal set with round disks of blue glass in a Celtic wave pattern. They made a majestic pair, though there was something almost skeletal about the horse's head. George could see through the nostril. He could see through several bits of the horse, in fact, because it wasn't solid at all. It was hollow. And then George looked more closely and saw that the sculptor had made both the man and the horse out of plates of armor. The Knight was a hollow man. Which raised the question—a pointed question, given the sharpness of the lance in the Knight's right hand—of whether he was a spit or a taint.

"Ariel," said George quietly, "why is the bell summoning me, exactly?"

A fine shower fanned out in a flattened halo around her as she shook the water out of her hair before speaking. George noticed that there was something theatrical about everything she did.

"I told you, boy. You chose your own fate. You picked the Hard Way. That starts here."

George was pretty sure the Hard Way had begun when he was knocked into the sky by Spout, if not even earlier, when the Gunner had been taken from them. He didn't like the idea that that had just been a warm-up for something much worse.

"And who is the Last Knight?"

"He is the Last Knight of the Cnihtengild."

She pronounced the strange word *Ke-nik-ten-gild*.

"The what?"

"They are a guild of knights. Spelled the old-fashioned way. That writing explains it," she said, pointing behind him.

There was a plaque on the shallow wall beneath the hedge that surrounded the Knight.

George walked slowly forward, keeping an eye on the Knight and his charger as he went down on one knee in a rain-splashed puddle in front of the plaque and read:

KING EDGAR (943–975) GRANTED THIS DERELICT LAND TO THIRTEEN KNIGHTS, ON CONDITION THAT THEY EACH PERFORM THREE DUELS, ONE ON LAND, ONE BELOW LAND, AND ONE ON WATER. THESE FEATS HAVING BEEN ACHIEVED, THE KING GAVE THE KNIGHTS, OR CNIHTENGILD, CERTAIN RIGHTS . . .

He got no farther because the horse blew an irritated harrumph and stamped its hooves. George looked up to see that the Knight was leaning forward, the dark shadows of his eye slits pointed at him. And as George stared back at the Knight, the shadows lightened and he could see a pair of dim blue lights beginning to kindle where the eyes would have been. Before George could decide whether to straighten up and run away, or stay where he was, the Last Knight spoke. His voice was deep and sonorous, and shared the brassy harmonics of the bell tolling in the background, as if his voice were the bell put into words.

"Will you stand?"

It was a simple question. George could see no harm in it. He straightened up and wiped the rain from his face. "Yes. Hello."

"And will you stand?" repeated the Knight.

George looked down at himself then back at the blue eye-lights staring out from within the blank helmet. The horse pulled against its reins and pawed the ground with a great metal hoof.

"Here I am. Standing," he answered, a little puzzled. The Knight pulled at the horse's bridle, which made it snort and stop pawing.

"And then will you stand?"

The repetition was getting strange. Or maybe just annoying. Or perhaps the Knight couldn't see very well out of the narrow slits in his armor.

"Yes. I'll stand. I am standing. I do stand. As you see." He spoke slowly, with exaggerated politeness, so as not to cause offense. "You've asked me that three times already."

The horseman's neck straightened, and his mount snickered through its curling nose holes.

"And you have accepted three times, good knight."

George decided the statue was a bit mad. As far as he knew, there was no reason why statues shouldn't be as mad as anyone else. He hadn't accepted anything once, let alone three times. He decided it was time to try much harder to get back to Edie.

"Yes. Well. Good night to you, too," he said, and turned away.

Clang! The toll of the bell was augmented by a simultaneous roar and clash of arms.

The sound hit him like a physical blow. It was so loud he saw rainwater bounce up out of the puddles around him. It was a shout of approval, and it came from many more throats than just the Last Knight. It was the sound of a great host shouting and hitting their shields with swords or lances. And in a flash of something like lightning or a sheet of flame, George saw the Guild gathered around him in a living frame, like ghostly projections on the rain. But these were no brightly colored fairy-tale knights from a child's book. These were grim combat-worn figures clinging to their saddle horns with the last of their strength. Their armor and chain mail wasn't shiny but hacked up and skeined with blood. Their sword edges were nicked and dinged, and their shields bore so many gouges that it was hard to make out the heraldic designs that had once been painted on them. Those that carried their helmets had faces grizzled with stubble, and dark, shadowed eyes stained with battle weariness. Several of the faces were bruised and bloodied, and many of them sat awkwardly on their mounts, shoulders dropped or curled over the pain of wounds George couldn't see. To complete the sense that they had all just paused in a battle, breath panted out of their mouths and the nostrils of their horses, pluming in the cold. They held drawn weapons in their hands.

George saw all of this in a flash, and when it was gone, the modern buildings reasserted themselves and he was staring at Ariel, still with his back to the Knight. One thing that had changed, however, was that there seemed to be hundreds of bright blue lights radiating out from behind him, making a starburst on the surrounding walls of the courtyard, like an intense disco ball.

"He meant 'good knight' with a K," said Ariel.

There was another flash, timed with the tolling of the bell, and he saw the other knights, the Guild, moving slowly in.

"Okeydokey," George said slowly, really not wanting to turn around and see where all those blue lights were coming from. "And what does that mean, exactly?"

"It means he's honoring you as a fellow knight, for accepting the challenges. It's chivalry."

"Er, no. It's rubbish," he hissed desperately. "I didn't accept any bloody challenges, let alone three!"

"Yes, you did, boy. You agreed to stand. You agreed three times."

"But I didn't know what he was saying! I thought he couldn't hear me or something. I thought that was why he was repeating himself"—he lowered his voice—"I thought he might be a bit deaf. Or mad . . ."

Clang! The bell tolled and there was another intense flash and the sound of a host shouting, and George saw the Guild again. They were moving in, making two long lines on either side of him.

"Good luck, boy," Ariel said, and walked backward away from him.

"What am I meant to do?" he hissed.

"Stand and fight. Three duels, three trials of strength, none to be fought on the same ground as any other. You must fight on the earth, under the earth, and on the water. You read the plaque. That is the way of the Guild."

"But why must I fight?"

"Because in choosing the Hard Way, you chose to remain. Now you must prove you are worthy."

"And if I don't?"

Another toll of the bell, and this time a flash with no shout, just the vision of the knights. This carried on every time the bell rang. It was like seeing the knights in a very slow strobe, a tempo dialed down to the funeral toll of the bell.

"Then you will not remain. Here or in any unLondon. This world will have seen the last of you."

She pushed up his sleeve and tapped the metal flaw twining out from the maker's mark.

"Each of these flaws will start to move toward your heart when you begin a duel. They do this to make you finish each contest; for if you run away, the flaw will continue up your arm and pierce your heart. So do not run from any of the duels. You must stand and prove yourself. Only in that way will you show what you are made of."

Desperation was making George's breath come faster. He clenched his fists and clasped at a last straw as he heard the horse behind him nicker and shake its bridle chain.

"But I can't fight. I don't have a weapon!"

Ariel smiled a sad smile of farewell and pointed behind him. "Then pray that your wits are sharper than his lance, boy, because here it comes."

He turned, and in the next flash saw that the Cnihtengild had hemmed him into a narrow jousting space that bristled with weapons and fierce-looking faces. And more than that, at the other end of the gauntlet he saw the source of all those lights. It was the Knight and his charger.

The blue glass disks that were interlinked in the horse's surcoat had each lit up, lancing blue light in all directions as the knight spurred the charger slowly forward off the dais. The lights bounced and waved hypnotically on the surrounding walls and windows, mirroring the sinuous rippling of the surcoat as the great horse stepped daintily over the low hedge, one hoof after the other, clopping onto the wet stone floor of the courtyard.

The Knight was shrugging his shoulders and rolling his head on his neck, like a boxer loosening up before a fight. He looked every bit as murderous and businesslike as the rest of the Guild in the flashes that George saw every time the bell tolled.

He moved back, roughly along the alley made by the now-visible, now-invisible knights. He wondered if they were actually there all the time, or only there when the flashes happened. He stepped sideways, planning to run into the low brick colonnades, where the Knight would be too tall to follow him easily. He could at least grab one of the metal chairs to use as a weapon.

Something hard, like the flat of a sword, smacked his head and made it ring, but not before he heard the jingle of a harness close by his ear, and the word *"COWARD"* hissed at him.

He held his ears and stumbled back across the now-obviously-more-than-imaginary jousting round. He must have staggered too far, because something big and flat and hard like a shield batted into his face and sent him sprawling back into the center of the narrow space.

And being hit in the nose was perhaps the thing that saved him. Being hit in the nose hurts a lot, but it also spikes adrenaline and makes you very angry, instantly. George got very angry very quickly, and a treacly black feeling surged up into his throat. He wiped his hand across his nose and wasn't surprised to see a thin streak of blood on it. He remembered the Gunner, just after he'd first saved George, way back at the beginning of their nightmare journey, when he'd looked down at him and said: "You're angry. Sometimes angry gets things done. This isn't one of those times. . . ."

But he also remembered the way the Gunner had channeled his fury when fighting the Minotaur. That had been one of those times when angry did get things done. This, he knew, was the same kind of time.

"Okay," he said to himself. "Fine."

And even though he was soaking wet and there was no point to it other than show, he turned, rolled up his sleeves, and set his legs a shoulder's width apart. The Gunner may have been physically absent, perhaps lost forever, but there was definitely something of him in the way George planted his feet and held his ground.

He spat into the puddle and faced the Knight at the other end of the courtyard.

"FINE," he shouted. "Do your worst."

There was a flash, and in it, George saw the Guild, again looking as if they were somehow both projected onto and made out of the pelting rain itself; and they were all looking at him.

They just didn't look like a happy band of knights in armor who were devoted to courtly poetry and rescuing damsels in distress, or slaying picturesque dragons.

They looked like a nasty, hard-nosed bunch of medieval muggers.

"Anyone going to lend me a shield or something?" George asked.

In another flash he saw no one moving. It just made him angrier.

"Good. Nice chivalry. To hell with you all anyway."

He felt the scar on his hand twinge badly, and he knew without looking that what Ariel had described had started. The metal flaw had jagged up his arm and was heading for his heart. He looked at this hand and held the maker's mark out for the Guild to see. Then he showed it to the Knight.

"I don't know what this means, but I am a maker. You might not want me to get my hands on you."

He was of course bluffing, but bluff was all he had going for him.

The Knight stopped and cocked his helmet. "Show me the hand."

George's spirits rose. Maybe the bluff was going to work; though he had no idea why it would. He held his hand up. "A dragon did this . . ." he began, hoping the extra detail might impress someone.

"You carry the mark," boomed the Knight.

"Yes I do," said George quickly. "I do carry it."

"The mark of the Ironhand," continued the Knight.

The bell tolled in the next flash of light, and in it George saw the Cnihtengild craning forward in their saddles for a closer look. He felt he was getting somewhere.

"Yes," he said, trying to sound as if he had a clue

what he was saying. "Yes. That's right. Um . . . I am the Ironhand."

Here was a pause. Nothing moved but the rain.

"No," said the Knight. "*An* Ironhand. There have been many. You have the mark that says you may be one. Only time, your ordeals, and how you face them will tell."

"But an Ironhand's a good thing, right?" said George, trying to catch up.

"It is."

"So . . ." George said hesitantly, realizing he should negotiate the next bit very carefully, because he might be at a very important junction where the right reply would send him down a road where he wouldn't need to fight the big statue with the even bigger pointy lance; whereas the other road would end with his being neatly—or probably not so neatly—kebabed.

"So," he continued, "so you're good. And I'm good. So me being an Ironhand, sorry—a maybe Ironhand— means what? That we don't have to fight, yes? I mean, it makes a difference, right?"

He injected an eager note into the last question, as if he were stating the obvious.

And then his heart suddenly bucked and soared as he saw the Knight slowly nod his great helmet. He made a doubly imposing figure sitting on a horse at the center of a moon-burst of blue lights radiating out from the horse's chain-mailed caparison. George forgot to breathe, waiting for the Knight to add words to his silent affirmation.

"Yes. It makes a difference."

"Great!" George exploded in noisy relief. "That's great. Just great. Brilliant—"

The Knight lowered his lance and aimed it right at George's chest. "It means you are a worthy adversary. Now."

George froze in horror. That "now" definitively pricked the bubble of his newly inflated hope.

"Now?"

"Now—à outrance!—Have at you!"

The Knight jagged his spurs into the horse's side, and the horse bunched its muscles and leaped forward. There was another shout and clash of arms, and a flame freeze-framed the Cnihtengild hemming George in, and all he could see was nowhere to run and the sharpened lance point barreling in toward him like an express train through the rain.

CHAPTER TWENTY-TWO

Black News

The Walker paced back and forth on the corner of Bury Street and St. James's Court. His hands were clasped behind his back, and as he walked, his head was cricked to one side, watching himself.

He was looking at his reflection in the highly polished black granite stone adorning the corner of the building.

The edge of the building had been sculpted so that a stylized steamship appeared to be plowing its way out of the corner and into the street. The Walker let his hand trail over the frozen bow wave the boat was making—a V of tight stone curls peeling off the facade like black wood shavings.

The Raven sat patiently, watching him from its perch on the bowsprit of the boat, the only thing blacker than the granite around it, apart from its eyes. The eyes flickered, and then the Raven hopped on to the Walker's shoulders.

"The eyes of Tallyman have seen something?" hissed the Walker.

The bird clacked its beak in the Walker's ear.

The Walker listened and then nodded. "Puddle Dock, they say?"

He turned on his heel and walked back in the other direction.

"A glint walking down Puddle Dock, seeking succor or knowledge would likely be on her way to see a friar. A Black Friar."

The Walker ran his hands over the black mirrored surface, as if testing it. Then he turned away with a snap.

"Black is a lucky color. Tell the Tallyman where she is bound. Now that she is found, it would pain me to have her lost again."

CHAPTER TWENTY-THREE

A Wilderness of Mirrors

Edie thought for a moment about the fact that she might just have betrayed George. It was a short thought, but a sharp one.

Then the Friar was talking and she was listening, and what he told her quickly pushed the uncomfortable thought to the back of her mind, into a place from which she could unpack it later.

"The mirrors are gateways. Not all mirrors, just mirrors that are set up parallel with each other. They work in two ways: firstly, by stepping into a mirror, a being may move himself from where he is to another place within the city, so long as there are parallel mirrors set up in them."

"That's wild," said Edie, despite herself.

"Oh, it's much more than wild, I assure you. It's much more than a mere 'transporter.' It's very powerful, and it's very, very dangerous. . . ."

"Why?"

The Friar stood up, the swiftness of his movements making Edie flinch. But he was only gesturing for her to take a position in the archway.

"Stand there. Between the mirrors. Do not touch them, because now that you know what they can do, they may be open to you. But look."

She saw the images of herself and the dimly lit bar multiplying away into the distance.

"You think you are seeing reflections of yourself, again and again. But you are not. You are seeing moments in time. Even a single reflection in a mirror is never yourself in the present, because it takes a thin slice of a microsecond for the light carrying the image to bounce off the mirror and back to your eye. A face in the mirror is always a face in the past, by that tiny fraction. And because of that, we never see ourselves as we are, only as we were—"

He smiled at her.

"Look at the images of your face, repeating off to infinity. Each separate image looks the same, but that's only because the images you can see clearly are the ones where the differences are so minimal as to be beyond detection. Travel farther through the layers and you travel deeper into the past."

Edie looked into the mirrors, trying to see where the differences began. She couldn't. But she felt uncomfortable, as if the mirrors were gazing back at her, somehow.

"How does it work?" she said, looking away.

"The 'how' of it doesn't matter. It's just something that *is*, the same way the sky or a sparrow just is. It's like that, and it's always been like that. London is a place of power, and it was a place of power before people built the first shelter here. It was a place of power before people built stockades or roundhouses or temples or huts on it; why, it was a place of power before the thought of temples had even occurred to man. It was a place of power when the wide arch of the sky was temple enough for all. Look along the river; look at the Tower of London. Ancient? It's a Johnny-come-lately. It was a Christian church, and before that a Roman temple, and before that a shrine to a Celtic crow god, and before that a god with horns on his head, and before that only the Raven himself remembers. All pasts are all still there, layered under the skin."

His eyes were shining. He ducked through the arch next to her.

She turned, uncomfortable in the thought that he might be trying to get behind her in the dark. "So the mirrors not only transport you through space. They can also move you through time, into past Londons."

"You're quick, little girl."

"I'm not a little girl. I'm a glint. I know all about the past."

"And of course it holds no terrors for you."

Edie rolled her eyes and blew her cheeks out at him in impatience. "It holds plenty of terrors for me. Don't be stupid. The past's not a nice place, is it? I'm just saying I understand about being able to go to the past because it's sort of what I do. I can get my head 'round that."

The Friar's face broke into an anticipatory grin, eyes flashing theatrically at Edie. "You don't seem impressed, child."

She shrugged. "Not really. I got enough trouble coping with this particular present. I don't need more."

"You don't *need* more?"

The more outrage he showed at her lack of response, the less she wanted to appear impressed by the vista of possibilities he was opening up.

"Nah. Sorry. I just can't really do the past layers of London thing. I mean, I hear what you're saying, but it's all a bit . . . crap."

She hadn't meant to say crap. She'd meant to say weird. Or maybe scary. But her mouth had taken control before her brain could hit the anchors, and she'd said it. The Friar looked shocked.

"A bit . . . *crap?*"

"Yes," she replied. She supposed she meant it, having said it, and all.

"You think different realities, layered pasts are a bit . . . *crap?*"

"Yeah." She just wasn't going to be bullied. "Yeah. No offense, but it's the sort of thing saddoes talk about when they've bonged a bit much or got all boozed up and out of it, you know what I mean? All that magic mushroom mumbo jumbo they think makes sense of what's going on in their messed-up heads, stuff like all the molecules in their fingernails being galaxies with little worlds spinning 'round them and all . . ."

As someone who had spent most of her life trying *not* to see strange and frightening things every time she accidentally touched something, Edie had strong views on people who voluntarily monkeyed with their heads in order to *think* they saw strange things. As someone who'd slept rough in the city and been in and out of more hostels than a young girl should have, she also had come across people who went to extreme lengths to get out of their heads, usually for the entirely understandable reason that they couldn't get off the streets and out of the cold.

The Friar rose to a height that seemed at least half a foot higher than normal. "Saddoes? You think this is something for *saddoes*?"

He spat the word, hissing the S's on each end in disgust.

Once again, she decided not to show she was intimidated by him. "Well. It all sounds a bit . . . crap, doesn't it?"

"What it sounds like to your young ears is something I have no control over, glint. What it is—" And here he raised his hands over his head and did something to the checkered circular mosaic in the ceiling. It looked as though he had moved two of the rings in different directions. "—What it is, I can show you."

There was a crump and crunch, and somehow, the world jerked a bit and felt suddenly a lot darker and more serious. And the Friar looked less like a monk and more like a demon, as shadows danced across his face, lit from below. The main reason he looked like a demon was because the light that was casting these sinister shadows across his face was red and dancing like flames, and there had—a moment ago—been no flames in the room. Edie turned to see where the fire was coming from and only got halfway to looking behind her, because she felt a great heat blast sear the side of her face. Her eyes stopped as they swung past the mirror to her right, the mirror that had contained the endlessly repeating reflections of herself, and now contained a blast furnace vision of hell and falling walls and screaming people.

The shock of it made her leap back—and for an instant she felt the cool glass of the other mirror behind her. And she heard the Friar yell, "NO! STAY AWAY FROM THE MIRROR!"

The cool hard glass at her back gave way as gently as a soap bubble popping. The world lurched as Edie started to fall through into a howling firestorm, and a blast lashed her face. Something grabbed her foot, and that's when things really started to go wrong.

CHAPTER TWENTY-FOUR

The Stroke Dolorous

The Last Knight barreled through the rain, his lance aimed unwaveringly at George's heart. George backed up until he felt a wall behind him, and then he ducked and rolled sideways.

He knew the invisible knights had him hemmed in; he had the throbbing nose to prove how hard it would be to try to barge through their cordon. It was a thick impenetrable wall of horse's bodies and shields and men with weapons. But he also noticed when the knights became visible at the next flash and toll of the bell that lower down, under the horse's bellies, there was plenty of space to escape at ground level.

So that's what he aimed for as he ducked and rolled for safety, hoping he wouldn't find a hoof in the way. As it happened, a hoof found him and gave him a glancing blow on his shoulder, but apart from that, his plan worked pretty well. As he rolled, the bell tolled in another flash, and he saw the belly of the horse above him. He hauled up onto his feet and sprinted across the courtyard to the relative shelter of the low brick colonnade.

He heard a roar of disapproval from the Cnihtengild, heard someone clearly shout "CRAVEN!" and turned in time to see the Knight hurriedly raise his lance to the sky and try to apply the brakes by leaning back and hauling on the reins. The charger's head came back, and its hooves locked into a slide. He could see why the Knight had raised the lance; because if he hadn't, he would have definitely speared himself a nice big office building.

George ducked sideways and flattened himself against the inside of a pillar and held his breath. In front of him was the plate-glass wall of a coffee shop. The shop was closed, but a girl was stacking chairs and wiping table-tops. She looked up, and George was sure she saw him, so sure that he was about to shout for help, when he heard a horse's hoof slowly clopping closer. He saw in the reflection in the plate-glass window the lights on the war horse's surcoat as it stepped slowly into the arch behind him.

He saw the Knight try to bend his head low enough to get into the colonnade, but there wasn't enough headroom. He looked down and saw the lance jabbing in beside him, tapping his leg.

And that's when he remembered that if he could see the Knight in the reflection of the coffee shop window, then the Knight could see him right back.

"You must fight," said the Knight. "You must come

out and fight, or you must forfeit as a craven varlet." His voice echoed ominously in the low-roofed space.

"I am fighting," said George. "I just don't have a weapon!"

A twinge of pain in the scar made him look down at his hand. He remembered how it had cut through the tentacled arm of the earth creature that had grabbed him in the underpass the day before. He remembered how the Temple Bar dragon had looked at his hand in a kind of wonder. He remembered making the bullet that had killed the Minotaur. He remembered the Gunner's look of awe as he had told him he was a maker.

And then he looked down at the lance that was tapping him on the leg. Somehow the tapping was too ignominious to bear. The Knight was cajoling him to fight as if he were a toddler having to be coaxed out of a hiding place in a playhouse.

He thought of the power in his hands. He thought of how he had just been called Ironhand.

And then he moved. His hand flashed down and grabbed the lance, about one foot six inches from the tip. He knew what he would do, and he tried to focus his mind in order to do it. He was going to snap the lance and then he would have a pointed weapon of his own, and the lance would be blunted. This would be a good thing on many levels, not the least because he was pretty sure the sculptor who had made the Knight had decided not to equip him with a sword.

It was an act of desperation, but somehow George knew from the pulsing pain in his scar that it would work.

His hand closed around the shaft of the lance and he tried to put every ounce of strength and will into it. At the very least he would bend the thing and render it useless.

It was a good plan, and he *did* put everything into it. He put so much willpower into squeezing and tugging at the lance that when it neither snapped nor bent, he remained clenched on to it for too long, and when the Knight kicked his horse so that it sprang backward, George was dragged out into the open, like a terrier refusing to loosen its grip on a particularly enjoyable stick.

As he was dragged out, he suddenly had a horrible vision of what his hand would look like if he slid down the lance and the blade sliced it open.

Without thinking, he flinched.

He flinched because he let the fear in.

And as he flinched, the Knight flicked his arm and the lance sideways and sent him skimming across the rain-slick courtyard floor as effortlessly as a man twitching a fishing rod.

George spun to his feet and looked for the next place to run.

The bell tolled, and he saw the Guild advancing behind him in a solid and ominous wall of armor and general-purpose grimness.

"You must stand. You cannot run. You must fight. Refuse to fight and you forfeit," bellowed the Knight.

"I am fighting," shouted George. "You've got a bloody horse and a weapon. All I've *got* is running!"

However, he was in a dead end. So he stood his ground, because when there's nowhere to run, and all the talking hasn't worked, that's almost all you can do.

And when the Knight pricked his horse forward and lowered his lance, George did the one other thing he hoped the Knight wasn't expecting: he ran toward him.

He didn't plan it, but it came to him as he was already kicking into a sprint. His dad in the park, a rugby ball, cold winter afternoons. And the words: "The trick is to zig when they expect you to zag."

The stutter step. The key to wrong-footing the tackler on the other team. His dad had spent hours trying to help him get the hang of it. Do it right, and a hefty opponent closing in on you at speed wouldn't have enough room or mobility to change his direction in time to catch you. It was the perfect tactic.

The only problem, he remembered five steps into the run, was that he'd never really been that good at rugby and was particularly crap at selling the stutter step. Often he just tripped up and tackled himself.

He erased the thought and focused on the tiny circle at the end of the lance as it sped toward him. When it was two paces away, he jinked left but went right, and the lance tip tried to follow him, and whiffled past his ear as he ducked and dug in, his left shoulder grazing along the side of the horse's chain mail as they passed.

He reached the safety of another colonnade and looked back to see the big horse outlined by the office building beyond, trying to one-eighty at speed; sparks flew from its hooves as its skid sent up a huge backlit wall of spray.

George didn't wait to see them get their balance again. The bell tolled, and he saw in the accompanying flash that the Guild were arranging themselves in another long line, cutting off his most obvious route of escape. But he also saw, at the end of their gauntlet, not a blank wall but the sentry-box-style gatehouses he'd flown in over with the golden girl. And beyond the gatehouses, the traffic and lights of the city beckoned.

He didn't think twice, just clenched his fists, ducked his head, and ran his heart out, tearing past the sporadically visible walls of knights. He had to get there before one of them positioned himself at the end of the line and cut off what he was pretty sure was his last chance of escape.

He ran so fast that his heart bounced alarmingly hard against the inside of his rib cage; but he saw that he'd made it.

None of the Guild was going to be able to block his exit. He didn't let up on his speed. He wasn't going to slow down until he'd put a lot of ground between the Knight and him. Or until he threw up or had a heart attack or something. He felt the jag of elation as he closed in on the open gate. Two paces out, he allowed himself to look back.

This meant he was facing the wrong way when the gate slammed shut.

He hit it in a pile-driving shoulder charge. He hit it so fast and so unexpectedly that the impact was somehow dulled with shock. He saw stars, bright tiny stars that whirled around in front of his eyes. It didn't really hurt so much as take all the breath and hope out of him in one bone-crunching impact. Except no bones crunched. The only thing that broke was his spirit.

He opened his mouth to say, "What?" but didn't have the breath to voice the word. He turned and saw a flash of gold beyond the tightly arranged black bars of the gate.

He couldn't believe it.

"Ariel?"

Her slender arm serpentined through the bars, and her hand found his upper arm. She squeezed it gently.

"You cannot run. You cannot refuse the duel."

He shook his head in disbelief, trying to shake some of the stars out of it.

"You closed the gate? *You?*"

She squeezed his arm again. Given the fact that he saw in the next flash of flame that the Knight was now aimed at him from the other end of the two long ranks of the Guild, it didn't give him the comfort he imagined she'd intended it to impart.

"Open the gate!"

She shook her beautiful golden head sadly. He was sure he heard real regret in the catch of her voice. Which made what happened next almost worse.

"I cannot, boy."

The Knight lowered his lance for the third time and kicked the horse forward. Its hooves danced through the puddles, sending up great sheets of spray as it bore down on George.

"Okay fine," he said desperately. "Let go of my arm and I'll climb over."

"I cannot do that, either." Her hand clenched around his upper arm like a manacle and pinned him to the gate.

"But why?" he shouted, heart freezing at the sight of the inbound knight.

"Because I am a minister of fate." The new note in her voice was as hard as a diamond and cold as ice. "And no one, absolutely no one, cheats fate, boy."

She spat that last "boy" as if she were getting something really disgusting out of her mouth. And no matter how hard he struggled, he couldn't break her iron-hard grip as it pinned him to the metal gate like an unmissable target.

Clang! The bell tolled its final note, and in the flash, George saw the Guild rise in their stirrups and shake their weapons at the sky, in celebration of his death, and the fatal lance tip sped in toward his heart—three meters, two meters, one meter—Game Over.

He reflexively jerked his head away. He actually sensed the wings of Death flying in to gather him as he closed his eyes and felt a tremendous impact. Something felt horribly wrong, and he heard his scream of pain as if it were already coming from outside him. He felt himself leave the earth in one brutal savage jerk, and his head seemed to explode. Then his spirit soared into the sky, and he opened his eyes, knowing he would see himself being drawn into the light. . . .

Instead he saw Spout looking down at him with his implacable stone eyes as he flapped into the night sky.

"Gack?" the gargoyle inquired drily and tightened its grip on George's chest. It swayed into another lopsided wing beat, circling north.

George looked down, still half expecting this to be an out-of-body experience, still imagining he was going to look down on his impaled body.

What he saw instead was the Knight and the horse and the lance thrust through the gate, up to the hilt. He also saw that the figure writhing on the end of the weapon was the source of the screaming—not him. Her golden shape was the last thing George saw before his eyes fluttered shut and unconsciousness swept in and anaesthetized him.

CHAPTER TWENTY-FIVE

Tyburn's Last Victim

In the darkness, in the cold, in the absence of hope, the Gunner dug on.

The scoop and scatter noise had been joined by a new sound, which was a hollow splash as he dug in. The Gunner had dug down into the gravel, below the level of the surrounding water in the tank. He was so deep that he had one leg inside the hole and was bending and stretching as he dug, waist-deep in a gravel-ringed pool of his own excavating.

The tiredness that he was now feeling was a real tiredness, the tiredness of hard work, not the wrong feeling that had been churning inside him in the absence of any distractions. It occurred to him that if he'd put all this effort into trying to dig upward, he might have reached a surface by now. Then again, he might not have. The roof was stone, and shifting a stone to start digging might have ended everything before he'd even begun.

"Could have brought the house down," he said aloud. The sudden sound of his own voice in the echoing chamber made him pause. He became even stiller as he felt something move around his ankles. It was the water in the pond.

There was the ghost of a current, barely there, but definitely there.

The Gunner didn't know it, but the current he was feeling was the pull of the Tyburn, one of the lost rivers of London, the one that gave its name to the place where London's criminals used to be hanged. And now it was exerting its dark pull at the Gunner's ankles. He didn't know that, any more than he knew that he was standing in a lost medieval water tank below Marylebone. All he knew was that moving water meant a stream, a stream meant a channel for it to flow down, and a channel might, just might, mean a way out of this rat hole.

If he'd been of a reflective bent, he would have said, like most soldiers, that the ideal way to die was at home in bed, surrounded by great-grandchildren. But since that wasn't an option, he thought he might as well die trying not to.

He doubled his efforts, and as he bent and shoveled, the urgency of his movements tipped his tin hat into the water in a great splash. It took him a moment to realize what had happened and to retrieve the helmet. And when he did, the obvious hit him.

"Must be getting stupid," he muttered, and started digging with the hat. Now he really was making progress.

The hole deepened, and he was even able to feel the top of a low arch in the wall beginning to appear. As he dug, he wondered why the hole had been blocked up. It's the nature of an underground stream, if blocked, to silt up with the debris it washes down, and this was how the bank of gravel in the tank had been created.

But something had blocked the exit pipe from the tank, and as the Gunner's hat suddenly skidded sideways instead of digging in, he found the reason. He put his hat aside and reached down. His first thought was that it was a tree root. Then it came away in his hand, and he felt it. He had a sudden horrible feeling he knew what it was. He reached into the water and found more pieces. And then his hand tangled in hair.

He carefully disentangled it and shook his hands dry before lighting one of his precious matches.

Although the flame reflected off the surface of the pool, he could see enough to be sure: staring back at him were the two wide-eyed sockets in the skull of a woman. He could tell it was a woman because there was a long hank of dark hair hanging off one side of the skull, and there was a gold ring glinting on a finger bone next to a small bundle. He reached in and moved the bundle and then he realized it wasn't a woman's skeleton at all, because another face smiled back at him. It was a crude face, carved out of some kind of stone, but it was unmistakably a doll's face.

The dead woman was no woman, but a little girl.

He knew without needing to be told that the girl was a glint, and that she was one of the Walker's victims, possibly even his first.

The little bone hand clasped around the smiling doll's face did something to the Gunner. It filled him with a murderous blackness, as dark as the chamber as the match guttered out.

"Right, you bastard. Fate or no fate, I ain't bloody dying tonight. I'm coming after you."

He lit another match and looked into the small skeleton's eyes. He didn't see anything gruesome in the bones and fragments of flesh and clothing that remained. He saw a little girl who had died clutching her doll for a comfort that never came. He imagined the sobs that had filled this stone chamber before she went quiet. His jaw clenched tight.

A statue can't cry, of course. Everyone knows that. It must have just been water from the splashing as he dug that rolled off the upper curve of his cheek and plopped into the Tyburn below. He reached gently into the water and began to move the bones, laying them softly on the gravel bank in as close to the right order as he could. Despite the growing clumsiness in his hands, he managed most of the time to be as delicate as a father putting his child to bed.

"Sorry, love. I got to move you. But it's only so as I can have him. And I WILL have him, straight up. I'll swing for him wherever he is."

CHAPTER TWENTY-SIX

Black Mirror

The King's Library sits off to the west side of the great circular courtyard of the British Museum. It's a long, elegant room, and the mixed collection of curios on display come from all ages and regions of the world.

There are delicate fossils and brutal Maori war clubs, exquisite alabaster vases as high as a man, and slender Native American spears tipped with meteorite blades. There are Greek sculptures and busts of the great men who had assembled the collections. There are ancient manuscripts and gold jewelry, savage flint axes, rude Roman wind chimes, and all manner of obscure religious relics and paraphernalia.

To most people, this looks like a charming hodge-podge of collectable objects from the Age of Enlightenment; only a very few people know that there are things in this compendium of seemingly mismatched objects that are there because they keep each other in check: things of power, dark things and light things canceling each other out by the careful way they are arranged around one another.

The lights were off and the museum was silent.

Then there was a very distinct popping noise, and the Walker stepped out of one of his small mirrors. He reassembled them, snapping them together, face-to-face, and slipped the disk into the pocket of his coat. He stood in front of a tall, free-standing display case and feasted his eyes on its contents. He pushed back the hood of the green sweatshirt he wore beneath his flapping overcoat, releasing the Raven that had been traveling with him. He leaned forward, both hands on the glass of the cabinet as he stared at the contents.

The Raven stretched its wings and flapped across the width of the room, finding a perch on the railing of the walkway that ran around the bookcases at first-floor level. It fixed its unreadable black eye on the Walker and the glass case he was engrossed in.

The contents were as follows: three big wax disks of different sizes—two small, one big, all thick as cheeses, decorated with magical symbols like pentacles and forgotten names of great significance. There was a "shew stone," or small crystal ball, not much bigger than a golf ball. There was a thin gold disk engraved with the same concentric circles and simple turrets that had been scratched into the surface of the pewter plate in the underground water tank; and perhaps strangest of all, there was a black stone mirror. The other objects looked just like the kind of occult paraphernalia anyone would expect to see in a magician's lair. The stone mirror was a different thing altogether. Its lines were so simple and unadorned that it looked timeless, simultaneously modern and irretrievably ancient. Carved and polished from flawless black obsidian, the label described it as being of Aztec origin.

"Aztec," the Walker snorted and spat derisively. Spittle dribbled down the sheer wall of glass between him and the offending label. "Collectors with the brains of pygmy shrews."

He knew this black mirror had been old long before the Aztecs in Central America had developed their strong taste for human sacrifice. It was into the highly polished face of the stone, which looked like a hand mirror with a handle and a hole for a long-perished thong, that the Walker stared so intently.

"Birds and butterflies. Imagine that . . ."

He looked up at the bird as he pushed up the right-hand sleeve of his coat.

"The Aztecs sacrificed them in the hundreds of thousands to their god Quetzalcoatl. Hummingbirds rather than ravens, mainly, so you, my friend, would have been fine. But I should liked to have seen that. It takes a particularly exquisite sensibility to think of sacrificing a butterfly. . . ."

The Raven, for whom the insect world was essentially

an all-day buffet, didn't think killing butterflies was especially unusual, but it kept its beak shut. The truth is, the Walker liked to talk, and the Raven was doomed to listen.

The Walker reached out and splayed his hands against the glass, opposite the circular crystal ball. He closed his eyes, spread his hand as if measuring it, and committed the size to his memory. Then he peered into the dark glassy surface again.

"The mirror is no use alone. Without its twin, it's little more than polished rock."

He smiled darkly up at the Raven. "An ordinary pair of glass mirrors will open a portal to wherever in this world you wish to go, anywhere in space or time, if you have the knack. But compared to what a stone mirror can do, that is a mere parlor trick for mewling infants. A pair of stone mirrors can open a portal into another world entirely. And from that dark world, a cunning man may bring and harness powers the likes of which this world has never seen."

If the Raven was impressed, it chose a strange way to show it, as it squittered a prodigious bird's mess onto the bald marble head of the eighteenth-century worthy below him. The Walker didn't notice.

"They thought they could clip my wings by separating my mirrors and hiding the other stone mirror where I couldn't find it. Yet it never occurred to them that with eternity spread ahead of me, I would have time to find a glint and a master maker to choose a stone and carve me a new one. Fools . . ."

The crystal ball was beginning to spin inside the case, answering a hidden force emanating from the Walker's spread fingers, and the faster it spun, the more it seemed to wobble on its axis.

A bead of sweat trickled down the Walker's nose and splashed to the parquet floor as he struggled to contain the powerful answering judder in his hand. With a gasp, his open hand snapped closed, and he lashed it back and forth, flailing it across the air in front of the cabinet. As he did so, the ball whipped and ricocheted around the interior of the glass cube, matching the movements of the fist, bouncing off the sides faster and faster, until the noise of the sharp percussive impacts sounded like the rip of a machine gun. Then all the glass in the cabinet shattered at the same time and fell to the floor like a dropped crystal curtain.

An alarm bell began to ring prosaically in the distance, and the dim lights came on. Ignoring all that, the Walker stepped over the shards of glass and deftly snatched the ball from its now-stationary position in midair in the center of the case and pocketed it.

His hands reemerged, carrying two crumpled and mismatched gloves. He speedily put them on, and then equally quickly, he spread a scarf out and placed two of the protective wax disks on it. He picked up the obsidian mirror and put it on top of the disks, letting go of it as soon as he could, as if not wanting to touch it any longer than he had to, even though he was wearing gloves. Then he sandwiched it with another protective wax disk and tied the corners of the scarf tightly together, making a bundle. He pocketed the gold circle with the dream of four castles on it and stepped back.

"Come," he said.

The Raven flew onto his shoulder. The Walker held the ends of the scarf, wrapping the bundle containing the stone mirror. He exchanged his gloves for the mirrors in his pocket; and then, just as the first museum guard was running through the door, he stepped into one of his small glass mirrors and disappeared.

CHAPTER TWENTY-SEVEN

Hunter's Moon

Edie fell into the mirror behind her. She felt the surface bend and pop as delicately as a soap bubble, and then she was falling into a fire. As she fell, someone grabbed at her ankle but wasn't able to hold it, and she hit the ground with a thunderous crash, like the gates of Hell blowing open.

She fell on her back and rolled, so that the first things she saw were her legs in the air above her, and beyond them, the dark sky and the bright disk of a full moon staring down at her, the pale night sun of a hunter's moon, framed for an instant between two familiar scuffed boots.

She felt the sharp dig of a broken brick in her back, and lost contact with anything familiar as she flinched and squirmed to her feet, just in time to see long, white fingers of light sweep across the sky, cutting it into jagged segments. And then she was conscious of the hungry crack and pop of a fire very close to her.

She realized that the crash she had heard was not her landing on the ground; it was the sudden continual hell storm of noise that shook the world around her, the world she had fallen into: it was the sound of a world blowing itself apart. There were deep explosions and crashes and screams. And behind the screams was the low moaning sound of a siren rising and falling; behind that, there was a rhythmic throbbing engine rumble from the sky itself. There was the sharper counterpoint of antiaircraft fire from a hidden battery nearby, and others farther off. Mixed in all of this were urgent shouts and jangling ambulance bells and more screams and huge earthshaking thuds that she could feel through the soles of her boots.

Unwilling to look around at the source of all this horrifying sound until she had to, Edie looked at her feet and saw they were on the step of a shop. There were fragments of brick and glass all around her. She looked to her side and saw a mirror on the doorpost. She saw her face staring back at her, a white smear of shock side lit by flames. Before she could see if there was a matching mirror on the other side of the door, there was a huge thump that knocked her to her knees as the ground kicked and buckled beneath her. When she looked up, stunned by the violence of the invisible blow, halfway back onto her feet, she saw something that stopped her from moving at all. She remained there, one knee on the ground, eyes wide, mouth open, staring at the infernal vision towering over the other end of the street.

It was a firestorm. Out of the very center of the flames rose the familiar dome of St. Paul's Cathedral, wreathed in conflagration and black smoke—but untouched. It was a vision of the end of the world. But from the heat on her face and the twinging pain in her shoulder where she'd rolled onto the half brick, Edie knew this was no vision. She wasn't glinting this.

This was real.

When she glinted, the past came in jagged slices, and she had no choice about what she could see. She never ended up with brick dust in her mouth. This wasn't glinting; this was being.

"Hey you, girly, get off the bloody street, get down the shelter!"

A voice shrieked at her from the other side of the road. She turned to see a middle-aged man in a suit, with a canvas bag over one shoulder and a tin hat like the Gunner's, except the Gunner's didn't have a white W painted on the front. He was waving at her angrily, thin mustache bristling like a furious hairy caterpillar.

"It's that way, down the end, you trying to get yourself killed or—"

The side of the ancient brick building behind him jerked as if it had been kicked by an unseen giant. The man never got to what came after the "or," because the front of the building just dropped on him in a brutally short avalanche of brick and stone.

Edie instinctively put her hand over her mouth as the dust cloud rolled out. It thinned, and she saw the white W of the hat slowly rolling toward her. It hit the curb at her feet and turned over. She got a glimpse of something wet inside, and looked away.

In the inferno surrounding the unscathed dome of the cathedral were plumes of water arcing futilely into the roiling mountains of fire. At their base were the dark outlines of small groups of men wrestling fire hoses. In the sky above, the fingers of the searchlights quested back and forth, and the intermittent lines of tracer fire squirted into the dark heavens like fiery echoes of the water jets playing on the devastation below.

Edie realized she had her hands jammed over her ears, trying to keep the jarring assault out of her head.

And then something grabbed her arm.

She spun to see the Friar. His normally jolly face was tight and worried.

"Come," he shouted over the sound of another building crashing to the ground on the next street. "Back into the mirrors. You don't want to die here."

For once in her life she didn't even think of arguing. She let him drag her back toward the shop entrance, where she saw, with relief, two mirrors facing each other on either side of a bookshop window. That was their way out of this nightmare.

The Friar stopped dead.

"What?" Edie began.

And then she heard it, an instant before it hit: a whistling sound from out of the chaotic sky overhead, shockingly, intimately close.

There was another sharp jerk on her arm, and the Friar pulled her to him and turned away from the bookshop and the safety beckoning in its mirrors just a pavement's-width away. He curved around, enveloping her.

The bomb hit, and Edie's feet were blown out from under her. Only the unbreakable grasp with which the Friar held her to his chest stopped her from falling. The very air seemed to punch them viciously, and there was a sudden jagged horizontal silver hailstorm as the windows of the shop blew out. If she hadn't been completely shielded by the arched metal back of the Friar, she'd have been just a red mist and so much ground meat blown across the cobbled street. The shop window was followed by the shop's contents. Whole books spilled across the pavement, and a snowstorm of pages from volumes shredded by the explosion swirled around them.

After a second the Friar straightened, and they turned to see that they were in the middle of a slow-moving blizzard of paper, some pages on fire, some not, but all whirling up into the night sky on updrafts created by the heat around them.

The Friar crossed the pavement in four fast paces, batting the airborne page storm out of his way as he went. Edie stumbled after him—and she stopped when he stopped.

The mirrors were gone, shattered by the same blast that had destroyed the shop window. Even through the maelstrom of the Blitz around them, Edie could hear the single sharp tutting noise the Friar made. It was more ominous than a building falling.

"Those were the mirrors," she said.

He tutted again.

"Those were our way out," she went on, voice rising.

He peered up at the sky. She tugged at his robe. Glass shards fell out of the folds and tinkled to the ground around his feet.

"What do we do now?"

The Friar looked up and down the street. Seeing him unsure made Edie more frightened than she already was. Finally he looked at her.

"Can you run?"

She glanced up at his great bellied bulk standing over her. "Can you?"

The ghost of a smile flickered across the flame-lit face above her.

"Lady, when my survival depends on it, I can practically fly. . . ."

He hiked up his cassock above the knee with one hand and grasped her hand with the other—and ran. And even though she would never have admitted it later, the fact that he held her hand did pull her out of her stunned state, and she ran alongside him, matching his every long pace with two of her own.

The details of that headlong dash through the firestorm and the falling bombs blurred together so that later she could not remember exactly what had happened. But single moments remained, disconnected with each other, one minute there, next minute gone. An old-fashioned taxi with spoked wheels was blown across the road in front of them, burying itself upside down in a second-floor bay window. They ran on. At some stage, a stream of fire suddenly flashed out of an alleyway, blocking their way. The Friar just grabbed Edie and hurdled through it. There was one point where she remembered running past a London bus, on its side, and she registered the curling staircase that ran up the back to a top floor that had no roof. She turned away before her brain could make sense of the twisted coat and hand sticking out from under the side of the bus.

They ducked down narrow lanes between vertiginously high walls, and at one point dodged through an old graveyard that appeared out of nowhere in the warren of streets. She remembered the whump of a bomb hitting the graveyard behind them as they left it, and turning and seeing a long box toppling back down out of the sky and dashing itself to pieces on a church wall, and turning away before she had to see what was in the coffin. She remembered the Friar saying:

"They'll be burying those poor souls again in the morning."

They were running on and on, through strangely empty and quiet streets one minute, then through flaming ruins the next. And it was only when she saw a street sign hanging off the corner of a building reading "Puddle Dock" that she realized where they were running to.

Though tired, she redoubled her effort, and they skidded around the final corner to see the Black Friar standing on the prow of his building above them. He didn't look down to see himself running past, or if he did, Edie was sprinting too quickly to notice.

The Friar pushed open the door, and they tumbled in. She had time to notice that the windows were crisscrossed with tape, before he yanked her forward in between the two mirrored arches.

"Right," he panted. "Home, I think."

"James who?" inquired a familiar voice from the alcove within.

Edie peered in but couldn't see him. What she could see was a poster, a finely drawn cartoon of two men leaning on a bar, talking—and the bottles, and even the beer-pump handles behind them, all had the familiar face of a man with an angular sweep of hair and a—in fact the—Hitler mustache, listening carefully. Below it, the message, "Careless Talk Costs Lives." It was a colorful and funny-looking poster.

"You're right," she said into the darkness, aiming her

voice toward where she knew Little Tragedy would be listening. "I do like the poster."

The Friar snorted and pulled her arm, and they were falling back into the mirror; she staggered and found she had different carpet under her feet and the world outside wasn't blowing itself to hell, only grinding itself quietly down with the traffic beyond the windows—windows no longer crisscrossed with antiblast tape.

"I think," said the Friar, "that that explains the mirrors."

"Yep," said Edie, trying to stop her legs and voice from trembling. "Got the mirror thing. Definitely not for saddoes. Definitely real."

She sat down suddenly, right there on the floor, because something had to give, and her shaking legs just did so first.

Chapter Twenty-eight

Eigengang

It was the football that woke George up—that, and a man's voice shouting energetically somewhere far away.

"Over here, my son, on the head!"

And then there was the unmistakable dull thump of a boot kicking a wet leather football. George opened his eyes and came out of the dark and saw a white-and-red ball spinning up into the air below him and then slowly drop away to meet a group of players rammed in around a crowded goalmouth. There was a tussle and some muddy skirmishing, and then the ball billowed the back netting. One of the players pulled his shirt over his head and ran off in a victory circuit, hand held high, and there was the sound of good-natured laughing and catcalls from the others. The only abnormal thing about it was that George was seeing it from a teetering bird's-eye view.

He felt the stone talon wrapped around his chest and remembered Spout, and the fact that he was meant to be dead, and the screaming golden girl on the end of the lance; and the past dropped back in and hit him like a bag of wet cement.

The floodlit green space below was Coram's Fields, an oasis of grass and trees just south of Euston Road. Spout was flying faster now, as if he were nearly home and didn't have to conserve his energy. The rain had eased, but was still coming down—a light drizzle instead of the downpour that had soaked him earlier.

George was wet to the skin, shivering badly, and trying to figure out exactly what had happened and why he wasn't dead.

Ariel had pinned and held him to the gate, so hard that he couldn't move. The Knight had thundered in behind the lance. George had looked away at the last minute and closed his eyes. And then he'd felt the colossal impact. He really should be dead.

Except now that he was conscious again, he replayed the final moment more slowly and realized that what had felt terribly wrong was not the impact so much as the direction it had come from. The lance had been about to punch heart-high through his chest, impaling him like a butterfly on a pin. But the impact hadn't come from the front. It had come from the side. He remembered thinking that he'd heard Death's wings flying in to gather him. But now that he thought about it, it hadn't been Death but Spout diving out of the night sky at the very last minute, snatching him out of the way so that the Knight's lance had punched past the empty space where George now wasn't, and through the gap in the gate railings into the space where Ariel still was.

There had been a feeling like his head exploding, and that must have been Spout clattering him up something like the roof of the sentry box as he snatched him into the sky, because George could feel a definite bump throbbing behind his ear.

So that was how come he was now being flown over Euston Road toward the lavishly ornamented roof scape of St. Pancras Station: Spout had snatched him back. Spout had rescued him, just as earlier Ariel had saved him from the gargoyle. Out of the frying pan, into the fire. The only thing was, he wasn't sure who was frying pan and who was fire anymore. He was pretty certain Spout hadn't suddenly changed from an enemy into a friend, so it had to be that the rescue was accidental, and Spout had taken him back for his own reasons. It was all too complicated, and he was hurting and cold and confused.

The memory of Ariel—her smile, her joy in just flying around the gherkin, pirouetting on the top of the world— all that hurt him too, especially when overlaid with the ice in her voice as she had gripped him and held him for the Knight. The hurt was because she'd betrayed him.

Spout was slowing as they flew up and around the tall illuminated clocktower on the eastern end of the building. He registered the green slate roof thrusting sharply into the sky above the clock faces on each of its sides, and the accompanying pinnacles decorating each corner, as they circled the massive exuberant confection of orange brickwork and clean white stone.

The engine shed of Kings Cross passed his right shoulder. Spout flapped down the roof of St. Pancras, over a sharp ridge with a narrow, flat runway on the very top. They flew west between tall chimneys that swept up from the vertiginously sheer roof slopes on either side. Before the building curves abruptly ended, in a squatter tower on the far end, there was another tower, and it was to this tower that Spout was flying. As it loomed ahead of them, Spout stopped flapping and spread his wings wide, making them act as air brakes, slowing their speed to a stalling point. Just when it was clear to George that flight was no longer viable and they were going to start falling, Spout reached out a talon and stuck to the corner of the wall.

"Geer!" he coughed, and put George down on the narrow space behind him. There was no question of George's running away from this position. Spout's aerie was a small space where three angles of roof met and then fell away sheer. There was a lead gutter box, a sort of inset tray with a hole, and a piece of broken masonry wedged in one corner that provided a place for George to squat and watch the gargoyle as he settled into position. Except, unlike all the other gargoyles on the building, which were facing out at the city, Spout turned in and looked at George.

George had no clue as to what was going to happen next. The gargoyle stared at him and then shook himself like a dog, slowly stretched his wings, and folded them neatly down around his back. It was the first time George had really had a chance to look at Spout properly, at rest. Every time he'd seen him before, he'd been moving, running, flying, or chasing. And George had been so busy trying to stay as far from the creature as he could that he'd never had a chance to really take him in, in all his glory.

Not that he was very glorious. He definitely had, as George's dad used to say, been hit with the ugly stick. He was a stringy feral cat with wings where his front legs should be. There was something strained and tortured in the way the sculptor had made him, and life on the roof had clearly not been kind to him. He was streaked with dirt; his mouth leaked green from where the old copper pipe had been that George had pulled out of his mouth; the weather had not only beaten him, but had shattered off the knuckle tip of one wing, which gave him a lopsided quality. In fact, George wondered if it were this missing bit of wing that made him fly so lopsidedly, too.

Spout bared his fangs, and George saw how deep the green staining went, curling out around the lower teeth like blood.

"*Gack,*" rasped the creature.

"Yes," said George. "Nice place you've got here." He had his arms wrapped around himself and was hunched down into a ball, trying to get some warmth trapped in his middle. "Shame you haven't got central heating," he said.

"*Gowk,*" said Spout, leaning in and tapping his own mouth, then prodding George back against the tiles. "*Gowk!*"

He was trying to say something, George realized. He was definitely trying to communicate. And he looked irritated at George's inability to understand.

"*Gowk!*"

"Yes, gowk," said George.

Spout didn't look impressed. His fangs ground against each other in silent irritation, and his throat worked as if he were trying to cough out a fur ball or a fish bone.

"Sorry. I don't speak Gargoyle," George apologized.

Spout shook his head and batted at his mouth again, wingtips clattering against the bared fangs. And George suddenly realized what he must be saying.

"You want the spout! The spout I pulled out of your mouth. Yes, of course, I'm sorry. . . ."

Now it all made complete sense. It explained why the creature had been so tenacious in his pursuit of him. He'd wrenched an important part out of Spout's mouth. In fact, before he'd done that, he couldn't remember the thing making any noise at all. These attempts to speak sounded so painful, George wasn't surprised that the gargoyle wanted it back.

His hands scrabbled in his trouser pocket and

disentangled the corroded metal pipe. He held it out like a peace offering.

And then he got clever just in time, and snatched it back out of Spout's grasp.

"Although . . ." he said slowly, thinking as he spoke. "Although, perhaps we can make a deal. You put me down on the ground, and then I give you your spout back. You understand?"

He mimed flying down and handing over the pipe. Spout cocked his head. His talon flashed out and back with surprising speed, and George's hand was suddenly empty. The gargoyle looked at the metal pipe he now held in his own grasp.

"Yes," said George. "Or you could take it now and then put me back on the ground. If that works better for you, I'm, um, easy. . . ."

He knew he was clinging on to the frayed coattails of a very forlorn hope, and so he folded his arms around himself and tried to look on the bright side.

"Still. As long as you got your spout back, I'm happy. You're happy, and—"

Spout stopped looking at the copper pipe and stared at George with a stony intensity that shut him up. Spout twirled the pipe once in his talon and then tossed it over his shoulder without the least interest. George stared at Spout as they listened to the pipe ping and clatter its way down the roof and onto the engine shed below. George swallowed.

"Gowk!" Spout clattered his wingtip against his chest and poked George insistently. *"Gowk—eigengang. Eigengang—gowk."*

Somewhere all this made sense, but not on any planet George was presently inhabiting.

"Sorry. I don't know what *eigengang* means."

Spout lunged forward, and for a moment, George thought he was attacking, but then the gargoyle grabbed the broken lump of stone in the gutter box under his feet and tugged it out. George tipped backward and his hands flailed against the tiles to stop himself from falling into the void below. When he looked up, Spout was thrusting the stone at him like a club.

He raised his hands to shield himself, but Spout hissed in frustration and sat back on his haunches. He waved the broken piece of stonework at George. Then he lunged forward again, put the stone fragment down, and grabbed George's hand. The scar with the maker's mark twinged as Spout pulled George forward so he was standing on tiptoes. Spout rubbed George's hand on the edge of his wing—in the place where the weather had shattered a large lump out of it.

"Ow," said George, his hand being sandpapered by the abrasive surface. Spout hissed angrily and stepped back. George was suddenly alone and unsupported; worse than that, he was on tiptoe, on the brink of a very long drop. He tottered and fell back into the gutter box. The broken piece of stone jagged into his side as he landed, and he arched his back and pulled it out of the way. But as the stone pressed itself into the soft flesh of his hands and fingers, he knew.

He knew without having to look at the shape lopped out of the gargoyle's wing that he was holding the broken piece. His hands felt the identical rough texture, his fingers knew that he was feeling the negative shape of the one he'd felt on Spout's wing. He knew it was the same rock, and he knew it would fill the space exactly. He knew that the two pieces of rock not only belonged but, in some way he couldn't explain, wanted to be together again.

"Oh," he said. And sat down. He looked at the piece of wing in his hand and then at Spout.

"Oh."

Spout squatted back in front of him and angled the broken wing knuckle toward George. And although George was more frightened of this stone monster than anything he could imagine, he couldn't help putting his hand out and feeling the stone wound again.

"You want me to mend you."

He felt the stone surface. He put the broken piece into the wing. It fit perfectly.

"Eigengang," said Spout, nodding.

"If *eigengang* means mend, I can't. I'm sorry. I mean, it's not just a matter of putting it back. It's got to be fixed."

His mind flashed back to the ordered mess of his father's studio; he heard his dad breathing in the sucking-air-in-the-side-of-his-mouth way he did when he was smoking but couldn't spare a hand to remove the cigarette. He saw his dad using two hands to hold a broken piece of sculpture together. It was a ballerina that had belonged to his mother. George had broken it, and they were trying to mend it before she noticed. It had been a conspiratorial moment between the two of them: boys together, working against the clock. He remembered his dad saying it wasn't just a matter of glue. That you couldn't just rely on glue. That for a repair to work, you had to make a mechanical join, too, as well as the glue. Especially if you were going to put pressure on the break. George thought of the immense pressure that Spout put on his wings every time he flapped, trying to keep his great mass airborne.

"It's complicated. It's got to be glued or mortared or something. I mean, it's probably got to be screwed or pinned. I'm sorry."

His hand squeezed the wing apologetically. And as he did so, he felt the stone becoming hot.

Spout looked at him sharply.

"*Eigengang.*"

George squeezed again. The heat became fiercer, and as he moved his hand along the seam between the two pieces of stone, it became hard to work out where the heat was coming from. He realized he wasn't feeling heat coming from the stone.

The heat was coming from his hand.

He didn't know, afterward, why his eyes had closed,

but he found he had blanked out the world and just focused on what he could feel. His hearing seemed to dull, too, as he felt the rough surface of the stone. He felt the tiny crackle and popping occurring within the crack, as split granules of stone found their sundered neighbors and knitted back together under the heat coming from his hand.

He slumped back, strangely exhausted and panting for breath, a dull empty feeling beneath his breastbone. Whatever he had done, it had cost him. He was drenched in sweat, and steamed slightly in the cold air.

Spout shook his wing as if testing it. The broken piece was solidly a part of him again. He nodded his head with enthusiasm. *"Eigengang!"* And sat back on his haunches.

George did the same.

"Wow. That was . . . something," he said. He looked up at the night sky, trying to concentrate on the tingling aftermath in his hand, and not the emptiness in his chest. "It's stopped raining."

Spout's head came up fast, his eyes wide, his ears back, all the hackled spines on his neck raised.

Something was coming.

CHAPTER TWENTY-NINE

Queen Takes Knight

After dark, the narrow streets in the City of London quiet down. City workers have all gone home, and the twisting canyons hemmed in by high-rises are not on the way to anywhere. Traffic passing through the city blasts past on wider thoroughfares, and the narrow streets that are so busy by day become a ghost town.

The Red Queen drove her horses slowly along the road, the ancient design of the war chariot beneath her feet strikingly at odds with the shiny modern buildings towering over her on either side.

Her daughters flanked her, scouring each side street and alley as they passed, looking for Edie—or anything that might give a clue as to where she was.

Both daughters had the intense look of their mother. They were fierce, mostly silent, girls. But when they needed to move, they did so firmly and decisively. They had her fearlessness running in their veins, but whereas their mother allowed her fire to blaze freely, the girls chose to keep that fire banked up quietly.

The one on the left heard it before the others.

She touched her mother's arm, and the Queen instantly reined in the horses.

Then they all heard it.

The sound of hooves, coming closer.

The Queen gripped her spear. The source of the noise came slowly around a corner. The three women stood stock still.

It was the Last Knight. He rode at a slow, funereal pace, his lance lowered in mourning, his head bent forward in sadness. Across the saddle in front of him was draped the limp golden body of Ariel.

The Queen and her daughters watched the Knight move toward them, as still as if frozen in a pocket in time. When it became apparent that he was going to pass without acknowledging them, the Queen spoke tightly.

"Sir Knight. A word, if you please."

He just carried on past.

The Queen nodded at her daughters. Without the need for words, they leaped nimbly from the chariot and ran toward the Knight, soundless on their bare feet. The Queen threw her spear to one of them, who caught it almost without looking and ran ahead of the Knight. As the Queen snapped the reins on her chariot and turned, the daughter with the spear stood foursquare in front of the warhorse and armored man towering above her, and jabbed the spear warningly at his throat. He stopped the horse. The other daughter grabbed the bridle reins and held them as the Queen trotted up.

She looked at the golden girl lying across the horse's neck. Then up at the Knight.

"What is this?"

There was a pause as the Knight slowly looked around at her.

"An accident."

"And what are you doing with her?"

He nodded ahead. "I had thought to scale the building and put her on her plinth before turn o'day. I would not have her die on my account."

The Queen looked at her girls. "Was it on your account that the accident happened?"

"It was," replied the Knight.

The Queen nodded at her daughters. The one holding the reins pulled Ariel off the horse and onto her shoulders.

"It is my obligation . . ." began the Knight in protest.

"You have done enough," said the Queen, seeing the large hole in Ariel's side. "If you had done but a fraction more, I could have ridden my chariot through the wound you have put in this poor girl."

"It was not meant," he protested.

"It never is," she snorted.

"Go back to your guild, Knight. And play your sword games with each other. That is all you are good for. We will take care of her from here and make sure she is on her plinth by turn o'day."

The Knight looked at her, then bowed his head and backed his horse into a turn and rode slowly away.

The Queen watched him as her daughter carefully laid Ariel on the back of their chariot.

"See, girls. It's as I always tell you. It never does to send a man to do a woman's job."

CHAPTER THIRTY

Deathslide

High on the roof of St. Pancras, George could hear them coming. He looked over the edge of his precarious perch and saw that a great many stone things were crawling over the green tiles and chimneys below.

In the middle of everything, George had forgotten what the Gunner had told him about gargoyles: that they might be taints and bent on his destruction, but they always had to answer their first purpose, which was to be highly decorative waterspouts.

This meant that when it rained, they had to go back to their places on whatever roof they came from and funnel water. It raised the question of why Spout alone had suddenly been able to fly freely through the rainstorm. George had a strong feeling that it had something to do with the fact he'd somehow changed the gargoyle by giving him a name and modifying him by ripping out the metal spout that had been gagging him when they'd had their first confrontation. It was, however, not a question that George was going to have time to concern himself with right now.

The question crawling, slithering, and hopping toward him at that moment was what he was going to do now that the rain had stopped and most of the gargoyles in the rookery of St. Pancras had come alive and were converging on Spout's aerie from all sides. That was the sound he'd heard—stone limbs and talons scraping relentlessly toward him over wet roof tiles and dripping smokestacks.

They moved slowly, but there was something much worse about that than if they had come in a rush. If they'd come in a rush, he wouldn't have had time to see them in all their brutal detail. They came in different shapes and sizes, but all had jaws stretched wide in gaping snarls panting through their mouths as if they somehow smelled with the backs of their throats. Some were worn and weather-beaten to a point where their features had begun to erode into almost abstract masks of hostility and threat. Some clearly had been carved more crudely than others, and several of them obviously had been recently restored, because they looked newer and their lines were more finely incised.

The larger ones dragged their wings after them like great capes, while the smaller ones hopped from perch to perch, leapfrogging one another from gable end to dormer window to chimney stack as they came.

George wondered if this was what Spout had intended, if this was his end, to be torn apart by this pack of blank-eyed taints high above the uncaring city.

Spout turned to him and held out a talon. *"Gung,"* he said urgently.

He was shaking like a dog when its blood is up and it smells trouble. George didn't understand why the arrival of his friends was upsetting the creature so much.

"Gung ear!" hissed Spout, motioning with his talon while keeping an eye on the approaching gargoyles. George had just enough time to wonder if he was trying to say "Come here" with a catlike mouth that wasn't designed for normal conversation; then something tumbled out of the sky above them and buried its teeth into Spout's shoulder. The momentum knocked him off his perch. George's eye met his for one appalled moment, and then Spout and the smaller gargoyle, who had dived on him from the spire above, fell over the edge and out of sight.

George scrambled to the lip and looked over, just in time to see Spout and his attacker crash down onto the flat roof below, landing on another gargoyle, who instantly joined the fight. The other gargoyles on the roof stepped back, and for a few moments, the three creatures ripped and tore at one another in a snarling hissing ball that rolled back and forth across the narrow space. At one point it looked as if they were about to plunge into the forecourt below, but Spout hooked a great talon on a protruding gutter and heaved himself and the two monsters back into the middle of the roof.

He slammed himself back into a chimney stack, stunning the small gargoyle on his shoulders. It fell to the ground, and Spout savagely back-heeled it over the edge. The other gargoyle, locked on to his front, tried to get its fangs into Spout's throat, but Spout struck faster and closed his fangs on the gargoyle's head.

The surrounding creatures hissed in fury as Spout shook the smaller gargoyle back and forth in his jaws. The circle of gargoyles closed in on Spout, and he spat the lifeless creature onto the tiles and grabbed the first new attacker that rushed in on him, stepping nimbly aside, using its momentum to throw it straight past into the solid brick chimney behind him. Then he grabbed the stunned assailant by a wingtip and whirled him around like a club, cutting a swath in the surrounding horde as they backed off to avoid being hit by the flailing gargoyle. George realized Spout was fighting his way back to the foot of his tower.

The wing of the creature Spout was swinging snapped off with a crack like a rifle shot, and the body spun away into the night.

The other gargoyles froze. Spout looked at the wing fragment in his hand and sort of shrugged. He hefted the improvised club in his hands as if to say, "Who's next?"

Three gargoyles, two his size and one bigger, rushed him from different points of the compass. He kicked the first one out of his way, but the other two tackled him, and their impact knocked the wing fragment from his grasp and took them all out into the darker air over the engine shed, and they were gone.

Half of the gargoyles below rushed to the edge, but the other half turned to look at something more interesting.

George.

He was staring down at them, wondering what to do, when a gargoyle blindsided him by crawling around the roof and grabbing him.

He found himself airborne again, but only for a short flight, as the gargoyle was one of the medium-size ones with quite stubby, not particularly aerodynamic, wings. It clearly didn't have the lift necessary to keep itself and its human prey in the air at the same time.

They crash-landed on the narrow ridge below. It happened slowly enough not to hurt too much, and awkwardly enough for George to end up lying on the creature's arm.

He had nearly dashed his brains out on the broken wing fragment that Spout had used as a club, but he jerked his head out of the way just in time.

The gargoyle tugged its arm, trying to get out from under George. Before George thought too much about what he was going to do, he grabbed the broken wing and scythed it into the gargoyle's face in a crunching haymaker. He could tell it was crunching because crunch is what he heard. The gargoyle looked at him, groggy and puzzled, then shook its head and snarled.

George just hit it again, a carbon-copy blow, and then once more, even harder. The gargoyle's head was smashed sideways in a ninety-degree arc with the first blow, but it came back around, snarling in fury—just in time for the second blow to send it one hundred eighty degrees the wrong way on its neck. The crunch this time was followed by a *thunk* as the head dropped off, onto the ground.

It wasn't just George who was shocked at the result of his despairing blow. The gargoyles on the roof were suddenly very still. He took advantage of this to roll to his feet and get the solid brick of a smokestack at his back. He figured he'd do better if they could only come from in front. He'd seen how far trying to fight a three hundred sixty–degree battle had got Spout.

The gargoyles began to hiss, starting quietly and becoming louder.

"Right," he lied. "I can do this all night. Who's next?"

His bravado didn't slow them one bit as they began to close in.

George didn't have a plan. He was outnumbered and out of options. The only chink of hope he might have, he realized, was the ray of light beaming straight up from the roof, about fifty feet away. It was a skylight, and though jumping through a window is not usually the most sensible thing to do, in this situation he thought it might be the safest option. Out here he was surrounded. If he could get inside the building, there would be corridors and rooms and places to hide. If he could sprint through the advancing tide of stone killers and hit the glass with both feet, and then roll like a parachutist when he landed, he might have a chance. Of course, the chance depended on A) not getting too sliced up by the falling glass, and B) the skylight dropping him into a room on the floor below and not somewhere else, such as, for example, an unending well that ran down the whole height of the building.

"I can do this," he said, trying to ignore the voice in the back of his head that told him he was still lying.

If he was going to do it, if he was to have any chance of getting off this roof, he would have to do it now, before the gargoyle horde closed any further in and became too dense for him to run through. So he gripped the fragment of wing and ran.

As he exploded into motion, the thought flashed that this was the second time he'd tried to get out of a tight spot by running forward instead of running away. The thought gave him strength as he remembered how well it had worked on the Knight.

The first gargoyle he came to reared up and snatched at him, but he ducked under its wings and powered forward. Coming out from under the wing, he found another gargoyle in front of him, and before it could move, he jumped at it. His front foot hit it in the chest and it went over backward. George went with it, using the gargoyle like a springboard as he jumped over it and raced for the skylight on the roof ahead. A small monster leaped at his face, but he managed to club it back with the fragment of stone.

And then there was nothing between him and the rectangular skylight, except four paces of clear roof. A big gargoyle had launched into the air on the other side of the glass, but it wasn't going to intercept George in time to stop his desperate para-jump through the glass.

George hit the edge of the skylight and leaped high. He registered, almost without time for relief, that on the other side of the glass was a drop the height of one room, onto a pile of old boxes.

He brought his feet together in midair and slammed his heels down on the glass in one mighty smash.

One thing about London is that the people in charge of how things are built have very strict ideas and rules about the materials that have to be used. One of the rules about skylights is that they have to be made from safety glass. And if the skylight is to be in a roof just below a tall tower that has stone decorations that may shatter in frost, or fall off in high winds, then that safety glass has to be as safe as safety glass can get. It has to be tough— the kind of tough that doesn't just go to pieces at the first sign of danger.

George's heels smashed down on the glass and didn't break anything except his fall.

The water on the rain-slick surface did, however, combine with his considerable forward momentum and turned the rectangle from a skylight into a skating rink.

George's feet flew out from under him, and he hit the slippery glass with his tailbone, only managing to get his chin down just in time to stop from dashing his brains as he fell backward. But that was where his good luck ended and the very bad luck began.

True, he did slide beneath the airborne gargoyle that had been leaping at him from the other side of the skylight, but only because he was now tobogganing at high speed toward the edge of a very steep roof and a long drop onto the engine shed roof below. He scrabbled and shimmied, desperately trying to get some friction going, some kind of stick that would slow him down or help him stop.

Hope flickered alive as a new gargoyle appeared over the fast-approaching roof edge. He stuck his feet out to brake himself against the roof, but the gargoyle was heartbreakingly quick-witted for a lump of stone. As he was about to impact, it simply flattened its ears and ducked.

And so George flew onward, over its head, off the roof, and into the void.

CHAPTER THIRTY-ONE

Three Challenges and a Betrayal

Edie had got her legs back under control, but she was still sitting on the pub floor, absorbing what had happened to her. Finding herself in the midst of World War II at the height of the Blitz had been quite different from the sharp pain of merely seeing slices of the past when she glinted.

Being in the past rather than just seeing it wasn't painful as such. It just left an overwhelming feeling of nausea and a kind of empty horror inside her. Maybe it was being there and coming back so suddenly that did it, she thought, concentrating on this idea rather than the twisted overcoat and hand she'd seen sticking out from under the tipped omnibus. Perhaps this was like jet lag only worse—time lag, in fact.

The Friar watched her from the bar, which he was leaning against, still getting his breath back. He pushed George's coat to one side and heaved his great bulk up on the bar, bare legs and sandals dangling out of the bottom of his cassock, somehow startling in their powerful nakedness. He looked as if he were sitting on the side of a river, about to paddle. He lacked only a fishing rod to complete the illusion. Instead he looked at Edie and flicked a question over her head like a fly.

"And the second question." The Friar spoke in a voice so honeyed and solicitous that, despite the shock flushing through her body, Edie felt her hackles begin to rise.

"Second question?"

"Apart from the mirrors and how they work. You said you had a second question."

Though it had been only minutes ago, it felt as if she'd asked that question in a different life. She shook her head to clear it.

"Yeah. Right. The Hard Way. You said if George didn't make his sacrifice by putting the broken head on the Stone, then he would have to do things the Hard Way."

"Indeed," he purred, and sat there with the kind of smugness that, in Edie's book, would have been asking—in fact begging—for a slap. Somehow in her present state, she didn't have anything approaching a proper slap in her—real or verbal. She took a deep breath.

"What exactly is the Hard Way? Is it why he just vanished off the face of the earth?"

The Friar twirled George's coat around on the bar top. Then hung it neatly on one of the beer handles.

"Maybe."

Somehow, having been dragged back from what very possibly was, and certainly had felt like, the end of the world hadn't put Edie in a mood for *maybe*'s.

"I need you to tell me a little bit more. Please."

The *please* stuck in her throat, but she got it out with a good attempt at a smile as sugarcoating. And to her surprise he told her. He told her that George must stand and fight the three duels, and that they all had to be fought above or below ground, in the air or in or on water. He explained that this was so because the challenge of three contests was one of London's forgotten rituals, but that just because it had been forgotten didn't mean that it didn't underpin the city in an important way.

"After all, my dear, who remembers the keystone that was laid beneath the cathedral or the church? But they are there, and though forgotten, it should be remembered that the whole edifice would tumble without them."

"You mean it's like tradition," she said.

"It's nothing like tradition. Tradition is like giving votes to the most obscure class of people, namely your ancestors. My word, no. Tradition is the democracy of the dead. No, this is part of the living warp and weft of the city itself. Nothing dead about it at all. He has to fight three duels to earn his place in the fabric."

"What if he doesn't fight?"

The Friar's eyebrows rose and fell, one after another in a small ripple of outrage at the very thought.

"He has to. To refuse a contest is a failure. To fail is to become a Stone Servant and walk in thrall to the power of the Stone for eternity."

Edie absorbed this carefully.

"So that's bad."

"So that, as you so perspicaciously put it, is bad."

"But if he doesn't know this, if he doesn't know the Hard Way is the way of three duels, he might refuse a challenge. He might. I would. I'd run away unless I couldn't avoid it!"

"Then you'd better find him and tell him, had you not?"

"But how can I find him?"

"Look."

Edie spluttered with frustration at the enormity of the task he was outlining for her. "In this city. It's like searching for a needle in a haystack!"

"Then don't waste time"—he hooked his thumb and jerked it toward the door—"be on your way. The first step in finding a needle in a haystack is to start."

She sat tight. "Will you help me?"

"I thought I just did."

"Help me find George," she added.

"Why would I help?"

"Because you're a spit."

His expression didn't change by a flicker.

"Okay, then," she amended, "because you're not a taint."

Maybe something ticked under his eye, but even if it had, Edie was pretty sure it had been irritation. He sighed shortly.

"Absence of hostility does not mean presence of benevolence, my child. It can also mean indifference, and I, uncharitable and uncharacteristic as it may be to admit, find that I am sublimely and ineffably indifferent."

"But why?"

He looked over her shoulder. "'Why,' she says. Why?"

There was a little needling "Tchah" of disbelief from behind her as Little Tragedy tried to express how extraordinarily dense she must be not to know why the Friar was suddenly, inexplicably changing tack.

"I mean it," she said, hating the plaintive note that had crept unbidden into her voice. "I don't know why you've gone all like this, why you won't help."

The Friar deliberately scooped George's coat off the beer pump handles and let it fall to the countertop with a distinct and giveaway thunk.

Little Tragedy scuttled out of the shadows and nimble-fingered his way into the pockets. In an instant, he pulled out the broken dragon's head like a conjuror producing a rabbit, eyes wide as soup plates.

"Ooooh," he said. "Look at that. It's little George's little dragon. Blimey."

"Blind you, indeed I should, You Imp, if you don't stay where you ought," barked the Friar, snatching the carving from his hands. "Blind you, indeed I should, were my heart not so damnably soft and sentimental."

Sentimental and soft were the last two words Edie would have used to describe the look on the statue's face as his eyes locked on hers across the dragon's head.

"Why? Because it appears that the boy did not trust me, and neither do you. And trust, milady, is a two-way street. That street is now closed. I cannot abide a liar."

He glared at her with an intensity she found hard not to blink at. She wanted him to turn back into the Friar who had shielded her from certain death and then run her to safety through the Blitz. But that Friar was gone. Too late, she realized, she hadn't thanked him for following her into the mirror and saving her life.

"Look, I'm sorry, and I should have thanked you—"

A tap at the window stopped all conversation. Edie followed the Friar's gaze. Three figures were outlined against the night beyond. Two of them had noses pressed to the frosted glass, so close that it was clear their eyes were black raven eyes. The figure behind them was less distinct, but he was tall and seemed to be wearing a hood.

"Tallyman!" piped Little Tragedy. The Friar cut him off with a look and slid off the bar, landing on the floor with an ominous thud. He paused to put the dragon's head back in the pocket of George's coat and then walked to the door.

"Keep her out of sight until I tell you," he hissed over his shoulder.

Edie felt Tragedy tugging at her urgently. "Come on, Glinty. Time to be somewhere else."

She let him pull her into the shadows behind the arch. They could see the bulk of the Friar blocking the door as he opened it, and then he stood like a roadblock, whispering earnestly to whoever was on the outside.

Edie's blood ran cold, in a way she'd heard talked about but never felt. If the figure on the outside was who she thought it was—the Walker, the man who'd sent the Minotaur after her, the man who'd calmly threatened to slit her belly and spill her guts on the floor like a bag of peas—if it was he who she'd glinted and seen drowning the girl at the Frost Fair, then her blood had every reason to turn cold.

Because if it was he, then Death had come to call.

CHAPTER THIRTY-TWO

Siege in the Sky

When George had slid pell-mell across the wet skylight and been launched into the void above the glass-roofed engine shed far below, there had been an instant of actual and momentary weightlessness that battled a sickening sense of disbelief, as his world went quiet . . .

—And then gravity took over and "off the roof" turned into "down toward the ground."

George had heard that people who fall off high buildings lose consciousness before they hit the pavement. It was one of those playground facts that kids tell each other, like the one about drowning, how gentle it is in the end. George had always wondered how anyone knew this stuff. It wasn't as if you could ask dead people how it had felt. He had fallen through the air like a flailing starfish, watching the humped-glass roof of the train shed come up to meet him with appalling finality.

He didn't lose consciousness. In the few seconds of free

fall, his mind remained as sharp as the glass panels he was about to hit. His life didn't flash before his eyes. He didn't experience a moment of relief, of oneness with the universe. He just felt alone. Brutally, sadly, and irrevocably alone. And he just had time to think what a terrible waste this was, how terrible it was to have wasted such a precious and extraordinary miracle as life. He felt ashamed at how little he had made of what he had been given, more ashamed of anything he'd ever done or not done in his life.

He wondered if this terrible pain had gone through his father's mind the instant of the car crash that had killed him. As George accelerated toward impact, his last thoughts tumbled after one another, and they were these: he knew his father had definitely felt all of this, and he knew that his last thought had absolutely been of George, and he knew that the pain of that last thought had been unspeakable, and he knew this just as surely as he knew he had gone to sleep every night since wishing for just one last word with his dad. He thought of his mother and remembered the good times and laughter and realized, just as he ran out of air and hit something solid, that she would now spend her life unable to say those last words to him. And the sudden pain of that realization was worse than the impact.

The impact wasn't too bad.

What took the edge off was the ton or so of flying sandstone that swooped in at a shallow angle and caught him, flattening off his downbound trajectory and slowing his velocity into a survivable deceleration. George had the air knocked out of him as the gargoyle almost fumbled the catch, and things went black for a microsecond, but then he saw the wing that was flapping above him, and he saw the mended seam. He twisted his head to see the gargoyle's face, which spared him a quick look and said:

"*Gack!*"

"Hello, Spout," said George, fighting a ridiculously inappropriate bubble of hysterical laughter that was rising in his throat. "We've got to stop meeting like this. . . ."

Spout swerved suddenly. A large gargoyle swiped a talon at them, and then a second one flew in from above. Spout only managed to avoid a collision by flying into the side of the building and bracing himself against the scaffolding. On reflex, George grabbed on to the plastic safety webbing that shrouded the cold tubing. Spout punched away another assailant with a snarl and then turned and slashed at George. For a moment, George thought the creature had perversely snatched him from death only to have the satisfaction of decapitating him. And then the talon whistled past him and slashed a hole in the webbing. Before George could quite realize what was happening, Spout had grabbed him and pushed him into the relative safety of the decking within. George sprawled on the splintery boards, then turned in time to see Spout reaching a talon inside the slash.

"*Ging,*" he hissed urgently. George held out the fragment of wing, and the talon closed around it.

The great stone mouth opened and produced the first clear word George had heard from it, probably because it actually *did* begin with a G.

"Go."

George was shocked by the clarity.

"You're saying 'go'?"

Spout nodded fiercely, one eye scanning the sky above him.

"Go, Eigengang, go!"

George got it.

"Eigengang? You're calling me Ironhand?"

Spout exhaled heavily and rolled his eyes as if George were actually denser than the rock Spout had been carved from—and then Spout was savagely yanked back into the blackness as a gargoyle dropped and tackled him around the neck.

George didn't waste any time wondering why Spout had started to talk. He just decided anywhere would be better than where he was right now. As he saw gargoyles buffeting the protective mesh around the scaffolding, he decided to try for anywhere with solid brick walls around it. He ran along the clanking aerial walkway, trying each window as he passed. Four windows along, he got lucky. The window was in the process of being replaced, so there was just a dark hole in the brickwork.

He vaulted in and rushed blindly through a room full of timber and workbenches. He saw a door on the far end, which he ran for.

As he burst through the doorway, something grabbed him in an all-enveloping tackle. For a jolting moment, he knew it was some fresh hellish monster, and then he got himself disentangled and realized he'd just run into sheets of plastic that had been hung to keep the workman's dust in one room. He pushed through into a long, dark corridor and stumbled abruptly, his foot—the one without a shoe on it—finding a void where the floor should be, and he crunched on a rough surface below. He looked down, and in the murk, realized he'd gone through the floor and onto the lath and plaster of the ceiling below, because half the floorboards had been removed and were stacked on the side wall of the corridor.

He got up and made his way forward, picking a path as quickly as he could, past the long holes in the floor— hoping he was going to find a staircase soon. He thought he could hear stone wings and talons keeping pace with him on the scaffolding that ran parallel with the corridor, one short room away. He was sure he heard great stone knuckles rapping on the windows behind him, testing them. He bumped against a bench, and something heavy thudded onto the floor.

It was a club hammer, the big heavy kind used for hitting cold chisels.

He picked it up. Having three pounds of drop-forged steel on the end of a stout hickory handle was just the confidence-booster George needed. There was a piece of rope looped through a hole in the bottom of the handle, and he put it around his wrist.

He remembered a comic book his dad had had in his workroom, a memory of his own childhood—*The Mighty Thor*. He'd been a superhero with a hammer like this. George didn't feel much like a superhero right now, as he teetered his way carefully along the skeletonized floor joists. The sound of gargoyles tracking him seemed to come closer and closer.

He pushed through another curtain of plastic sheeting and found himself in a great, long room. It was so full of builders' equipment that in the dark it felt like an obstacle course: scaffolding towers and ladders hugged walls that were in the process of having the plaster scraped off, back to the brickwork beneath; big sacks of plaster and stacks of paint cans were piled next to blocks of Sheetrock panels; and there was even a cement mixer in the middle of the floor. George closed the door behind him and locked it for good measure. He stood there, shivering and wet. Now that he was still for a moment, he had time to realize how very cold he was.

The room had windows on both sides. George was pleased to see that the ones where the outside scaffolding was were all boarded up. So were many on the other side, facing Euston Road. He moved slowly around the edge of the room and wondered if he was safe. He couldn't hear any more noise from the gargoyles outside; though maybe that was because they, too, were keeping silent and trying to listen, so as to figure out exactly where he was.

If that was so, he gave them a big clue by almost immediately knocking something off a table, something that clashed like a cymbal as it hit the floor. He bent down and stopped its rolling before it made any more noise. It came apart as he lifted it back up, and nearly spilled its contents out the bottom. He caught the lid awkwardly because his free hand still had the club hammer in it. It was a biscuit tin, and George was holding it upside down. He put the hammer down on a tabletop, turned the biscuit tin the right way up, grabbed a handful of biscuits, and ate them greedily, almost on autopilot as he moved away from the table, scanning the room for anything else useful. He wondered if there was a heater in among the jumble, and whether, if there were, would he be able to warm up in front of it. He squeezed between a stack of cylinders that looked solid but then gave and wobbled as soon as he touched them. They were rolls of soft roof insulation. He reached a hand out to stop them from toppling.

And then he went very still, as out of the edge of his vision he saw an ominous group of men behind him, their faces standing out in the relative darkness of the corner of the room.

He didn't look directly at them, but carried on as if he hadn't seen them. They were so still that there was definitely something not right about them. He didn't know why a line of men would wait in the dark, just watching him, but he knew it couldn't be for any good reason. He drifted slowly back to table where he'd left the hammer. He wanted the reassuring heft of it in his hand before he confronted them, and he figured the way to do that was to act nonchalant. His mouth was suddenly dry as he reached for another biscuit. He crunched into it and then put the lid back on the tin.

He reached toward the tabletop, hoping the men would think he was just going to put the tin down. He placed it on the table, then grabbed the hammer and whirled, ready to lash out if they tried to rush him.

"Okay," he hissed. "What do you want?"

As he pulled the hammer from the table, he caught a coffee mug, which went spinning off the edge. The only answer he got was the sound of it smashing noisily in darkness.

The men didn't move. He was now facing them directly, so he could see this clearly. They just stared at him, great white moon faces impassive in the gloom.

He tried to swallow, but the biscuit had gone to sawdust in his dry mouth, and he choked. He stepped toward the line of men, determined that it was better to face them than turn his back and run away. There was something very unnatural in their stillness.

He dry-swallowed the biscuit fragments.

"Seriously, who are you—?"

One step closer and then he stopped dead.

They weren't anyone. They were just a line of white hard hats and overalls hanging on the wall. It was only his fear and the darkness that had turned them into people.

He lowered the hammer in relief. Better than not being people, they were dry clothes. He quickly rummaged through and found two work jackets and a padded shirt jacket. The shirt jacket had the flat, slightly sour smell of plaster, but George was in no position to be choosy. He stripped off his wet shirt and shrugged into the padded one. The quilted interior was cold against his skin, but he buttoned the jacket up and tied the arms of his wet shirt around his waist to keep his body heat in. He put the smaller of the two work jackets on top of it. It was rough, dark wool with some kind of plastic covering on the shoulders, but it was warm. Almost immediately he could feel the heat returning to his outer body. He stumbled over something at foot level, and was pleased to see it was a pair of paint- and plaster-covered workman's boots, like leather Wellingtons, without laces. He jammed his bare foot inside. The boot was big, but not unwearably so. He put the other boot on and stuck his other shoe down the back of his belt, cinching it tight. He rolled up the sleeves of the shirt, went back to the table, where he filled the jacket pockets with the rest of the biscuits and looked for something to drink.

There was nothing except a paint-splattered plastic kettle, so he drank the water from that, all the time keeping his ears open for any sign of gargoyles trying to get in. The only sounds he could hear were normal nighttime city sounds: traffic, the occasional thump of a car stereo in the street below, the high-pitched whine of a scooter, and in the distance the wah-wah and shrill electronic chirrup of a police siren. He crossed to the street side of the room and looked out one of the windows. No sign of trouble.

A gust of wind blew cold in from the window space next to the one he was looking out of, and a rattle of chains alerted him to the fact that it was somehow open to the night air. He hurried over and found that it was open but blocked by the huge circular mouth of a rubbish chute. It was one of those long segmented tubes that you see attached to the side of buildings under renovation. The kind that are essentially made from many bottomless dustbins chained together to form a long snakelike slide that drops all the builders' debris into a Dumpster below. This one was slightly curved, and George couldn't see what was at the bottom.

He stuck his head out of the small triangular gap at the side of the chute to see if the angle was shallow enough for him to even think of using it as an escape slide. The bad news was that it wasn't, really. The worse news was that something hissed on the wall to his right. George looked up to see three gargoyles flattened like geckos on the exterior of the building, all staring at him.

He ducked away fast, but not fast enough to miss seeing that the outside of the building was swarming with stone creatures, all listening at windows or scanning the brickwork. He ran back to the door, knowing he had to get out of there. He bumped into obstacles as he went—sending a teetering pile of felt roofing rolls scattering ahead of him. He hurdled one and then caught his shins against the sharp, hard edge of a paint can and reached the door in an ungainly stumble, dropping his hammer as he reached out to steady himself. It clattered loudly on the floor. He figured that the gargoyles must know where he was by now, so he definitely had to get somewhere else fast.

He tugged at the dead bolt on the door. It was stuck. He'd rammed it too tight when he'd locked the door. He gritted his teeth and pulled harder. It wouldn't budge, no matter how hard he pulled—then something hit the other side of the door, which freed the bolt, and the door flew open, sending him flying backward.

Two stone talons appeared on either side of the doorjamb, and as George scrambled to his feet, a gargoyle that had once had two horns but now only had one and a stump snarled into the space between them. The gargoyle was too big to get into the room without ducking and edging sideways—and that was what saved George.

He knew he was too far from his hammer to get it, but his hand closed on the wire handle of one of the paint cans he'd tripped over. As the gargoyle was ducking sideways and starting to unfold one wing into the room, George lunged forward, swinging the paint can in a desperate haymaker.

The weight of the can developed a powerful centrifugal force as he swung it over his shoulder, so that by the time it was coming back around on the upswing, it was going at quite a speed. The gargoyle snarled and launched a wild bite at George—and thereby stepped into the blow. The can caught it right under the chin. The force of the blow jarred George's hand, but he managed to keep hold of the can as the gargoyle went cartwheeling backward out into the corridor and ended up flat on its back. It lay there stunned, then shook its head and tried to right itself.

George felt adrenaline spiking in his nostrils and heard his teeth grind as he clenched his jaw and went after the creature. He swung the can left, and hit it hard on the side of its head, and then he caught it on the backswing. The can burst as the gargoyle's head bounced on the floor, and sprayed red paint all over its face and wing.

George saw its neck go slack, and backed up fast, rebolting the door behind him. Something else was rattling the boards that obscured the windows on the opposite side to the street. As the bolt slammed shut, the thought occurred to George that unless he came up with a plan for getting out of the room, he might just be caught like a rat that had locked itself in its own trap.

He wondered if he could survive the five-floor drop by sliding down the rubbish chute. He thought of the Dumpster that it must empty into, and all the lethal, hard, and sharp rubbish it could be filled with. Bad idea.

His legs were starting to shake, wanting to run but having nowhere to go. And now something started rattling the boarded-up windows on the chute side of the room. It really was time to go. He kicked out in frustration, to stop his leg from shaking as much as anything else, and connected with a soft roll of roof insulation. It thudded across the room, and as it did so, George knew what he was going to do. He picked up the nearest roll. Although it was unwieldy, he ran across the room and threw it down the chute. It just fit, with about four inches on either side. He turned and grabbed another, threw it after the first, and then went for another one, working fast and methodically so he wouldn't have time to listen to the second thoughts banging insistently on the back door of his consciousness.

There was an alarming splintering noise from the blocked window behind him, and he saw that the creature on the other side had managed to get one corner of the boarding free. It was definitely time to leave.

He took a deep breath and swung one leg into the chute. Then one of those second thoughts got through. If he reached the ground in enough of one piece to walk away, exactly how was he going to do that? The gargoyles on the outside wall would recognize him and swoop down.

He swung his leg back out and ran across to the hooks where he had gotten his jacket. He quickly jammed a second work jacket over the one he was already wearing. It was a tight fit, but when it was done, he felt bigger and fatly padded. Then he pulled a hard hat onto his head, snatched up the gloves he'd left on the table, and hammed his hands into them as he ran back to the chute, trying not to look behind at the new banging noise that was rocking the door on its flimsy hinges.

He didn't let himself think twice this time; though he did grab the hammer and another roll of insulating felt as he passed. He tossed the roll down the chute and swung straight after it into the yawning plastic gullet.

As his hands released the rim of the chute, he heard a loud crack from the window on the other side of the room—but then he was gone, plunging groundward at speed.

He could feel his stomach leap skyward as he fell in the opposite direction. Everything happened at once as he tried to remember to keep his mouth closed so he wouldn't bite his tongue on impact, as he'd once done on a high flume at a water park. His hard hat bobbled off and fell after him as he attempted to slow his descent by braking with his shoes and elbows and gloves, bracing his back against the curved interior of the pipe.

The outward friction didn't seem to slow him much, but he hoped it was enough to do more than turn a clean but fatal free fall into a juddering death-slide. His attempt to slow himself down kicked dirt off the sides of the tube, so he was falling into a blinding cloud of choking dust as he went. He stopped breathing and was trying to think how he'd know when to stop his feet from pushing outward in time to bring them together and attempt a parachute landing, when it all became academic: he hit bottom with a slamming jolt that knocked out all the air left in him as his knees pistoned upward toward his chin, and he stopped dead. But alive, he realized with a wave of elation that didn't diminish half a beat later as his hard hat caught up with him and bounced off his head.

He stayed very still, surrounded by the soft pink plug of roofing felt that had cushioned his fall, trying not to cough and splutter in the dust cloud his impact had kicked up. Once he'd really believed the evidence of his senses and ascertained that nothing was broken, he grabbed his hat and gripped the hammer tightly as he squeezed himself down through the roofing felt and into the half-empty Dumpster beyond.

It was covered with a tarpaulin and tied down against the wind, but he found a gap and managed to serpentine, headfirst, out of it. He risked a glance upward, and saw that all the gargoyles were massed around the windows of the room he'd just left, five stories above. He darted into the protection given by the overhanging scaffolding and walked as quickly and quietly toward the corner of the building as he could manage.

If the gargoyles hadn't heard him falling down the chute, he was sure they must be able to hear his heart hammering. He remembered to put the white hard hat on his head as he came to the end of the scaffolding, and walked out into the street with only the slightest hesitation. Not looking back and up was almost the hardest thing he'd had to do, but he knew he couldn't. Because any gargoyle who looked down mustn't see his face and realize that the bulky man walking away beneath the hat was, in fact, a boy.

His shoulders itched and his ears strained for the sound of anything whistling out of the sky behind him, but by the time he had walked halfway past the next building, he thought he might have gotten away with it. As he passed the cascading fonts announcing the entrance to the British Library, he gave himself the luxury of twirling nonchalantly on his feet. He saw that the coast was clear, and his knees almost buckled with relief as he hurried down Euston Road.

He didn't notice a huge statue turn its head and look at him from a vantage point set back in the piazza outside the British Library. The huge male figure was bent over a large pair of dividers, as if measuring the world. He looked as though he had been made, cut up into chunks, and then badly reassembled, with gaps where the joins didn't quite meet.

The giant looked at him, then up at the rookery on St. Pancras. He put his fingers in his mouth and whistled.

Chapter Thirty-three

Escape to Silence

"Come on, Glinty, time to be somewhere else," said Little Tragedy, tugging Edie back through the mirrored arches, into the dark alcove beyond.

At the front door of the pub, she could see the Friar talking earnestly to whoever was on the other side. Being somewhere else seemed like exactly the right idea. The only thing was that once she looked around, she realized there was no door out of this cloistered space. It didn't feel like a place of escape. It felt like a dead end. She suddenly felt like a rat in a trap.

As if reading her thoughts, Little Tragedy put his finger up to his lips and monkey-swung up onto one of the wall lamps and did something to the mosaic roundel in the ceiling. He dropped to the ground, nimble as a cat.

"Trust me. I know somewhere the Tallyman won't find yer."

He beckoned her to the parallel mirrors. Edie's feet

braked on the carpet. She had no intention of going back to the Blitz. Little Tragedy shook his head impatiently.

"'S all right. I changed the wossit in the ceiling. We ain't going to the past, just somewhere else in the city, somewhere they can't find yer. It's an 'ouse, a safe one, don't worry. Look, it's nuffink bad."

He pointed into the mirror. Edie let her feet take her close enough for a look. There was no conflagration on the other side of the mirror. There was just an empty gray room, bare gray walls meeting dusty gray floorboards. The only relief from the plainness silvering everything was the crisscross lattice shadow thrown across the floor by the window in the moonlight. There was nothing else in the room, and no shadows where danger might lurk.

She heard the Friar raise his voice in the doorway. She heard the words "walker" and "stone," and that alone evaporated any misgivings she was having about reentering the mirrors.

She nodded at Little Tragedy. Her eyes slipped over his shoulder and were caught by the sight of George's jacket hanging on the beer-pump handles. Little Tragedy saw what she was looking at and nodded.

"You're right. Don't want to forget the dainty, do we?"

He nipped out into the barroom proper, and quick as thought, had snatched the blazer and was back at her side.

"Ladies first," he whispered.

Just before Edie stepped into the mirror, she hesitated. *What if—?*

Before the thought could go further, Little Tragedy had clucked with impatience and pushed past her, into the mirror, tugging her arm as he went. She stepped in after him and felt the surface tension on the mirror stretch and pop as before, and then she was in the room beyond.

This time, instead of her ears being assaulted by a hellish barrage of noise, she experienced the opposite— complete quiet. It was the sound of a city at peace with itself. It was so silent that she could hear her heart begin to slow from the panicked tempo it had risen to when she had been in the pub only an instant before.

It wasn't just the lack of explosions and fire that was different from the last trip she'd made into the mirror. It also wasn't hot. In fact, it was the opposite. The air was still, so there was no draft, but it was not even warm.

"It's cold," she said, watching her breath plume as she turned to look at Little Tragedy.

"Sometimes it's cold, sometimes it isn't. It's a funny old room," said the boy. He was looking at her over the top of George's jacket.

There was something in his eyes that she hadn't seen before. He still had the cocky urchin's grin, but his eyes didn't match the look. His eyes weren't grinning. They were saying something completely different, something not cheery, or chirpy, or cheeky.

They were saying sorry.

"'E's not a bad man. 'E's always looking after glints. 'E told me. 'E said no one looks after them better."

Her heart froze and her hand was already in her pocket, closing around the well-worn disk of her sea-glass. Even as she pulled it out into the gray room, she knew what she would see, because it was already hot to the touch, already blazing with warning light. And as the light shone out and cast her finger shadows on the gray walls, she completed, too late, the thought she'd begun in the pub, just before Little Tragedy had pulled her into the mirror.

The thought was this: if the Friar had shielded her from a bomb blast and saved her from the Blitz, why wouldn't he save her from the Walker? Of course, the answer was that he probably *would* save her from the Walker. Which raised the question of why the boy-imp had pulled her into the mirror behind the monk's back, and why he was looking so wrong—

"You're not talking about the Friar, are you?"

His eyes swiveled this way and that, anywhere but at her face, at the shock and rising horror in her eyes. He held out the jacket, as if making a peace offering.

"'Ere, take your coat. It's chilly in here."

Edie looked at the mirror behind Little Tragedy, calculating how she could get to it without his stopping her.

"Thanks," she said slowly, taking the jacket. She knew how to do it. She'd take the coat and throw it over his head and jump past him in the confusion. She remembered the broken dragon's head in the pocket and thought that she'd better take that with her, but suddenly she realized the heavy weight wasn't in the pocket at all. She hesitated, confused for an instant, then looked up and saw it.

Little Tragedy had the broken carving in his hand. He took advantage of her shock to back up to the mirror in two fast steps.

"You can't take that," she said, her voice hoarsening. "Don't do this."

His smile was really just hanging on by a thread, and his eyes looked so sad peering out from the mismatched face, that he might have been a tragic boy wearing the mask of Comedy, rather than the other way around.

"Don't leave me here," rasped Edie, looking at the bare gray walls. Something moved slowly beyond the windows, and a new terror gripped her.

"'E's not a bad man. 'E told me," the urchin insisted. He put one leg into the mirror. He paused as if he wanted to be gone but his conscience wouldn't let him make a quick exit, as if what he wanted was for her to tell him that what he was doing was right.

"Tragedy, no, please—!"

He shook his head. Something glinted in his eye.

"'E'll be along in a while. You'll be hunky-dory, no bother."

As Edie leaped for him, trying to get in the mirror, he

jumped back and out of the room, and she hit nothing but hard, cold glass.

Her first impulse was to smash her fists into the mirror, but sense took over and halted her in midpunch. For some reason she couldn't get back in the mirror, but if she calmed down, maybe she could find a way.

She stepped back, trying to clear her head, pushing the panic and outrage at Little Tragedy's betrayal down far enough so there was room for her to think.

She spun around. There was a door, four walls, and a window. The door was the obvious choice, but a thought was becoming more and more insistent at the back of her mind, and she didn't want to open it or even touch it.

She crossed to the window and looked out. It was, of course, barred. The thing that she had seen moving beyond the window was still moving, and the warning bell it had triggered jangled louder and louder in her head.

It was snow.

The rooftops it was falling on were not the rooftops of the London she had just left. There were no sodium streetlights, no TV antennas, no satellite dishes—no lights or flickering from TV screens in the windows beneath. There was no hard-edged electric light out there at all.

It was quiet way beyond the fact that the snow was deadening every sound as it blanketed the city. There was simply no traffic noise. No cars, no buses, no whining motor scooters. There was a distant sound of a barrel organ, and the jingle of a harness.

She looked down through the bars. In the narrow slice of street that she could just make out, she saw a horse pulling an old-fashioned hackney cab, its wheels slowly cutting twin furrows through the deep snow. The driver sat on his high seat, cracking his whip at the horse's hindquarters, a short top hat tied onto his head with a scarf, his legs swathed in a horse blanket. Then he was gone, leaving nothing but wheel marks in the snow.

She knew then that the imp had lied about more than one thing; she knew she was not in present London. She was in an older London, a London deadened with snow, an icy London where horses made wheel furrows through white streets, a London where it was cold enough for rivers to freeze over and for girls to be drowned in ice holes.

She knew, too, that he had lied about this being a safe house. This was not a safe house, because she could always tell if stones held sadness or anguish or horror, and this was why she didn't want to touch the gray walls or even the door handle several feet away.

She knew all this even without hearing the distant sound of a woman sobbing, which came from a lower floor, beyond the door.

This was no safe house. This was the House of the Lost.

CHAPTER THIRTY-FOUR

The Euston Mob

George hurried west on Euston Road, leaving the British Library behind him. He had just heard an urgent, earsplitting whistle, and though he hadn't seen the whistler, he had a nasty feeling that whatever it was, he'd do no harm by quickly getting as far from it as he could.

Now that he wasn't actually fighting for his life, he was able to focus on his urgent worry about Edie and the Gunner. As far as Edie was concerned, George was pretty sure that she would continue on to the Black Friar as they'd planned. One of the things about her was that she didn't go to pieces when things got hard. The Black Friar would surely be able to help her. He hoped she would find the broken dragon's head in his coat pocket and use it to bargain with the Friar if necessary. He couldn't believe how much time had been wasted since they'd sat together in the shelter of the Dumpster, working out the first step in their probably futile plan to save the Gunner. Now that George was safe, the whole business of being picked up and flown all over London seemed like a desperate inconvenience. He still had no idea how to find or save the Gunner. The frustration of it hit him with the intensity of a blow, and he stopped, trying to think straight now that the adrenaline was flushing out of his system.

He realized he was walking with no sense of where he should be going. He should be heading for the Black Friar's pub. Of course, going to the Black Friar's pub meant crossing back into the City, and that meant finding a way past the dragons that stood watch on each thoroughfare leading across the old boundary; but he'd have to deal with that problem when he came to it.

He was level with the entrance to Euston station. If his sense of direction was working, then he needed to turn south and east. His London geography was a bit sketchy, but he thought if he turned south he would eventually hit the river, and then all he reckoned he'd have to do was to head east.

So he turned, and the scrape of his oversize plasterer's boots on the gritty paving stone was echoed by another stony scrape in front of him, and then a hiss. And as he looked up, he saw two massive stone bat wings blocking his way as the gargoyle he had hit with the red paint can dropped softly in front of him. The red was splashed across it like blood, and its head was cocked.

One paint-spattered eye was screwed shut, while the other seemed to bore into George, despite its stony blankness.

He looked around for somewhere to hide. To his left was a big blocky gatehouse, one of a pair leading into the station. Unfortunately it would be too far for him to reach before the gargoyle got to him, and even if it wasn't, there was no door that he could see in the facade, which was carved with the names of battles fought long ago in faraway places.

With nowhere to run, George knew that his battle was about to be here and now.

He knew it from the look on the gargoyle's face as it scraped one talon forward on the paving stone and dragged the other one after it. He knew it from the painful twinge in his hand, from the dragon's scar, and the three flaws entwining his forearm.

He gripped the hammer, ready to go down fighting.

The pain in his hand gave him an idea. The scar had bought him a moment with the Knight. If it bought him a moment with the gargoyle, maybe he could think of something that would stop the gargoyle from tearing him to shreds.

"Hey," he said, holding his hand out. "Back off."

The big taint cocked its head and then, amazingly, stopped.

George saw his wrist extending out from the work-jacket sleeve, and caught a glint of metal reflecting the streetlights on a part of him where he should just have seen his skin. He realized with a sickening jolt that the stone and brass grooves braiding around his arm had definitely moved farther toward his elbow. He decided he didn't have the time to worry about that now. He had to keep his advantage over the gargoyle.

"Yes," he said, submerging the shake in his voice. "A maker's mark. An Ironhand. You back off, or I'll—"

He couldn't think of what to say. So he took one step forward, brandishing his hand in front of him as if it were a magical talisman.

"Back off, or I'll . . . I'll . . ."

"Most likely bleed all over him, like."

The voice from behind George was not one he'd heard before. It was a Geordie voice with the flat, hard matter-of-fact vowels of northeast England.

"I was you, bonny lad, I'd lower the hammer and step backward,"

George wanted to look behind him, but he didn't want to take his eyes off the gargoyle.

"Big Red there's not fussed about your 'and, Sonny Jim. He's fussed about four Lee-Enfields pointing right at his ugly mug," rasped another voice, which sounded as if it came from South London and had smoked way too many cigarettes along the way.

George realized that the gargoyle wasn't looking at him at all. It had stopped because of something that was behind him.

"Now, why don't 'e step back to us, lad. Be safer, all things considered," said a third voice, humming with a west-country twang in which all the S's sounded like Z's.

George turned.

Four bronze World War I soldiers were behind him, tall men in long flapping army greatcoats. Three stood and one knelt, resting his elbow on one knee. They wore soft peaked hats instead of tin helmets, and they all had rifles leveled unwaveringly at the gargoyle. One of the standing riflemen's jaws was in constant motion, as if chewing tobacco.

The kneeling soldier took his trigger hand off the weapon and beckoned George toward him, nodding slowly as if to say it was going to be all right.

George backed up fast. The standing soldiers made space for George, without taking their guns off the taint, as he walked between them and turned to see what happened next. The rifleman who was chewing stepped forward into the space that George had just vacated and spat a large gob of something dark onto the paving stone at the gargoyle's feet, splashing its talons as he did so. The chewer gestured to the sky with his gun.

"Haddaway, ya greet sackless cuddy!"

When the gargoyle didn't move, the soldier took another step forward and prodded it in the chest with his gun. The gargoyle flinched, hissed, and threw itself backward into the air. Its great wings beat downward, causing the soldier's greatcoat to billow behind him like a cloak. It pulled itself higher and higher into the sky, until it disappeared behind the rooftops. There was a general easing of tension and uncocking of guns, and the soldier next to George turned and nodded at the chewer.

"It's all right; we never know what he's saying either."

George looked at the soldiers as they all crowded around him, looking down with interest.

"You'll be the boy we heard about, most like," said the one called Westie. "Us got a pigeon tellin' us to keep a sharp eye out. Friend of the Gunner's, it said?"

George nodded. The chewer looked around.

"Said tha was wi' a lass too, kiddar?"

"Edie," said George. "We got split up."

The soldiers tutted and sucked their teeth.

"Who are you?" said George.

The soldier nearest him paused in the action of lighting a cigarette.

"Rifleman South," he said, his accent turning "South" into "Sarf." He thumbed introductions over his shoulder without looking. "These are my oppos. Corporal North's a Geordie bastard, as you can tell, so we don't understand hardly nothing what he says; Westie here's a bit of a wurzel, but once you get used to him he's all right. And Private East there don't say much anyway, but he's a nugget, lets his fighting do the talking, so don't you worry about him. They're all good men in a scrap, none better. They call us the Euston Mob."

He jerked his thumb at an obelisk with four empty plinths at its base.

"That's where we stay. We was railwaymen, see, before the war, so they put us in front of the station. That's our billet. Plinths on points of the compass, as you see; hence the names. Come on, out of the street."

He led George back toward the obelisk.

George looked into the night sky, where the red gargoyle had disappeared.

"You think he's really gone?"

South hunkered down against the stone, rifle across his knees, enjoying his smoke.

"He won't hang about. Westie here may seem slow, but he can shoot the eye out of a running squirrel without breaking a sweat; leastways that's what he's always telling us, eh, Westie?"

The other soldiers joined them sitting against the monument's base, except for East, who seemed edgier than the others and stood apart, keeping watch on the sky toward St. Pancras.

"'E won't be back, not if 'e knows what's good for 'im," agreed Westie, taking a light from the end of South's cigarette.

"The Gunner's in trouble," said George. "I need help."

"Everyone needs help, Sonny Jim. Why don't you start by telling us what's going on, then," said South.

In as few words as he could manage, George sketched everything that had happened to him since his nightmare began. The soldiers didn't interrupt him, but he was aware of their looking at each other at certain points in the story. And when he told the bit about how the Gunner had broken his word and had been taken by the Walker, even East turned away from his scouring of the night sky and looked at George intently. George finished, and was conscious of nothing so much as that he just seemed to have wasted more time.

"So anyway," he concluded, "I started out to help the Gunner, and now I've got these three duels, or contests, to fight as well!"

"Oh yeah, you gotta fight them. You can't duck 'em. Duck 'em and you're done," said South. "Them stripes on your arm, they're the marks of your task. Each stripe is different, see, like the contests are. And they're on the move, right?"

George stared at the flaws corkscrewing toward his elbow. Two were slowly moving up his arm, but the metal one had just started to circle in a tight coil. As if it couldn't go farther. He nodded.

"Ay, well, it'd be worse than the black dam if you let one o' they buggers get to your heart."

"What do you mean?" George asked, knowing he was going to hate the answer.

"Why, you'll likely croak or worse, lad," South said flatly, looking at him through a skein of cigarette smoke.

"What's worse than croaking?" asked George in horror.

There was a pause.

"You met the Walker, yeah?" puffed South, and widened his eyes as if no further explanation were necessary.

"'E just must face up to the three contests, and one by one they'll clear," Westie explained. "That's why you must stand. If you don't, you'll lose anyway, because you won't stop the line reaching your heart, see."

Now George was panicking, despite all his intention to keep a clear head.

"Wait, but with the Knight, I didn't finish the fight. I mean, am I already doomed?" He stared at the soldiers' faces. "Am I going to croak?"

North reached over and took George's arm. He pushed the sleeve back and examined the scars. He looked at South.

"Well," exhaled South, "that's a matter of opinion. It seems to me you didn't duck a fight as such. Seems to me you were on the point—a very sharp point—of losing one. And then this gargoyle, the one you called Spout, he flies in and snatches you, yeah."

North and West nodded.

"Reet. Wasn't tha' running away, like. Was a *deus ex* wotsit . . ."

North snapped his fingers, trying to conjure the word that was on the tip of his tongue.

"*Machina.*" South cleared his throat and pulled a watch out of his pocket. "You didn't run, is what I'm saying. Worst you could say is rain stopped play."

"I don't follow."

"Maybe you don't follow, chum, but I reckon the Last Knight will. I think he'll follow you until the fight's all done. It's your fate, mate. Your first duel ain't over, it just got cut short. Postponed, as it were. I'd say you're half a scrap down and two more to go. Look at how that metal vein must have started to move, but then stopped. If you'd chosen to run away, it would have continued on and split your heart, and we wouldn't be wasting valuable time talking. It's just coiling around and around, like it's marking time until you meet the Knight again and finish the duel you started. But that ain't the problem right now."

He tapped his watch. "This is."

George stared at the timepiece. If he'd felt sick before, he felt sicker now.

"You're saying I'm out of time. The Gunner's out of time. It's nearly turn o'day."

"Exactly," said North.

"Ar, and if 'e isn't there, if his plinth is empty by midnight—"

"The Gunner's a goner. . . ." finished South.

George felt the night closing in on him, as the rising claustrophobia of hopelessness began to take over.

"But I'm out of time. I'll never—"

"You want to talk less and listen more, chum," said an unfamiliar voice. It was East. He pointed at Westie. "What did he say?"

George reran the conversation in his head. He heard

the soft west-country burr saying *If 'e isn't there, if his plinth is empty by midnight* . . . But it didn't make sense, and they were all looking at him . . . and then he got it.

"If he's plinth is empty—you mean?"

North nodded. "Canny lad."

George was on his feet. Urgency took the place of rising hopelessness and squashed it back down into place.

". . . You mean, if someone takes his place on the plinth, he won't die?"

Four bronze faces nodded solemnly at him.

"Well, why didn't . . . That's easy . . . I'll do it!"

South shook his head. "Standing to ain't easy, Sonny Jim. It's not just standing there—"

"Fine, but I'll do it!" George was almost giddy with relief.

"Nobody 'ere doubts that. That ain't the question."

"What is the question?"

Rifleman South held out the watch. George looked at it and started doing a horrible calculation in his head.

"Question is, how fast can you run?"

George didn't waste any time answering, because he had no time. He just nodded and sprinted westward. He did remember to stop when he got to the edge of the traffic—and he took advantage of the enforced second's pause to turn and hurl a hurried "Thank you" over his shoulder as he did. A hole opened in the cars, and he dashed across the road, vaulted the central divider, and jinked west, running at full tilt.

He was running so fast he didn't see the homeless man in the doorway track him with raven-black eyes. And he was too intent on finding his way to Hyde Park corner to hear the tramp saying, "Boy maker running west on Euston Road."

CHAPTER THIRTY-FIVE

The House of the Lost

Edie stood quietly for a long time. After the distant fit of sobbing, the house was still, but not quite silent. Outside the window, the snow-deadened city continued to leak the sound of a distant barrel organ. Apart from that, the only noises she could hear came from within the house, and they were the sounds of the house itself: a door with hinges that needed oiling opened and closed somewhere below. There was a short sliding noise and then a sudden thud as if an unseen hand had opened, or perhaps shut, a heavy bolted lock. Floorboards creaked as something moved across them.

And then there was silence, a silence that Edie added to by not moving at all.

One reason she didn't move was because she knew that when she did, the dusty floorboards beneath her feet would creak, and she had the distinct feeling that the silence she was listening to was *exactly* the kind of silence that was listening right back.

It was a silence that was patiently waiting for her to make the first sound.

The other reason she stayed still was that she was in the middle of the room, as far from the walls as she could get. A normal person wouldn't have noticed it, but Edie was a glint, and being a glint, the walls growled at her with a kind of low-frequency hum, a horrid magnetic attraction enticing her to touch them and release the stored trauma from the brick and plaster. It was the same intensity of sadness she felt as she passed cemeteries and churchyards and old hospitals, somehow willing her to reach out and draw it from the stones.

She steadied her breathing and tried to keep her mind off the tug of the stored distress by calmly checking the room for anything that might help her. The insistent pull of the walls made her bunch her hands deep into her pockets, in case they wandered off on their own and touched something without the permission of her conscious mind.

There really was not much to see. There was the barred window, there were the two mirrors, and there was a thick layer of dust over everything. And that was it.

Having reviewed the contents of the room, and keeping her ears on alert for the slightest noise beyond the door, Edie turned her attention to the floor.

She realized that the sick tug of pent-up anguish that

came at her from the walls also dragged at her from below, like a dark undertow. She was glad she was wearing shoes. She had never been in a place that held so much potential malice and sadness, so much that there was a foretaste of it in the air; she could tell it was bad in the same way that you can tell what certain foods will taste like just by the cooking smell. It crackled invisibly all around her, like static electricity.

She had never been in this house, but it felt like home.

It didn't feel like home in a warm way, not like the few tattered happy fragments of home she remembered from the good parts of her childhood; nor did it feel like some idealized vision of home—a place of security where everything would always be all right, everything understood, everything forgiven.

It felt like the other one, the home she'd never been to, the one where secretly—ever since she'd killed her stepfather—she knew she belonged: the dark home where yesterday's secrets were exposed so that today's pain could be justified and tomorrow's punishments planned.

A single tear makes little sound as it falls to the floor, but the sight of it splashing in the dust jerked Edie out of the paralysis she had fallen into, and she remembered to breathe, sucking in a deep and desperately needed lungful of air. She angrily wiped the back of her hand across her eyes, determined that the one treacherous tear would have no company.

Then she focused on the floor again: it was thick with dust but there were distinct footmarks, which she could see were hers and the bare feet marks of Little Tragedy. There were also paw marks that had nothing to do with either of them. They were like dog paws, but bigger than any Edie had seen; and then there was a swirling drag mark serpentining into the room from the door. It came about a third of the way inside and stopped, as if some-one had started sweeping and then given up the idea when the thickness and the pervasiveness of the dust had dispirited them.

Edie was standing there, trying to piece together the evidence in front of her eyes, when she became aware of a tickle in her nose.

It wasn't a bad thing in itself, but it was going to lead to a sneeze. A sneeze is also not a bad thing in itself. Edie had once spent a summer's afternoon looking up into the sun because it made her sneeze, and sneezing, on that day, had made her feel good. On this night, sneezing was not going to make Edie feel good. It was going to make her feel very bad, because on this night, she knew she would be sneezing into a listening silence that was just waiting for her to break it.

On this night, Edie knew one sneeze could well be fatal.

Before she could think how to stifle it, it exploded. She grabbed her nose and clamped it shut and jammed George's balled-up jacket over her face to muffle the sound—but the noise of the air convulsing its way out of her just redirected out the side of her mouth in a sharp detonation.

She stayed where she was, bent over her hands, ears straining for a reaction to the noise. For a moment she thought she'd gotten away with it—but then she heard floorboards creak. It was the unmistakable sound of someone coming up stairs. She could hear a dragging noise, too, a sort of rustling, and the counterpoint of smaller clicking footsteps.

There was an especially sharp crack from a floorboard that seemed to be the larger thing or person reaching the landing, and then the sounds moved closer to the door. Edie had time to see a golden strip of wavering light appear in the crack beneath it, as if the figure approaching were carrying some kind of lantern— and then the footsteps and the scuffling stopped suddenly.

Edie grimaced and very quietly slipped her arms into George's coat again. Whatever was going to happen, she thought, another layer couldn't do any harm, either offering protection or warmth.

Then she heard the sniffing.

Two dark shadows broke the golden strip under the door, and from them came hungry intakes of breath, as if whatever was outside were trying to inhale the inside of the room in big hungry nasal gulps of air.

Edie looked down and saw the warning stone blazing

a shaft of light out of her pocket. She closed her hands around it, extracting some faint support from the familiar sea-rounded edges and accompanying heat.

The door opened.

A woman stood in the opening, a tall woman in an old-fashioned gray dress that covered her from her neck down to the floor and beyond, where her full skirts belled out and trailed around her. She wore a wide belt tight around her middle, and her hands were covered by thick protective gloves made from rough suede, which reached up to her elbows.

Edie couldn't see her face, because the woman held a candle in front of it, and all she could make out was the impression of a high forehead and dark hair scraped back into a severe bun.

"What is your name?" the woman said in a disturbingly quiet voice.

"What's yours?" said Edie, reflexively defiant.

There was a pause. Edie saw the woman cock her head as if adjusting to what she'd just heard. When she spoke again it was almost a whisper, as light and dark as a raven's feather, but not so quiet that Edie couldn't hear the rising note of surprise in her voice.

"You are a young girl?"

Edie looked down at herself. "Er, yeah . . . What are you? Blind?"

The candle lowered as the woman answered. "No. I'm not blind, child. I just choose not to see."

It was the word "choose" that made what Edie saw so much more disturbing than it already was.

The woman's face was gaunt and almost ageless in its severity, but the most striking thing was the eyes above her high cheekbones.

They were sewn shut.

Four workmanlike stitches closed each eyelid with thick black cobbler's thread. The only thing that made the sight worse was the hint that the woman had done this to herself.

"Why would you do that?" said Edie, despite herself. "Why would you let someone do that?"

The woman sighed as if the answer to the question were so obvious that it was a waste of preciously hoarded energy.

"Eight short stitches? It's nothing, child, not if you wish to stop seeing. . . ."

"But why?" Edie couldn't stop herself asking in outrage.

"Come. You know why. You know what happens when we do what we do. You know willpower is not enough to keep our eyes closed. You know however hard we try, the eyes always open, and then they see what is stored in the stones. You know that the shards of the past stored in the stones are seldom happy and almost always terrible—"

The meaning of what the woman was saying hooked into Edie's gut like a sucker punch.

"You said 'us'. . . . You mean you're a glint?"

"I was. And it is my lot to live in this house. Can you feel what is in this house?"

Edie nodded, her mouth too dry to answer. Then she realized that the woman couldn't see her; but before she could reply, the woman was speaking again.

"Of course you can. You'd do the same to yourself, girl: close your eyes, wear thick gloves and sturdy boots to avoid any contact with the fabric of a building whose every touch invites an agony a hundred times worse than a mere needle prick. . . ."

Her foot kicked out from beneath her skirt and stamped sharply on the floor, making the dust jump. Her voice remained unnervingly quiet in comparison.

"Now. Enough talk. You must come with me."

Edie had a very strong sense that she was going to be taken somewhere even worse than this. And though they hadn't worked, she wanted to stay close to the mirrors and the door. They might open back into her normal world and time.

"Forget it," Edie said. "No way."

"You must do as I say, girl. You must not say no."

"Watch me."

There was a low growl. For a moment, Edie thought it had come from the blind woman. Then she realized it had come from behind her. It was the kind of growl that you feel through the soles of your feet. It was the kind of growl you ignore at your peril.

"I cannot. And I am not used to being disobeyed. . . ."

said the Blind Woman in a voice as dark and delicate as beetles scuttling across a black silk shroud.

Edie knew that if she gave in to being scared, she'd go to pieces; and she knew that if she went to pieces, she was done for. So she set her chin and dug her heels in.

"Well, get used to it. I'm—"

Edie didn't even get as far as "not" before the growls started again, and then the Blind Woman's skirts billowed out on each side. Two brindled mastiff dogs the size of small ponies came into the room, heads low to the ground, ears flattened, teeth bared, hunched and ready to spring.

"You can come now, or you can beg to come later."

The Blind Woman's voice was pale with disinterest as the dogs prowled forward, their great heads six inches above the dusty floorboard, eyes rolled up and fixed on Edie. The spittle leaking out from their snarls left a trail in the dust as they moved across the floor.

Edie stood still until they were close enough on either side for her to feel hot breath on her hands. She clenched and pulled them higher in a subconscious but futile effort to keep them out of harm's way.

"Look—" she said.

The dogs leaped at her, teeth clashing, loud, angry barks hitting her with the force of actual blows. Dog spittle ribboned across her eyes as her hands reflexively snapped up to protect her face from the sharp fangs clashing inches away.

Despite herself, her survival mechanism kicked in, and she was pushed back by the enraged barking and snapping teeth as the dogs herded her across the room. Her hand touched the wall, and there was a jolt as the wailing past flashed into her.

She went rigid with shock, and dust billowed out around her like a mini blast-wave from an unseen detonation. What she glinted in harsh jagged slices was:

The room in summer.

Sunlight shafting in through the windows, making diagonal beams of light in the dust.

A short-haired woman in a light blue sundress with a sprigged daisy pattern was crouched in the center of the room. She was staring around herself in bewilderment. Her feet looked defenseless in a pair of white flip-flops.

Time sliced, and the woman was suddenly shouting "No!" at the door, with such intensity that the tendons on her neck stood out like whipcords.

Another slice, and Edie saw the woman's hands scrabbling something hanging on a chain around her neck, to protect it from someone standing in the door. She clutched it tightly, almost hiding the telltale light blazing out from its sea-rounded edges.

It was a brown piece of sea-glass: a heart stone.

Edie saw the short-haired woman go very still. She saw her clench her jaw—saw it in a way that she felt her own clenched jaw.

She saw two huge brindled shapes leap into the living frame, barking furiously, and she heard a scream—

Time sliced again, and on the floor where the woman had been was nothing except the sea-glass and a white flip-flop upside down in the dust.

Edie jerked her hand away from the wall, and the glinting stopped abruptly.

She saw the Blind Woman working her mouth as if choking down a rising wave of nausea. The dogs had taken a half step back. But only half.

"Whatever you saw, child," whispered the Blind Woman. "Whatever you saw, it will be worse when it happens to you."

The dogs snarled.

Edie thought of George. She thought of the Gunner. She saw the Gunner smile, and she saw George smile at her, too. She knew that giving in was betraying them as well as herself.

She felt the dogs' breath on her hand. Hot and wet and meaty. She decided she wasn't going to give in. She would live to fight another day.

"Fine," Edie said. "Fine."

She reached into her pocket and folded her hand around her heart stone before stepping carefully past the dogs toward the Blind Woman. The dogs moved with her, growling more quietly now, eyes still locked on her.

"If you try to run, if you do anything other than what I tell you, they will bite," the Blind Woman murmured as gently as a midnight breeze caressing its way through a cemetery hedge. "Now come to me."

Edie stood in front of the woman, shadowed by the dogs. She stared into the whipstitched eyelids.

"Happy now?" Edie gritted.

The Blind Woman didn't move. It was as if the unseeing eyes were somehow seeing Edie. She slowly pulled off a glove, and an unexpectedly soft hand traced the contours of Edie's face. She found the wet tracks of Edie's tears.

"Spirited," she said, and put the glove back on. "I was spirited once."

"Tell me what you want," said Edie, swallowing something bitter at the back of her throat.

"I want nothing that you can give me. I want my warning stone," the Blind Woman said simply. "He stole it."

"The Walker?" said Edie.

"Who else takes our heart stones?" sighed the Blind Woman. "Follow me."

"No, wait," said Edie, desperately trying to make sense of what she was hearing. "Why does he take our heart stones?"

"He wants the power in them, the power that makes them blaze, the power that gives us just enough strength to cope with glinting the past." She let a bitter half-laugh escape. "It's such a small piece of power, but it means everything to each of us individually. Whereas, the only way he can use the stones to get enough strength for his needs is to collect *all* of them and add their little powers together to make one big one."

She turned and walked to the door.

"Why does he need this power?" asked Edie, dry-mouthed, measuring the distance to the door to see if she could get past and put the woman between herself and the dogs.

The Blind Woman turned and looked at her, pausing in the doorway for an instant. It was hard to see if her smile was pitying or just sad as she replied:

"Ask him. He's coming. . . ."

Chapter Thirty-Six

Road Runner

For the first time in a long time, George felt he was running toward something. It made a difference. Fear was pretty good at getting him moving, but that was running fueled by the flight part of the fight-or-flight reflex. This running was taking its fuel from the fight part. Maybe that was why he was able to dredge up the reserves of strength he needed.

He stopped worrying about taints swooping down on him; not because he wasn't scared of them, but because worrying about things he couldn't possibly stop was an obvious waste of energy, and he had none to spare. Every ounce was going into keeping his legs and arms pistoning forward. He would just have to deal with any attacker, if it happened, as it happened. He had one shot at getting to the Gunner's plinth, and he wasn't going to let anything distract him from it.

He ran in a kind of fugue state. Somewhere he knew all this was hurting and that he had run through several stitches in his side, and that his breath was tearing out in great ragged gasps that would have sounded like sobs if anyone had noticed, but he didn't care. He just ran, clutching the hammer.

And as he ran, he realized that his mind was clearing all the things he didn't understand, and leaving only the things that mattered, only the things he could deal with. First he was going to be able to buy more time for the Gunner, if he could just make it to the plinth. Then he would find Edie, and she would tell him what the Black Friar had said, and they would find a way to get the Gunner back. There was no doubt in his mind, because there was no room for anything that would slow him down.

Unfortunately, he turned into a narrow alley and suddenly found there was no room in it for him and the low sports car that was heading straight toward him.

It honked its horn and flashed its lights, but George kept on running. Luckily, the alley was so narrow, the driver was going slowly in order to not scrape his expensive side mirrors. So when George didn't stop, the driver had enough time to slam on the brakes without skidding or running him down. The car came to a stop, entirely blocking the alley.

George didn't miss a step. He jumped up on the hood of the low-slung muscle car, over the roof, onto the trunk, and off into the empty alley beyond, before the driver knew what was happening.

Of course, the moment the driver realized that the boy had run over his car, he went berserk. George could hear a torrent of shouting from behind him, then a series of angry blasts on the horn, and finally the sound of someone trying to slam an expensive gearbox into reverse, managing to engage the gear at the third shrieking try, and then the boom of exhaust as the driver tried to back up and catch George.

George took the time to glance backward for an instant. He saw reversing lights approaching at speed as the driver wobbled to keep straight in the narrow alley. He had just enough time to see one side mirror explode into expensive shards against a drainpipe, and then he turned away and ran on, pausing only to pull a rubbish bin into the alley to discourage further pursuit from the driver, now leaning out of his window and screaming.

He ran out of the alley and adjusted his bearings as he crossed the road and carried on. He could see trees in a park beckoning at the end of the road.

Seeing the park reminded George of Edie, of the first time they'd met in an underground garage. She'd been sparky and aggressive and had hit him when he'd tried to be nice to her. But she'd turned out to be a brave and resourceful ally in all the adversity they'd had to face together. He wondered suddenly if she might already be there at the Gunner's plinth. Of course, the Friar had probably told her the same thing George had been told by the Euston Mob. The thought of seeing her again put more energy in his legs, and he hit Park Lane with a renewed burst of energy. He chicaned through the late-night traffic and slipped into the park.

Running on grass, beneath the fluorescent-lit tracery of the trees, was a lot easier.

He saw a clock face on the side of a building on Park Lane, and as he ran under the tall modern tower hotel, his heart was pumping like a trip hammer, but now it was because he knew he was going to make it to the plinth before midnight.

Hang on, Edie, he thought. I'm almost there!

CHAPTER THIRTY-SEVEN

The Makers and the Stone

The Blind Woman led Edie down two flights of stairs as calmly and precisely as if she could see.

The house had no carpets, no pictures, and no furniture: no decorations of any kind. Dust had grayed it all into nothing more than a background. There was no sense of a life lived within its walls.

The woman stopped in front of a door and reached for a large key ring hanging from her belt. She took off her glove and felt the various keys, searching by touch alone for the one she needed. She found it, and Edie noted that she put the glove back on before she inserted the key in the door and turned the lock.

"There is a chair," the woman said softly. "You will walk forward and sit on it. You will wait. If you move? The dogs will bite."

Edie saw that the Blind Woman stood to one side as

if afraid to enter the room. Edie heard a low growl behind her, and walked through the door.

There was a chair in the middle of the room. It was solidly built and rested on small iron wheels attached to each leg.

The room was lit by a single candlestick on a desk in the center of the floor. The room had been designed to be used as a library, but it was now a library without books. There was no furniture except for a high desk and shelves covering every inch of wall. They weren't, however, empty. Instead of the regular ranks of leather-bound volumes that might once have peopled its shelves, there were irregular lumps and bundles filling the space from the bare wood of the floor to the dangerously sagging lath and plaster of the ceiling.

Edie walked to the chair and sat in it with a shiver.

She noted that the windows were a lattice of diamond-shaped glass pieces joined with lead. Edie saw no obvious way to open them, so there was no question of throwing herself out one in a desperate bid for freedom. The dogs padded in after her and lay at her feet, eyes locked on her.

The Blind Woman stepped back from the door, into the hall, and sat on a high-backed chair against the wall facing the doorway.

For a long time, the only sound was the dogs' breathing and Edie's heart beating. She shifted in the hard chair, and the tiny creak immediately made both dogs growl sharply to their feet and raise their hackles at her.

Edie looked through the door at the stiff-backed figure staring sightlessly at her.

"What were you?" she asked.

"What was I when?" replied the Blind Woman, in a
voice scarcely above a whisper.

"Before this happened," said Edie. "What were you?"

More silence answered her. And then, just when Edie
had decided the woman wasn't going to respond, she did.

"I was a teacher."

"That figures."

"What do you mean?"

"Never liked teachers much," said Edie. "Never seemed
to tell you the stuff you really need to know."

"And what do you need to know, child?" murmured
the Blind Woman. "What could someone so young and
unaware possibly want to know, when any knowledge
will blight and not enlighten."

"That's rubbish!" snorted Edie. "Knowing stuff, the
right kind of stuff, is good. In fact, it's all good, isn't it,
even the bad stuff, because, how can you make a plan or
keep yourself safe without all the info?"

"You can't keep yourself safe with it either, child."

"Yeah, well, excuse me for living, but I haven't given
up yet."

The Blind Woman allowed the pale moth of a smile
to flutter across her face, and then it was gone.

"You will. Everybody does."

There was something pulsing at Edie from the shelves,

exerting a stronger force than the background pull from the walls. She looked at the strange assortment of indeterminate shapes lumped together around the room.

"What's on these shelves?"

"Stones."

"Why?"

She wanted the Blind Woman to keep talking. The silence left her mind too empty—a blank canvas for the malign hum of the house and its contents to bleed their promise of terror onto.

"Because he collects them. Like he collects our heart stones. Looking for the power hidden in a very different kind of stone. A much stronger and darker stone."

"What—" began Edie. Then she stopped and reformed her question. "Why is everything about stones?"

"Because it is," said the Blind Woman shortly. And then said no more.

Edie waited, and when it became clear that that was all the woman was going to say, she grunted in disgust.

"Typical teacher."

The Blind Woman's head came up, bridling at Edie's tone. "What?"

"It's like I said. Never tell you anything useful. Ask them a difficult question and you get 'You don't need to know that,' or 'That won't be in the exam,' or 'Just because.' You must have been a really rotten teacher."

The Blind Woman sat so stiffly upright that you could almost hear her spine crack.

"I was a good teacher," she whispered, soft as dust. "I was a very good teacher."

Edie stared at her. Unless she was mistaken, there was a single tear cutting a pink trail through the dusty skin at the edge of the Blind Woman's sewn lid.

"Then tell me why this is all about the stones," said Edie, just as quietly.

"It can't help you," the woman replied.

"Maybe it can help you," said Edie carefully.

"Nothing can help me, child." She laughed almost inaudibly. "I am lost, so mired in darkness that I cannot turn back."

"Then don't turn back," said Edie. "Stay where you are. But why don't you be a good teacher again? Tell me why everything is about the stones."

In the silence, one of the dogs turned and looked at the Blind Woman. She worked her mouth as she thought.

Her hand rose and smoothed nonexistent stray hairs back into her tight bun, and then she just started to talk.

"Long ago, before history began, before things had names, a darkness walked the earth. It fed on fear, and wherever it walked, it spread terror and hatred and ignorance."

She paused and listened, head tilted toward something she might have heard near the front of the house. After a moment she relaxed and carried on.

"There was a light that also walked the earth, encouraging life. It couldn't bear to see its children live where terror and hatred spread pain and violence, like a sort of dark canker. So it fought the darkness, and after a great struggle, it won, and bound the darkness deep into the rocky heart of the world, imprisoning its evil in the stone below, so that it could never walk the earth again.

"Time passed, and humankind, who are the sons and daughters of life, spread across the earth, and they built and lived and loved and laughed. . . ."

The Blind Woman paused, caught by her own words as if she had only just remembered there were things like love and laughter outside the House of the Lost. Edie waited while she took a thin breath and then resumed.

"And as well as building, humankind made things. At first the makers—the artists and sculptors—worked with wood and clay, but their children began to dream of making things that wouldn't rot or perish with time. They began to create out of stone and tried to work metal in the fire. But making sculptures out of stone and metal was much harder than working with wood and clay. And because they knew that nothing hard can happen without tears and sacrifice, they began to believe that a sacrifice must be made to the stone they wished to use, to make it easier to work with."

She looked blindly at Edie as if uncertain whether to go on.

"Although many ages had passed since life had imprisoned the evil in the rock, there were still people who had a memory that there was some ancient power in the stone. These women—for they were women, the memory handed from mother to daughter—these women had the sense of the power and memories that lived in the rock—"

"Women like us," said Edie.

"Women like us."

"Glints."

"Glints."

Edie wanted to scream at the woman. She wanted to ask how she could be so calm, so very quiet, so evilly doing the Walker's bidding in this terrible house when she and Edie were, or had been, the same thing. She clenched her jaw and kept the scream inside. She wanted to know how the story ended.

The Blind Woman cleared her throat and continued. "But time had made them forget that the power in the stone was dark. And when the makers came to the glints, the women told them of the power, confirming that it was a living thing, and the makers were happy, because they knew how to appease living things; they made a blood sacrifice.

"They drew lots, and the chief maker's son lost. He was taken to a stone that the glints had chosen, and a stone knife was used. Now, because these were children of life, the blood sacrifice was to be just that: not a death, just a little finger merely nicked with a flint knife, the tiniest of wounds, and then the makers would swear an oath to the stone. The child might cry for a moment, but then he would be surrounded with flowers and laughter and a celebration where he would be given the first of the food and the sweetest of the honey to make up for his short second of pain. . . ."

The woman's hands fluttered up and passed over the stitches in her eyes. Edie knew that she was feeling the pain of her own sacrifice.

"And did it work?" Edie said.

"You know it did. The oath between maker and stone was that the stone would not resist the makers, and the makers would use the power to work stone—to make, not mar. But the flint dagger had betrayed them— perhaps because it was a blade of stone and so had some of the evil hidden in it—and it turned in the father's hand, and the nick in the finger became a gash in the wrist, and before they could seal the wound, the child was dead. Although it was an accident, his life's blood had run to the stone, and the bond between maker and stone was sealed."

"The man killed his own son?" interrupted Edie.

The Blind Woman nodded. "He killed his own son. By mistake, tricked by the stone. Sadness and wailing came to the maker's house. But time passed. The makers made, and the stone didn't resist, and what they made had power. They made idols and gods and devils and gargoyles for their temples and churches, and these, though the makers didn't know it, were the first Servants of the Stone. They were made to frighten and to awe. And they were known as 'taints,' because wherever their shadow fell, the children of light were tainted with fear."

"But they made the spits, too," prompted Edie.

"They did—likenesses of living things, of animals and people. They made things with a new intent: to represent people loved and admired, or even just to feel the sheer joy in recording that which they found beautiful and pleasing."

"And that's why spits aren't Servants of the Stone?"

"Yes, child. They were called spits because they were made as a spirit and image of real men, and so had a sort of spirit inside them that stood free of the darkness and fear in the stone."

"And that's why the taints, the Servants of the Stone, hate them? Because they're free?"

"It's more than that. It's because the spits are the maker's revenge on the stone for taking the life of the innocent child. They found a way to banish a fragment of the darkness and put a spark of life back into the world with every spit they made. And—"

She stopped. The dogs' ears pricked up. Edie heard the floorboards creak in the hall and a voice she had hoped never to hear again—a thin supercilious man's voice ended the story.

"—And in this way the battle between light and darkness, between fear and joy continues. The darkness in the stone always waits for the makers to tire, so it can return to the earth and rule again."

264

The Walker appeared in the doorway, smiling humor-lessly at Edie.

"And you know what? Fear always trumps joy, and darkness is so much more reliable than light. . . ."

He tapped the long shiny blade of his jeweled dagger on the door frame.

There was a whimpering noise. Edie's first fear was that it was coming from her. But it wasn't. It was the Blind Woman. She was bent straight forward over her knees, sobbing quietly. The Walker turned and looked down at her. Her hand reached out beseechingly, although she didn't look up. She had taken off a glove. Edie heard a single word sift through the sobs.

"Please . . ."

The Walker reached inside his coat and pulled out a bright piece of sea-glass, blazing a bright orange light, sending grotesque shadows around the room. It was on a chain. He dangled it into her hand.

The hand closed on it greedily, and the Blind Woman shuddered and sighed with relief.

Edie had survived by herself on the streets. She knew that shudder. She'd heard the junkie's sigh before. She knew how the Walker kept the Blind Woman just alive and hungry enough to do his bidding. He was using her heart stone like a drug to control her.

Edie's hand closed over her own stone hidden in her pocket.

The Walker looked at her as if he could read her

thoughts. He bared his teeth in a sneer. "You're thinking you'll never be like her."

Edie kept her face blank.

He jerked the glass out of the Blind Woman's grasp and caught it in his hand. She screamed. Despite herself, Edie started toward her.

The dogs erupted into action and barked and snarled her back into her chair.

The Walker snapped his fingers. The dogs went silent and just stood there, looking at Edie.

"Stay calm. Stay still. I do not want to hurt you. I do not want to harm you. I do not, in fact, even want your warning stone. I do not want a thing from you except for your help in one small matter. I want you to use your gift for me."

"How?" said Edie.

"I want you to test some stones for me. Just touch them and tell me what lies within. Do that and you may go free, unharmed and safe."

"What kind of stones," Edie said carefully, not believing a word he was saying about letting her go free.

"Ah." He grinned. "There's the catch. That's why you may keep your heart stone with you as you work. You will need all your strength."

"What kind of stones?" she repeated, her voice snagging in her suddenly very dry throat.

He smiled wider.

"Dark stones. Very dark stones indeed . . ."

CHAPTER THIRTY-EIGHT

Substitute

George ran behind a giant statue of Achilles, heading south. He was aware of the naked giant with a sword in one hand and a round shield held to the sky in the other, as if warding off an attack from above. George looked up in case something was howling in from the night sky, but his luck seemed to be holding. He ran across the level crossing on South Carriage Drive, ran through the left hand of the triple arch alongside Apsley House, and finally took a breath as he had to wait for the lights to change and allow him across the final road width and onto the central island of Hyde Park Corner.

He could afford to allow himself this luxury because right in front of him he could see the huge stone cannon pointing to the sky, and two of the four bronze soldiers that stand, or in one case lie, on each side of the base. He couldn't see the Gunner's side, but he could see the soldier lying on a stretcher and the one facing into the center of the grassy space, with two huge shell holsters hanging pendulously on the side of each leg.

The light changed. And he ran. He felt the gravel spitting under his feet as he powered toward the huge memorial plinth. Then he was up on the surrounding dais, around to the Gunner's side, sure he was going to see Edie.

But no one was there.

Where the Gunner usually stood was only a slab of bronze plinth and a blank wall of smooth-cut, weather-stained slabs, broken by the words RUSSIA—PALESTINE—CENTRAL ASIA.

George stopped dead and bent over as if the disappointment had hit him physically. He braced himself with his hands on his knees. The truth was, now that he had arrived and his run was over, he was finally letting his exhaustion catch up with him. He was disappointed too, no doubt, but he told himself it didn't matter. He'd find Edie later. Right now he had to stand on the Gunner's plinth. By the last clock he had passed on Park Lane, he had a good five minutes to spare.

He looked down and saw a bronze helmet on the chest of the figure at his feet. The sculptor had made a body lying on its back, a covering thrown over his face. His booted legs stuck out from the covering, and a coat was thrown over him so casually that you could see a portion of the side of the soldier's face and a hint of hair, but not enough to get a good look. The boots were missing some of the hobnails, and showing signs of hard wear. George noticed that the laces in one boot had snapped at the bottom of the lacing and had been quickly tied together in a rough-and-ready knot. Somehow this personal detail made the anonymity of the unknown soldier more poignant.

Having gotten enough oxygen back into his lungs, George looked at the soldier with the shell canisters on his legs.

"Excuse me," he said, not knowing how to begin a conversation with a statue that might not know George could see him.

"Excuse me," he repeated. "I can see you. I know about spits and taints and everything. I'm a friend of the Gunner."

The soldier didn't move an inch. George decided not to waste time. After all, he knew what he had to do.

"Okay," he said, "I'm going to go on the other side and stand to for the Gunner. On his plinth. The Euston Mob told me all about it."

There was still no reaction, so he shrugged and hurried around to the Gunner's empty place. As he walked toward it he realized he was passing relief scenes of trench warfare carved into the white limestone of the memorial—men in shaggy sheepskin jerkins and tin hats wrestling weapons and shells and wounded bodies against a background of shattered trees and broken trenches. He saw a gunner struggling with a terrified team of horses, and then he was up on the Gunner's stand, and felt the cold wall at his back.

On the other side of the street, a homeless man was pushing his belongings past in a tattered red-tartan shopping cart. His eyes weren't on the pavement in front of him. They were staring blankly across the traffic. They were black eyes with no hint of white.

The traffic was too loud for George to have heard him speak even if he had noticed him, which he didn't.

"One boy maker. Hyde Park Corner. On the war memorial."

George, oblivious to the eyes of the Tallyman, wasn't sure what do, but since it was nearly midnight, he leaned back and spread his arms in the way he remembered first having seen the Gunner do. Something moved at his feet as he trod on it. He bent down and picked it up. It was a horsewhip. The Gunner had obviously left it here when he'd taken George under his wing and begun the first stage of the gauntlet George now suspected he had been running forever.

He put down the hammer, picked up the whip, and felt the solid heft of the thing in his hand. He noticed that once he took hold of it, the rigid bronze lash, casually wrapped around the haft, became flexible. It was as if the sculpted item were becoming real in his hand. He kept his feet on the plinth and shook out the lash. Somehow, having something of the Gunner's in his hand made him feel more secure. He was going to be able to do this. How hard could it be? All he had to do was stand here until midnight was over, and then he'd have bought the Gunner another day.

"What the hell do you think you're doing?"

The voice was tired and cultivated and mildly irritated, and it came from the left. George looked that way and saw a statue of an officer from the other end of the monument standing there, looking at him as though his very presence were some kind of unforgivable insult. He wore a tin helmet and a pair of binoculars in a case high on his chest. He held his hands together with a heavy greatcoat loosely folded over them.

"Er . . . I'm standing here . . ." he hesitantly replied.

There was a slight snapping noise as the Officer sucked his teeth in irritation. He had a small mustache neatly trimmed above his top lip, and it twitched as he looked at George.

"You're a boy," he observed.

"I'm George."

"Yes," sighed the Officer, opening the lid on a wrist-watch and then snapping it shut again. "Yes, I'm afraid you are. You're the one got the Gunner gallivanting off his station in the first place. You know where I found him last night? Half melted by the Temple Bar dragon, facedown in a pond over there in Green Park. Had half a mind to leave him there, but you know." He sucked and snapped his lips again.

"That's why I'm here!" said George. "Exactly. He's down. He got taken by the Walker. He's not going to be here by turn o'day. So I'm going to take his place. Then we'll have another day to rescue him!"

"Poppycock!" the Officer exploded.

"It's not poppycock," George said levelly. "I'm going to do it."

The Officer tipped the front of his tin helmet down and scratched the back of his neck in amazement.

"You're going to stand to, in his place?"

"Yes," said George.

As he said it, he felt something shift on his arm. It was a ripping burning sensation, as if his skin were splitting, and he doubled up, cradling the painful arm with his good one. The whip clattered to his feet.

The Officer lost his veneer of coldness as he dropped his coat and darted over to George.

"What's wrong, boy?"

"My arm," George gasped.

The Officer checked his watch, sucked his teeth in worry, and knelt by him. "Quickly, boy, show me."

George held out his arm. The Officer took it with surprising gentleness and turned it over. Another tutting noise escaped his lips as he saw the scar of the maker's mark and the three lines spiraling down from it to where they disappeared into his cuff.

"Right. Jacket off, look sharp."

He helped George get his arm out of the two jackets

he was wearing, then pulled his shirt open and revealed the arm from shoulder to wrist.

"Not much of you under these layers," he said quietly, turning George's arm outward in order to look at it better. A loud tut greeted the sight. "Still, you're a plucky one, no doubt about that. You carry the mark of the Hard Way."

George looked in horror at his arm. One of the flaws, the marble one, had suddenly lanced its way beyond his elbow and braided itself around his bicep so that the sharp questing point of the fissure was now dangerously close to his armpit. The other two flaws were still twining below his elbow.

"That happened, the long one, just now?" asked the Officer.

George nodded, biting his lip, not trusting himself to speak steadily.

The Officer tapped the in-grooved vein. The sound of bronze tapping marble made George queasy. It was as if someone were reaching inside him and tapping his bones. The Officer pulled George's shirt back up, hiding the arm. When he spoke he was all business, the veneer of mild irritation gone.

"Right. Cover up, jacket on, fast as you like. You're right, no question, you *definitely* have to stand now."

George shrugged into the coats and fumbled with the buttons, happy not to be able to see his arm and the twining stone and metal veins that disfigured it.

"What?" he asked.

"What what?" replied the Officer, eyes scanning the street in front of them.

"What changed your mind?" said George urgently.

The Officer looked into his eyes. Then he bent and picked up the whip and put it in George's hand. "Because if you don't, that crack is going to continue up your arm and into your body, and when it gets to your heart . . . I'm very sorry to say you'll be dead."

The Officer smiled encouragingly. "*Nil desperandum*. It's not all gloomy. You take the Gunner's place, like you said you would, stand to until stand down, and you should be right as rain."

George saw what he was saying and suddenly discovered that his mouth had gone dry. "You mean this is one of the contests, one of the duels? But how does just standing here at midnight . . ."

Then he felt a sudden wash of relief.

"No, that's brilliant. I mean, that's great. Just stand here? That's easy, right?"

"Not as such. There's a little more to it that that, old son."

He clapped George encouragingly on the shoulder and pushed him gently into place on the Gunner's plinth. George didn't like the smile on the Officer's face. It was the smile parents show you as you are pushed inside the dentist's room to have something painful done to your teeth, only worse.

"What more?" George asked. "Please, what exactly happens when you stand to?"

The Officer gestured to the tortured relief carvings ringing the monument.

"All that, I'm afraid. Carnage, slaughter, screaming fear, bloody waste of good men and horses. We stand to and relive it every night. It's who we are, and it reminds us why we're here. It's the maker's purpose."

He cleared his throat as if there were a great deal more he would like to have said about the maker and his purpose, but good manners prevented him from doing so.

George found himself grasping at straws. "But it can't be that bad. I mean, you know you're going to survive, right? I mean, you do it every night, so . . ."

"Doesn't quite work like that, young 'un." The Officer shook his head. "Not like that at all. We don't relive it as statues. We relive it as the men we were made to represent. And while we're reliving it, it's real. We don't know that it happens every night. None of us do. Not even him, poor devil . . ." He nodded at the dead soldier with his covered face at the end of the monument.

"Who is he?" said George.

"Depends who's asking," he said, checking his watch. "He's whoever people want him to be. He's the Unknown Soldier. That's why his face is covered, so the bereaved can come and imagine he is their lost loved one. Good idea, if you ask me. Jagger, the man who made us, knew a thing or two about loss. Mind you, he was a soldier, too. Now you're about to be one, if you're really going to do this . . . ?"

The way he made it a question offered George a way out.

"I'm doing it."

He was doing it for a lot of reasons, but in the end they all boiled down to a simple one: he wouldn't be able to live with himself if he didn't.

The Officer nodded. "Good man. Be strong. Stiffen the sinews and all that good stuff."

He gave George one final firm clap on the shoulder. "Do it for yourself. Do it for the Gunner. Do it for who-ever you like, but just do it. Don't step off the blasted plinth. You'll be tempted. And if you still believe in any-thing, pray to it."

"Pray?" said George shakily, clenching the horse-whip. "Why?"

The Officer checked his watch and moved back toward his own plinth, scooping up his coat as he went. He smoothed it over his arm and looked at George before disappearing around the right angle in the stone.

"Because for the next hour, old son, you're going to be eye-deep in hell."

CHAPTER THIRTY-NINE

Happy Ending

"There are no happy endings," said the Walker. "But then I expect you already know that."

Edie watched him place a scarf-wrapped bundle on the desk in the middle of the room and turn to smile humorlessly at her. All her muscles were tensed, ready to run or fight, but the fact that the door was locked and the dogs were waiting outside severely limited the likelihood of success, whichever of the two options she chose.

"Is that right?" she said, suppressing the tremor in her voice.

"It's a, in fact *the*, fact of life. . . ." he replied. "Now, please don't do anything sudden or stupid."

He thunked the point of his dagger into the desktop and walked over to her. She stared at the jeweled handle and the long blade as it reflected the candle flame. She remembered how he had been carrying it when she had glinted the scene on the frozen Thames, when she had seen him chasing the girl he had finally drowned in an ice hole. The girl with her face. That had certainly not been a happy ending.

"That's good, then," she spat. "That means no happy ending for you either."

She could feel his breath on her face as he leaned in and laughed quietly, strapping her right hand to the chair arm.

"Oh, there's an exception to every rule, and in my case, being cursed to walk forever has the one advantage of also meaning I have no foreseeable end. So I'm sorry, but I can't oblige you by fulfilling your kind wish."

He took her left wrist and jerked her hand out of her pocket. She let go of the heart stone just in time, as he quickly tied her arm to the chair with the efficiency of someone who'd done it many times.

All Edie had left was her feet.

"At this point," he murmured, "some of you decide that kicking me would be a heroic final gesture."

He reached back without looking and pulled the dagger out of the desktop. The blade flashed, and he stabbed it into the arm of the chair.

"It's never particularly heroic, and I can always let the dogs back in. They're not nearly as understanding as I am."

Edie relaxed her foot. Everything he said was a kind of threat. Even the gloating was a threat. The smile. It was all designed to make her scared. And suddenly she thought she knew why.

It was designed to stop her thinking. Fear can do that, make you freeze like a deer in the headlights of an oncoming car; it can dazzle you and take out your first line of defense, which is using your brain. So instead of coming up with a reply, she shut up and thought.

And as she thought, she took an inventory of the room in the candlelight: the shelves, the stones on them, the desk, the leaded, unopenable windows, the piles of paper on the floor around the desk. And as she did so, she forcibly shoved the fear to the back of her mind, in the same place she had earlier put the feeling that she was going mad when she had found that George had just astonishingly vanished. She could always unpack the fear and madness later. Right now she had to keep all her energy focused on there actually being a "later" in the first place.

Only one thing mattered now: she was going to do everything she could to not die in this dusty room.

The Walker was busying himself at his desk with the bundle he'd brought from the British Museum.

"You want me to touch some of these stones," she said, pointing with her chin toward the shelves.

"You're a bright spark," he said sarcastically, turning the wheeled chair so that it faced the desk.

"I'm a glint," she replied. "It's what we do, isn't it?"

"Indeed it is." He smiled. He walked around to the opposite side of the desk and made room amid the papers to unwrap his bundle. Edie watched as he carefully laid out its contents. As he took the thick wax disks out, they looked so like cheeses, Edie thought for an unsettling instant that he was unpacking a picnic. Then she saw the arcane magical symbols that were scratched all over them, and realized they were something else entirely.

"You'll forgive my good humor," he said, without looking up, "but these are old friends, and I have waited a long time to retrieve them. It is thanks to you and the boy that I have reason to be so happily reacquainted with them."

He carefully placed a thin gold disk on top of a smaller circular wax tablet, taking great pains to align its design with the marks scratched on the surface. Then he placed a little crystal ball at the center of it. Edie thought it would roll off, but there was an almost inaudible "snik" as he let go, as if a magnet had been engaged. It not only stayed in the dead center of the arrangement, but rotated slowly as it did so.

The Walker exhaled in satisfaction and turned his attention to the black mirror sandwiched between the two larger wax disks. He retrieved gloves from his pockets and put them on. He lifted the top disk and placed it on the edge of the desk, close to Edie. He picked the mirror off the second disk, holding it gingerly by the handle and placing it on top of the disk that was inches from her bare hands.

She felt the black surface suck at her hand, so strongly that her hand began to move toward it without her thinking. When she did think, and tried to pull her hand back, it was with an effort that had her gritting her teeth at its intensity.

The Walker saw this and nodded.

"It's strong. Touch it."

She shook her head, horrified at the way the shiny blackness was pulling at her hand.

The Walker came around the table and pushed her closer to the edge of the desk. The blackness dragged her hand across the rough wood toward it. She dug her fingernails in, but it did no good.

She had no idea what was in the stone, but its pull was far stronger than any other she'd ever glinted. She couldn't begin to imagine what kind of terror or pain she would experience when her hand completed its inexorable journey toward the mirrored surface, but she knew it would be worse than anything she had ever experienced.

With a final effort, she threw her whole body weight backward, and her feet lashed out, sending a dusty pile of papers skittering over the floor. But it was no use. The black mirror suddenly seemed to exert a stronger pull in reaction, and her hand flipped across the arm of the chair and slapped open-palmed across the center of the mirror, splayed like a white starfish on a plate of ink.

The jolt of contact detonated through her body and out into the room, sending a silent shock wave through the layers of dust, blowing them into the air all around her. It blew out the candle, too, and for an instant all was as black as the mirror. Then there was the scrape of a match, and the Walker relit the candle and coughed at the airborne dust. Edie did too.

And as she did so, she noticed an extraordinary thing.

She wasn't glinting.

Not as she had previously experienced glinting.

The past was not slicing into her in jagged shards of recorded pain.

Normally, glinting tore at her and left no room for thought until it was over. This was different, and it didn't immediately hurt. She could notice things—like it not hurting, for example.

The treacherous instant of surprise and relief lasted about as long as the match in the Walker's hand. Then she realized this was worse.

She wasn't feeling the past in the stone.

She was feeling nothing.

Absolutely nothing.

The stone was not a recorder of past pain. Whatever it had been used for, whatever it had witnessed had gone into it and out into the void beyond. And touching that void was purely terrifying. It was as if Edie were touching the exact opposite of everything in the world around her, because everything around her was *something*: whereas everything at the end of her hand, sucking at her splayed fingers, was *nothing*.

It was such an alien feeling that, given the choice between it and the foulest, most terrifying person that had ever lived, without a second's thought she'd have taken the side of the human monster and not what was touchable through the mirror. The void stripped everything down to a very simple equation—human or inhuman.

What was at the end of her hand was the possibility of something so vastly, cosmically bad that she couldn't begin to get her head around it, and didn't want to.

"You feel it," said the Walker.

"It's evil," she whispered.

"It's just different." He smiled. "The world is full of people who are too stupid to understand, and use words like 'evil' and 'unholy.' It's a third thing, a way to power that only the cleverest and bravest can take. And it will set me free and let me rule. . . ."

Edie gasped as something else edged into her consciousness.

"Can you feel them?" he asked.

Horribly, she realized she could. The thing about an absence or a void is that it should, by its very nature, be empty. Edie was slowly becoming aware that all around the edges of this black hole at the end of her arm were things like shadows in the dark, shifting and peering at her over the rim of nothingness. She tried to see what they were, but every time she did so her mind and vision just slid off them as they ducked out of sight.

"Do you see the Presences?" he asked eagerly.

"No," she gasped. "But they're there. . . ."

"Precisely," he said exultantly. "Don't worry. Not yet.

They can't come here unless a gate is opened, and for that to happen we would need another mirror to set up the reflections out of which they could step. I had the two mirrors once, but a meddling fool stole one before I had understood how to use them safely, or work out how to contain the Presences within bounds on this side, once they emerged from the emptiness. He thought I was going to unleash the end of days or some such nonsense. . . ."

He scowled at the memory and pulled his dagger from the chair arm, looking at it before slipping it back in its scabbard on the back of his belt.

"I caught up with him and gutted him in a field outside the city, but I have never found the twin mirror again, and I have searched this metropolis from top to bottom ever since."

He smiled suddenly. In many ways it was much worse than his scowl.

"And now I have a glint and an Ironhand at one and the same time . . . so I shall cut through the obstacle that I have been blocked by for three centuries and open the gates in the mirrors in one bold slash. . . ."

With that, he jerked the gold disk out from under the crystal ball so quickly that the crystal was left spinning furiously on the spot just above the wax surface of the protective tablet. In the same movement, he sliced it under Edie's hand, between it and the black mirror, and as it severed the connection between Edie and the void, she felt a savage, blunt pain as if a limb had just been brutally chopped off. Then her hand was free, and she jerked it off the gold disk with a sob.

She curled over the pain as her hand twitched like the jerking nerves of a dying fish.

"There," he said. "That wasn't too bad, was it?"

It had been so bad that touching the loathsome otherness in the mirror left her feeling shocked to the core of her being. She had just touched something behind the scenes, something that humans were not designed to be conscious of, let alone contact. It hadn't been pain, but if her hand had been free, she would have taken the dagger and killed the Walker simply for making her touch it.

"It was worse," she panted. "It wasn't like glinting. It wasn't like touching a stone normally is."

"Of course. And part of that is because the mirror is not really stone. Scientists, these new magicians of your age, they say that it's not a stone at all. It's obsidian, which looks like a stone but is a kind of glass, a volcanic glass."

"It's a glass. Like—?"

"Like your precious heart stone, yes. Don't worry." He smiled thinly. "Keep it for the moment. You will need all your strength."

He waved an arm at all the wrapped bundles of stone on the shelves.

"I will have you touch all of these pieces of black stone. I have spent a lot of time collecting them, as you can see, in the hope that one day I would be lucky enough to find a master maker and a glint who could tell me which one of these rough items most closely matches the feel of the dark mirror."

It all came clear to Edie in one flash of understanding. "You think George can make you a new mirror?"

"I know he can."

"He's not a stone mason, or anything. He's just a boy."

"It's not a learned skill. He will feel the shape of what is to be made in the obsidian you choose, and he will know how to bring it forth. It's not a skill. It's in his bloodline."

She shook her head. "No. He won't do it for you, even if he does have this ability you think he has. He just won't do it for you."

"He will do it for you," the Walker said simply. "He will do it to save you."

And with a plummeting feeling inside her, she knew he was right.

He roughly freed her right arm and pointed to the shelves. "I will unwrap these rocks. You will feel them. You will tell me which one feels most like the obsidian mirror. You will glint for me. . . ."

Edie forced the fear back and tried to think straight. "Okay," she said. It would buy her time. And now she had one hand free, even if the other was tightly tied to the heavy chair.

"I have freed your hand so you can reach all three levels of shelf. Do anything other than as I tell you, and I will have the Blind Woman set the dogs on you. Understood?"

She heard the hungry snuffling of the two mastiffs under the door and nodded. The Walker started along the shelf, unwrapping package after package, revealing black stones of every shape and size.

"Some of these are obsidian, some are flint. I did not know the difference when I began my collection. Don't worry about the flints. Just touch the black glass," he said as he moved away.

It was the word "flint" that made Edie know what she was going to have to do. She pulled against the strap pinning her to the chopping-board arms of the seat. The strap was only half an inch wide, but there was no question of breaking it. She would have to bide her time until it was the moment to act. All would depend on the Walker's being in the right place.

"Go on, then," he said.

She took a breath and touched the nearest slab of rock. It was about the same size as a roughly hewn telephone directory.

She jerked slightly as the memory in it flowed into her.

A weeping red-haired woman in a green coat sat in the chair Edie was sitting in.

She clutched a blazing heart stone that was pinned to her lapel as a brooch.

She had big hair, like an astronaut's wife in a 1960s newsreel.

Her thick mascara was running.

She screamed as the Walker reached in and ripped the heart stone out of her hand and off her jacket.

Edie convulsed as she felt the irreparable wave of anguish tear into the older woman as it was taken.

She heard the Walker say:

"Try another one, and you shall have your dainty back."

Then the vision of the past was over, and it was she who was strapped to the chair. She tried to understand what she had just seen.

"You have had other glints testing these rocks."

He nodded. "Ignore the memories of them. Their pain is . . . a minor distraction. Find me the rock with the possibility of a gate in it. Try them all."

He tapped the dagger handle.

"Try to thwart me by choosing the wrong one, and I will open the boy in front of your eyes and you can watch his life puddle away through the cracks in these very floorboards."

"But why do you need me if you've already had others test the stones?" she asked, in a final attempt to stave off the inevitable.

"Because the nature of the void in the mirror changes in time. It's as if whatever is beyond the gate in the mirror moves. As if it has been floating loose since it was separated from the second mirror. Two of them together seemed to hold each other steady. The uncut stone that was a match for the mirror ten years ago won't be right now. That's why having a glint and a master maker on hand at the same time is so very fortuitous."

She nodded slowly, turned, and felt the next stone. And the one after.

So began the longest hour of Edie's life. Most of the stones held at least one anguish-soaked memory of an earlier glint, sometimes more than one. She lost track of the pain and the faces in a mounting accretion of despair as she dragged her wheeled chair after her, trying stone after stone. The pain didn't make her numb. It just went on and on, wearing different faces that all blurred together. She began to feel she couldn't breathe, as though she were drowning in a never-ending sea of tears.

Eventually she became so punch-drunk that she just assumed this was going to go on forever. Only the closeness of the heart stone in her pocket kept her going, because in her mind it was where she'd hidden her last hope, her one desperate plan for escape, a plan that could only happen when everyone was in the right place. It was so unending, this onslaught of women's and girls' despair that when she came to the empty stone, she wept with relief.

He didn't have to ask her if it was the one. He just looked up from where he was bent over the desk, and smiled.

"Good."

Edie leaned against the shelf as the Walker reached past her and took the slab over to the table. As soon as he walked away, her hand closed on the obsidian next to the place where the empty one had been.

She checked that he was still moving away. And once he was at the desk, carefully putting the empty stone next to the dark mirror, she took a fast deep breath and closed her eyes.

She lifted the heavy slab and smashed it down on the stone on the shelf.

She heard a sharp cracking noise and felt chips of rock fly past her face.

Something stung her ear, but she ignored it and opened her eyes.

Sure enough, the obsidian had shattered, leaving fine shards all over the shelf.

"What are you doing?" the Walker shouted, and the noise started the dogs on the other side of the door barking furiously. Edie didn't spare a millisecond to see if he was going to get to her before she did what she had to do. Her free hand darted into the stone debris and grabbed a long, thin shard like a straight razor. It was the wrong way around, but she spun it in her hand in midair so the blade edge faced out as she slashed it at her trapped wrist.

The obsidian blade, sharper than the sharpest scalpel, seemed to whistle as it cut through the air and hit the taut rope, severing it almost as if it weren't there at all.

Without pausing, she kept the momentum of her

slash going and rolled out of the chair, spinning to her feet and whirling the heavy wooden seat on its wheels so that it was between her and the approaching Walker.

He was diving forward, and hit the solid chair hard, knocking it off its wheels as he tangled in it and fell. Edie jumped out of the way as he and the chair crashed to the floor.

The candle on the table fell over with the impact, but it didn't go out. It rolled in among some of the loose sheets of paper that Edie had disturbed.

The Walker managed to reach one hand out and grab the edge of her jacket. His normally sneering face was crimson with rage and pain.

"You will pay, you little hellcat!" he shouted in a voice like a thunderclap, dragging her toward him.

"You too—" said Edie calmly.

And with all the power and cold fury in her body, she slashed the obsidian razor across his face.

"—And don't call me little."

She didn't wait as he screamed and his hands flew to his eyes.

She vaulted over his hunched body, ran across the room, grabbed another big lump of stone from the nearest shelf, so heavy that she could hardly lift it, and with the last of her strength, hurled it through the leaded diamonds of the window. Snow billowed into the room as she jumped out into the night without a second's hesitation.

The only thought she had time for as she fell through the air was that, for all she knew, she was going to break her neck; but anything was better than what was in that room, pulling from the black mirror.

CHAPTER FORTY

Chimes at Midnight

George clenched the horsewhip in his hand and braced his back against the Portland stone stacked massively behind him. He had a thousand questions that he wanted to ask the Officer, but before he could think which one to call out, he heard the sound of a deep familiar bell tolling, reverberating high in the night air.

It was the sound of Big Ben, marking the turn of the day from its position three hundred feet above the city. Though he had heard the old bell on the radio marking the hours before news broadcasts, now that George was hearing it directly through the night air, it felt like the first time.

He heard the warning carillon ring one, two, three, four times, and then after a pregnant pause, he heard the majestic lonely bongs of the great bell counting out the hours. And as he listened, he thought of something his dad used to say when they'd return home after an adventure or a treat of some kind. He'd look rueful and tousle George's hair and, no matter what time of day it actually was, he'd say, "Well, we did that, didn't we? We heard the chimes at midnight."

The memory faded as George became aware of something else.

With each *bong*, he felt himself changing. And not only himself, but his surroundings. As the darkened city paled into a harsh winter light, he felt his body stiffen and become more ponderous. He wondered fleetingly if he was turning into a statue. His feet felt massy and increasingly clumsy, and his clothes seemed to become heavier. And then not only heavier, but less comfortable. They scratched and itched at him. And then he forgot his clothes and the heaviness as he focused on what was happening to the four-story white stucco building opposite. With each sound of the bell, it was fading, and in its place was a clear sky seen through a lattice of black-and-white silver birch trees. There were no leaves on the slender trunks and branches, and George felt a chill breeze cut through him. As he instinctively reached to fasten the plastic buttons on his reefer jacket, his hands met stiff tarpaulin canvas, metal buttons, and leather straps. He looked down in time to see the dark bronze rectangle of the plinth fade away and leave his boots standing on a muddy crisscross of wheel tracks punctuated by hoof marks.

Except they weren't his boots. They were the

Gunner's boots, the Gunner's leg protector on one side and the tight twine of puttees on the other. Although, they weren't exactly the Gunner's, because the Gunner's had been bronze, and these were real: leather boots, canvas puttees, wool army britches, canvas and leather bags and holsters hanging off him, as real as the stiff crackle of the thick canvas groundsheet he was wearing as a cape. He looked down at his hands and saw that they were flesh and blood; but they were not his hands: they were a man's hands—perhaps the hands that his would become one day, but weren't yet. Strong wide hands, grubby and calloused by work.

Somewhere at the back of his mind, the sense that he was a boy of nearly thirteen standing on a traffic island in London was fading away like the vision of the bronze plinth at his feet; but before it retreated to a point where he couldn't connect with it anymore, he was able to notice other changes as they happened.

His fingers rose to his face, and even without a mirror, he could tell it wasn't George he was feeling. The chin was covered in a strange rough bristle, the nose was longer, and all the planes of the face were wider, flatter, and wrong. The skin that covered them somehow felt thicker and more rubbery as he kneaded it against the bones of his skull. In fact, his whole body just felt denser and blunter. It was as if his center of gravity had moved lower, and the pull of that gravity had doubled. He no longer felt light on his feet, and it wasn't tiredness that made him feel that—it was a reconfiguration of his muscles and a thickening of his bones. He felt bulkier and stronger, but he also felt in a way that was as tinged with sadness as it was full of wonder, that he'd lost something irretrievable in this growth. Like something you don't notice until it's gone, he was missing the green ease and lightness in his body. It didn't feel like a body that could run full tilt and without much thought all the way from St. Pancras to Hyde Park, for example. His body had just fast-forwarded fifteen years. It wasn't that he had become fat; it was that he had become strong, like a flexible tree sapling that grows into a solid trunk, which can't bend as easily but carries more weight.

What he felt was simple age, and the inescapable weight of growing up.

He was also feeling an insistent itching, and he realized he was scratching at those itches without thinking about it. He looked up at the clear winter sky through the birch branches and wondered at the brightness. He heard the wonder in a deep voice saying:

"I thought it would be midnight."

He realized that the voice had come out of his mouth. He heard it all, the sounds of this new world dialed up around him. He heard a distant cracking and popping, and behind that an even fainter whine like an engine. Much closer, too, he heard the rattle of harnesses and wheels, men moving about, metal sliding against metal, and the sound of someone coughing his guts up close by.

And then he heard the Officer's voice right beside him saying:

"Thought what would be midnight, Gunner?"

George looked down from the delicate fretwork of birch branches against the pale winter sky and saw the world he had fallen into, and realized that he was, as advertised, eye-deep in hell.

A horse's body hung upside down from a tree, frozen and unmoving on the sharp stump it had been blown onto, its legs pointing skyward in an obscene imitation of the branches it had replaced. The other trees around it looked as if they had been hacked and slashed by some wayward giant, randomly splintered and shattered trunks jagging up out of the plashed earth at crazy angles. Below it, the earth was torn up in senseless ridges and random shell holes, strewn with barbed wire and the smashed detritus of war.

The Officer was standing in front of George, still carrying his greatcoat, and he too was now flesh and blood, no longer a statue.

"Nothing, sir. Sorry, daydreaming."

The words came out of George's mouth as if he were partly on autopilot. It certainly hadn't occurred to him to call this man "sir" on a conscious level.

"Well, snap to and get those nags into some kind of cover before that spotter plane gees Fritz into lobbing a wake-up call our way."

George looked at the horizon and saw a tiny

twin-winged plane moving slowly against the light, like a paper cutout. He realized that was the source of the distant whine.

"Sir," he heard himself say, and he saw his hand rise to the overhang of his tin helmet in a sketchy salute. Again, he hadn't thought of doing it, but some part of him was like a passenger without control of the body he was in. He didn't feel detached from it, just not wholly at one with what it did. It was the same feeling when he found he had reached back over his shoulder without looking and patted the muzzle of a horse that he hadn't really known was there.

"Come on, then," he heard himself say. "Let's find a better 'ole."

He turned and gathered two leading reins in his hand. A pair of chestnut-colored horses stood there. Behind them he could see a pair of field guns being set up for action by teams of gunners working fast to manhandle them into position just behind the lip of a shallow ridge. Some wore greatcoats and mufflers, others wore shaggy sheepskin jerkins, but all wore tin helmets and looks of fierce determination as if they were working against the clock.

George could feel his heart thudding with adrenaline. He realized there was a huge sense of apprehension churning in his gut, as if something very, very bad were about to happen. He could see by the tight faces around him that everyone else felt the same. It was as if someone were playing a single unending note on a violin, a note so high that you almost couldn't hear it, but just audible enough for it to be painful in its persistence, in the way it underpinned everything. His mouth was dry, and he felt he would murder someone for a cup of tea. Which was strange, because George—normal George—didn't much like tea at all.

Two artillery spotters were receiving orders from the Officer. One had a trench periscope strapped to his back. They nodded and set off over the lip of the ridge, keeping low. They held a spool of telephone cable on a bobbin between them that unwound as they ran. Then one stumbled and lay still. The other man kept hold of the bobbin and carried on, running until he disappeared over the ridge.

The Officer swore and trained his binoculars on the fallen man.

George felt the horses pull against the reins and found himself jogging away from the guns. He led them toward a dip in the landscape that had two walls of a ruined farmhouse at the bottom of it. He ducked them under a low arch, and wasn't surprised to find two more horses already hobbled and waiting, faces obscured by nose bags, contentedly chomping away at the contents. Except for the lack of a roof, the protective walls of the ruin made for good cover. High above them, George heard the distant engine whine getting louder.

There was another soldier crouched by a wall, trying

to get a fire going under a large blackened teakettle. His helmet lay on the ground beside him, and he was wearing one of the shaggy sheepskin jerkins.

"Char'll be up in half a mo'. Tell them to keep their hair on," he said.

George found he was hobbling his horses as if he'd been doing it all his life, but the watching part of himself in the back of his mind was looking at the shoulders and hair of the soldier hunkered down in front of the small fire. He had a cigarette parked in the side of his face, and George could hear the pop-and-suck of his smoking without using his hands as he squatted before the meager blaze, looking at something held in front of him.

Maybe because he was trying not to think too hard about why the man carrying one end of the telephone wire spool had not gotten up when he had stumbled and fallen, George concentrated on the back of the man's head.

The soldier had dark hair, the same color as George's, cropped short on the back and sides. When he swept his hand back through the unruly longer hair on top, George felt something tug at him in the pit of his stomach at the familiarity of the gesture. He suddenly and fiercely wanted this moment to freeze. He didn't want whatever was going to happen next to happen; because whatever was actually going to happen wasn't going to be the thing that tug had so treacherously hinted at. Because that was impossible.

The man picked the ragged stub of his cigarette out of the side of his mouth and spun it into the fire, then stood up, stretched, and turned.

George's heart stopped.

Any heart would stop if it saw the impossible happen.

Any body would forget to breathe.

Any throat would choke up so tight that there was only room for one small word to escape.

A word as small as:

"Dad?"

The eyes that he knew so well, the eyes he'd known he'd never see again, crinkled at him, and one brow rose higher than the other in an expression George not only remembered but had himself practiced to death in front of the bathroom mirror in the weeks after the funeral, so he would not ever forget. The doors of his heart burst open, and he felt light again as he started to run toward him.

"Who you calling Dad, mate?" The soldier laughed. "I reckon I'm younger than you. . . ."

George stopped dead as he realized that though the eyes were smiling good-naturedly, there wasn't a hint of answering recognition in them.

Then the ground skipped beneath his boots as the first bomb hit.

CHAPTER FORTY-ONE

The Gunner's Last Laugh

The Gunner was up to his neck in water that was filling the hole he had dug in the gravel spit. Now that he had moved the skeleton of the girl from where it had been blocking the outflow at the base of the water tank, he was definitely feeling a small current moving past his ankles.

He held his breath and submerged himself. Sure enough, water was moving through a low arch that came up to just below his knees. He closed his hands on the flaking bars that blocked it. They moved. He stood up and hacked at them with his boots. He kicked and kicked at the ancient metalwork. As he did so, he thought of the Walker's sneering face and imagined his boot was pounding into the center of it. It allowed him to rise above the exhaustion that was sucking at him just long enough to make a space he might have a chance to crawl through. He reached down again and confirmed that this was so.

He scrambled carefully to the top of his hole and gathered up the bundle of heart stones wrapped in his cape. He pulled out his matchbox and lit a final match. The skeleton of the young girl gleamed whitely back at him. He had arranged the scraps of her dress over her as decently as he could, and he had covered her face. He looked at the long hair and thought of Edie. He remembered how pale and shaky she had been when she was separated from her heart stone, how the life seemed to drain from her and be replaced by an enormous, all-pervasive fear. The match guttered out, and he thought how scared Edie would be if she were left in a dark place like this, without even her warning stone for comfort.

He paused for a moment to reach into the scrabble of sea-glass in the bundle and picked one at random. He reached for the skeleton and found a shred of dress by touch alone. He tore a piece off and wrapped the heart stone tightly inside it, so no light would blaze out if the Walker were to appear. He wrapped it in several layers, because the main point of all the digging he'd done was to make sure that if the Walker used his mirrors to come back here, the absence of warning lights might make it impossible for him to ever get out again. The Gunner reckoned if he couldn't see into the mirrors, he might just be stuck here forever.

He reached into the skeleton and placed the tight parcel of cloth where he thought her small heart would once have beaten.

"Sleep easy, little 'un," he said. "He can't hurt you no more."

He grasped the bundle and dropped back into the hole with a splash. Even though he knew he could move underwater without needing to breathe, he didn't actually feel that he could. He knew this was because there was a gap between what he was—a bronze statue—and what he had been made to represent—a man. The man side that had been instilled by the maker would go through all the agonies of drowning, even though he, as a statue, wouldn't die. Although, since he was sure it was nearly midnight, that was going to be something of a technicality, as he was about to die as a statue for entirely different reasons.

He was going to do it anyway, he decided, since the point was to get the heart stones that the Walker so clearly valued out of his clutches forever.

"He who laughs last, mate," he said into the darkness. "He who laughs bloody last . . ."

He grasped his helmet in one hand, the bundle of heart stones in the other, and took a deep breath. He ducked below the surface and pushed himself into the narrow water duct.

He kept his eyes open, but he might as well have closed them. The jagged shards of bar he had kicked out from the crumbling stonework rasped against the gravel in the pipe. As he pushed himself deeper into the pipe, the gravel spill thinned out, and he was crawling over a water-smoothed layer of slime on top of something that gave way as he moved on it.

As he pushed forward, he felt the acid burn of oxygen starvation scorching up from his lungs and tightening across his throat and gullet. His eyes bulged and his mouth began to strain against itself, the automatic reflex to breathe fighting the willpower he was using not to do so.

His teeth ground together, and he pushed blindly on. He knew in the part of his brain that was not occupied by the horror of the searing lack of oxygen that he was crawling away to die like a rat in a hole, but the fact that he was hiding the Walker's precious stash of glass gave the otherwise futile gesture a point. He held on to that thought as his willpower finally gave in to the inevitable, and he reflexively opened his mouth and breathed in water.

And as he did so, he squirmed around and made his screaming body face the unseen sky above the ground, so that he would not die facedown, but looking upward. After all, since this was the last choice he was going to make, he wanted to look toward a place where maybe a happier ending than the lonely death that would come for him at midnight was possible.

CHAPTER FORTY-TWO

The Broken Lace

The ground jumped as the bomb hit, and George was knocked onto one knee. The horses were pulling and bucking at their restraints. The soldier with his dad's face was running across the ruined space, swearing as he looked up into the sky. He grabbed the Lewis Gun set up on a stand against a low wall and squinted through its sights as he knelt beneath it and aimed almost completely vertically.

As he opened fire, George found he was grabbing the horses' bridles and pulling their heads together, automatically stroking and shushing them. His calming noises were drowned in the rip of heavy-caliber gunfire as the Lewis Gun rattled through the bullets held in the circular drum mounted on top.

George looked up and saw a yellow-and-black biplane turning overhead, so low that he could clearly see the goggled face of the spotter sitting behind the pilot as he leaned out and dropped a bomb by hand.

He had a sickening sense of the world going slow as the tiny bomb seemed to fall straight toward him; but slow as it felt, he didn't seem to have time to run. Or maybe it was something else: maybe it was the impulse in the body that was not his, the Gunner's instinct driving his movements. Whatever it was, he found that instead he was turning his back to the blast and protecting the horses' heads with his outstretched arms.

The second bomb fell somewhere beyond the walls of the ruin, and though something smacked into the other side of the wall and made the dust bounce out of the cracks between the stone, George and the horses were unhurt. The Lewis Gun was suddenly silent. George looked over and saw with relief that the soldier was still in one piece, just trying to snap on a new drum of ammunition.

"Bloody spotter plane," he swore. "We'll be in for a pasting now."

The soldier stared after the aircraft that was already a diminishing shape, heading for the horizon, and shook his head, sick at himself for missing.

"I don't know why they let me waste rounds with this thing. Couldn't hit a bloody barn if they locked me inside and made me let rip with a full drum of ammo."

He locked off the weapon and turned to George with a rueful smile.

George realized that the soldier had been right. He was impossibly younger than George. It was his father's face, but it was the face from photographs from before George was born and when he was a baby.

The soldier saw something on the ground between them and bent to pick it up from where he had dropped it on his run to the Lewis Gun. It was a thin pocket-size book with a scuffed red leather binding. Several black-and-white photographs had strewn themselves across the ground. George picked up the ones nearest him before the restless horses could mash a hoof on them. One picture was of a bright-eyed girl in a wide hat, smiling coyly to someone out of the frame, showing a lot of teeth and neck and shoulders and sitting in front of a potted aspidistra plant. Another picture showed the same girl on a chaise longue in front of a painted backdrop of trellised roses, holding a tightly wrapped bundle on her knees and rather awkwardly tilting it forward so that the camera could catch the bug-eyed outrage of a small baby being shown to the world.

"You see the horse in the tree?" asked the soldier.

George nodded, not trusting himself to speak.

"Bloody shame, that. I mean, I've seen some things out here, but animals? I don't know. This isn't their fight, is it?"

George shook his head and then realized that the soldier was holding his hands out for the photographs he had retrieved.

"Sorry," George grunted, and held them out. The soldier took the pictures and looked at them. He grinned ruefully.

"The wife."

"Very pretty," George swallowed.

The other man beamed proudly. "She should be. She's on the stage."

"Right."

George was somehow limiting himself to short words, for fear that he might betray himself if he allowed anything as complicated as an actual sentence.

"She's a sing-a-bit, dance-a-bit girl, really. She's different, you know."

The face that was impossibly his dad's face crinkled in thought for a moment, and George saw something raw and vulnerable that he wasn't used to seeing.

"I mean, I got pals think she's a bit flighty, but they don't know her. She just . . . likes attention. No harm in that."

George realized that he was asking for reassurance, and he felt embarrassed at the vulnerability in the very face he had gone to for comfort.

"No." He shrugged, out of his depth. The man looked at the picture with the baby. He coasted his thumb over the grimacing little face. He looked up into the sky.

"Maybe the nipper'll be enough. Maybe slow her down a bit."

"Maybe not."

The words came out of George's mouth before he could stop them. They sounded flat and rank and bitter.

"Yeah, well. If not, it doesn't matter. We'll have something good to show for it, eh?"

He waved the picture of the baby and then slid both photographs back between the printed pages of his book.

George nodded. His dad's eyes found his.

"You got nippers, chum?"

The question took George by surprise.

"'Course not."

"Takes you funny, it does. By surprise. It's like this." He waved the small, much-thumbed novel over his shoulder before pocketing it as he went back to crouch over the kettle that was now coming steamily to a boil. He carried on speaking without looking around. "It's like a book, isn't it—one minute you're the hero of your own story, and then your girl produces this little atom and, even though he's ever so tiny, everything moves a bit, and you see you got it all wrong—you ain't the hero of the story at all. And what you took for the center of your own stage isn't the center of any stage, it's just a space on the edge of a much bigger place that was there all the time, only you didn't see it. . . ."

His voice trailed off in wonderment, and for a while, all that George heard was the soldier tinkering with tin cups and the kettle and billycans. Then he turned with a face that was brightly smiling and so obviously trying not to be scared that it hurt George to look.

"But it's all right, it's good. It makes all this easier. I mean, it makes it lots worse, too, worrying and all, but you know even if some bloody whizzbang's got your number on it, at least you had a speck of a hand in something that carries on, right?"

He held out a steaming tin cup to George. George took it and nodded. He took a swig and gasped as the liquid burned his mouth. The soldier seemed not to notice as he continued earnestly.

"I mean, I ain't ever seen the little mite, not to hold, but if I was to stop one and never get back to Blighty, she'd tell him all about me, right? I mean, he'd know that I . . . you know, how much I—"

A giant sledgehammer slammed into the earth with an impact that knocked them off their feet, and the shock wave made George's ears go momentarily deaf to anything except the sudden panicked pounding of the blood in his head.

His hands scrabbled down his body, and he was appalled to find wetness all over it. He waited for the pain of the gushing wound to hit him, but all that happened was his hearing slowly returned and he saw his father's face looming over him as it fumbled on a tin helmet.

"Waste of good tea, chum." He smiled and reached a hand out.

George let himself be pulled back to his feet and looked down to discover no red pumping horror disfiguring his torso and legs, just the dripping contents of his tin mug.

Another slamming impact hit the ground, this time farther away on the other side of the ruin. The soldier grimaced. It was such a heartbreakingly familiar expression that George couldn't help believing this was his father in front of him. It was deeper than thought; it was flesh calling to flesh and recognizing itself.

"Ranging shots. Fritz has got us bloody bracketed. This is going to get hotter before it gets better."

Astonishingly, now that they were in action, George saw that all the doubt and vulnerability had gone from his father's eyes. He looked solid again, more like the dad George remembered. And then George's body took over, and he was a soldier, not a boy caught in a good dream about to go bad, and he was busy comforting his horses as a new series of explosions began.

"That's our mob hitting back. We'll have to see if we can't hit them before they plaster us!" his father shouted, ducking as something whirred past his head. "Call them artillery duels, but I'll tell you what, there's nothing gentlemanly about them. It's kill or be killed and devil take the hindmost or the one whose gun-layer can't cut the mustard."

BOOM. A shell clipped some of the remaining thatch off the top of the wall and left them ducking reflexively under a hail of dry rushes and plaster dust.

"And a happy Christmas to you too, Fritz." His father grinned, a fierce light in his eyes.

The horses were bucking and pulling at their hobbles

in terror, and then there was a sharp crack and a whump as something hit nearby. Something flew past George's head, and something else glanced off the leather protector on his leg, kicking him hard. He had to hold on to the horses' tack to keep his feet. One of the horses was neighing and shaking and trying to wrench itself free, and when George looked down he saw something smoking sticking out of its leg.

The sight of blood, the rising thunder of the barrage, and the nearness of the miss jolted George, and somewhere in the back of his mind he remembered that he could end all this by just stepping off a plinth in a city far, far away. It was a strong temptation, an instant ticket home.

He felt the shocked quivering of the horse's nose, soft as down beneath his hand. He didn't think as he dropped into a crouch, fumbling at one of the bags hanging off his belt for a field dressing.

"Here, give me a hand!" he heard himself yell. "Grab his head!"

The soldier with his dad's face grasped the horse's head and started trying to calm it. George saw himself reach down and grab the red-hot shard of metal protruding from the horse without a second's hesitation, and he felt the shock of his fingers burning as he gripped on to it and yanked it out of the shaking leg muscle. As the redness gushed from the wound, he jammed the thick pad of field dressing over it and pushed down hard to stop the bleeding. With his other hand he shook loose the bandage and looped it around the leg, cinching the free end snug against itself as he did so.

He ignored the fact that the ground was bucking and heaving around him, and wound the bandage tight over the dressing pad, passing the roll to himself on either side of the leg until he ran out. As his hands worked, he noticed how very white the bandage was, and how well it looked against the deep chestnut of the horse's leg. He inhaled the clean healthy smell of the wood smoke from the fire. He'd never smelled anything so good before. He leaned down and tore the end of the bandage against his teeth, and twisted the double end he'd made back on itself and tied it off securely.

The horse's leg was shaking, but George was pleased to see the blood wasn't yet leeching through the gauze.

"Good job," said the soldier, smiling grimly down at George from where he was holding on to the bit below the horse's widely dilated nostrils.

George stood up and put his arm around the horse's neck, stroking and calming it.

Suddenly there was a hole in the thunder, and George and the soldier stood there on either side of the horse's neck, still and waiting. George saw the horse's eyes with extraordinary clarity, and thought he'd never seen such a deep and beautiful brown. Then he was distracted by something red, and his focus shifted to a ladybird calmly walking up the leather of the bridle toward his father's hand resting between the horse's ears. Beyond the ears he saw the sky, and he realized that it was not a pale white sky as he'd first thought, but a delicate blue that had an exquisite green tinge to it. It was as if the moment of silence and the fact that death could come smashing in from that sky at any moment was making him see everything more intensely.

He suddenly knew, in a kind of extension of this heightened awareness, that this was an extraordinarily precious moment, and that he had to take advantage of it before it was eviscerated by the next salvo of shells. He had something to say to this soldier who was and was not his father, more than a once-in-a-lifetime opportunity, a never-in-a-lifetime chance that he mustn't squander.

He turned to look into his father's eyes, his mouth opening to speak, but the horse's neck obscured his father's face, and all he could see was an untidy tuft curling up and off the front of his head. As he moved to make eye contact, there was another explosion, not too close, but enough to make them both duck their heads. And then the shells began dropping all around them, and the day split open and hell blasted out in a thunderous series of hammer blows that slammed into the ground and seemed to suck the air out of their lungs as they clung to the horse's neck and kept their heads down. Flying shrapnel and earth and stones blew past them.

This time, there was no more silence, just incessant noise and a relentless pounding that made the hard earth beneath their feet buck and roll like a ship's deck in high seas.

George didn't see much of the barrage they were stuck in the middle of. Every time there was an explosion, he ducked his head, and when he opened his eyes, all there was to see was the air full of dirt flying around. All he could do was bury his face in the horse's neck, one hand clenched over it, the other rhythmically stroking it as he heard his voice saying:

"Easy now, easy now."

The bombardment was shaking more than the foundations of the earth on which he was standing. It was shaking his grasp on everything. Every time he heard an explosion he flinched, and he knew the next one would be the one that blew him apart. When it wasn't, the anticipation of the following one made him wish it had been.

Some distant memory of a plinth and the fact it would just take one step to free him from this hell again tried to make itself heard in the back of his mind as the endlessness of the horror took his legs out from under him; but he closed his ears to it.

He realized that it was only the other soldier's arm gripping his over the top of the horse's neck that was keeping him upright. He tried to brace his boots and set his legs, but it was like trying to stack jelly. He gritted his teeth, and then he heard his father's voice saying:

"Good boy, good boy, you're going to be fine."

And even though the soldier was saying it to calm the

horse, he was also gripping George's arm as he did so, and George's heart opened again, despite the cacophony of the world coming to an end all around him. He found the iron in his soul and made his shaking legs do their job. As he looked down and saw them braced and supporting him, he noticed the thing, the last bad thing before it happened.

His father's boots were like his.

The only difference was that his father had broken a lace and had hurriedly mended it by knotting it at the toe end.

George knew what was going to happen even as his hand clenched on to his father's sleeve and he started shouting—

"No! Dad! Listen, please, I didn't—"

The soldier's head jerked up and met his eyes across the horse's neck. He was smiling.

"It's okay—"

The wall came in as if another giant had just kicked it down. The horse kicked sideways, and they both flinched. George felt the hand that had been gripping his go limp, and suddenly it was his turn to support the whole weight of the man on the other side. Then the horse tumbled over as a gout of flame rolled over them.

George didn't let go of the arm even though they were suddenly enveloped in a cloud of dust and smoke that was impossible to see through. He felt the horses' hooves lashing about in panic and heard their screaming neighs, and with his free hand he found the hobbles and released them, and then the horses were gone. He pulled his father's limp, heavy body onto his shoulders and staggered out of the burning debris into the open.

He shouted for help, but none came, so he staggered forward up the hill, the weight on his back heavier with each step. He heard himself sobbing, and then the wind whipped away the smoke, and the barrage stopped. He saw the hill ahead of him, and he dropped to one knee at the horror it revealed.

The two guns were destroyed. One was pointing crazily to the sky, the other was just not there. In its place was a crater with the gun team neatly splayed around the rim like petals on a flower. Bodies were blown into the barbed wire, some of which were not moving. Something was trying to crawl out of a shell hole. The impaled horse was gone, as were most of the birch trees.

George's scream for help turned into a question, and he heard the word "Why?" convulse repeatedly out of his throat. All that time he clutched his father's dead arm tighter and tighter as he felt the weight of the body buckle his legs and start to drive him into the ground.

And then something clattered at his feet; it was a stretcher. He looked up and saw the Officer and a bombardier looking at him with infinite sadness in their eyes and heard the Officer say:

"Put him down, Gunner."

He shook his head and tried to straighten his legs

despite the crushing downward force on his shoulders.

"Can't carry him forever. Put him down."

Again George shook his head and clenched on to the arm all the more tightly.

"It's my dad."

One of his hands twined fingers into the dead hand's fingers, and he held on for all he was worth. But there was no answering flicker of life. Then the hand seemed to grow bigger in his, and his fingers slipped out of it. He heard the fast percussive *wah-wah* of a police car roaring past, the rumble of London's traffic dialed back up as the sky dimmed, and his knees gave way. He fell off the bronze plinth and felt himself being caught in two bronze arms. He hung there, looking down at the Officer's boots. The light dimmed down to black, and he let it close over his head like the sea.

CHAPTER FORTY-THREE

Gunner's End

The Gunner lay in the dark water, waiting for death. The human part of him was numb with the constrictive horror of drowning, the bodily outrage, the pounding claustrophobia of the pipe, the terrible impossibility of taking a last breath, and the choking wrongness of it all.

The statue part of him knew that turn o'day was upon him, and that his death as a spit was coming. He had spent his whole existence marking midnight and standing to, and as with any habit, the rhythm and timing of it was hardwired into his body clock.

He would cease to walk, cease to talk, he would just be an inanimate lump of metal. Somehow dawn would see him winnowed to the elements and reconstituted on his plinth, never to move again. He had often wondered if the spits who had died were dead inside, or merely unable to move or express themselves. He hoped they were dead. Otherwise it would be like being buried alive forever, with a tiny window to view the passing world but no way to communicate with it other than an unending scream that sounded only inside your head.

Death, he hoped, would be just nothing. A big blank, a full stop, a balance where the absence of life and hope was counterweighed by the absence of pain and despair. A final equation where nothing equaled nothing, and all calculation ceased.

He managed to squeeze his arms so that his hands could lie calmly across his chest. He closed his eyes and composed himself as he waited for oblivion.

The trouble was he didn't feel composed inside, because, as the seconds ticked away, he couldn't help thinking that the whole oblivion thing was an easy way out. George and Edie would still be in danger, no matter whether he was conscious of it or not, and that felt bad. He grimaced as he realized he was not going to go gentle into any good night; rather, he was going to go feeling like he'd betrayed them by checking out early.

His eyes snapped open in the blackness. Well, he thought. Forget this composing yourself lark. Go down fighting.

He kicked his heels in and started pushing himself farther into the pipe. As he did so, a savage smile played on his lips. He was smiling because he knew this was a doubly futile gesture: he was going to be dead any second, and no one would ever know he had tried. He was smiling because he was just doing it for himself. He was going to die living his last moment exactly as he was, and not a damn thing less.

It was a good plan. It was tough, it was valiant, and it was, in the finest tradition of all good plans, destined to fail.

He didn't die fighting.

He didn't die being who he was meant to be.

He didn't die at all.

Somehow in the middle of kicking and pushing his way along the narrow pipe, shoving the bundle of heart stones ahead of him, he realized that he knew the day had turned, midnight had passed, and he was, unexpectedly and extraordinarily, not dead.

He didn't know that this was because George had stood his watch and kept his place on his plinth alive; he just knew that not only was he not dead, but he was feeling stronger with every foot that he moved along the narrow pipe.

And the pipe was narrow. It was definitely getting smaller as the debris on the floor got thicker and the Gunner's nose began to scrape along the roof.

But instead of his dying, the pipe came to an abrupt end. He was reaching ahead of himself to push his bundle onward when it met an obstruction and all progress ceased.

The fact that his vigor and strength were unaccountably returning had the contrary effect of making his predicament feel much worse. When he was winding down into what he thought was an inevitable death, his weakness had enabled him to ignore the claustrophobia. Now, having all his energy crammed into a blank pipe end buried under who knew how much city earth was unbearable. The pressure building up in his head and body made him want to scream and kick, but you can't scream under water, and there wasn't really room to kick. So instead he tried to ignore the fact that he had been worming his way forward only to jam himself into a coffin of his own making. He tried to think clearly. He had gotten into this pipe because there was a small but definite whisper of a current running through it. If there was a current, it meant the pipe was not a dead end. So he reached ahead of himself and ran his hands over the roof. He felt nothing but stone. He moved the bundle, and his hands felt the sidewalls. And there it was—a void. It wasn't a dead end, but an angle. He squirmed until he could get his arm farther into the angle, and was amazed to find he could feel nothing but water, no sides at all.

He realized that the narrow duct he was in must be a side tributary to a bigger underground stream, and in this he was right. The underground water tank was an ancient spur of the Tyburn, diverted for the very purpose of providing an underground reservoir. The water he was feeling against his fingertips was the flow of the main channel of the stream itself.

He shoved the bundle of sea-glass ahead of him and

wrenched himself around onto his side. He couldn't quite get his body around the angle, but because he was gaining strength, and because when you get a second chance at life you grab it with both hands, he wrenched away the crumbling cornerstone and pulled himself into the wider stream.

He felt the pull of the water tugging gently at him. He could easily have gone with it and seen where it took him. But something pulled him the other way. He scrabbled for the bundle, took a firm grip on it, and pushed his way against the mild current. It was a contrary thing to do, but if anyone had been able to see his smile in the black tunnel, they would have seen it was not only contrary but obstinate and fierce and somehow exulting.

If he wasn't going to die, he was certainly going to live, and live his way—and he was not going to do that by taking it easy and going with any damn flow.

CHAPTER FORTY-FOUR

Unquiet Death at Ghastly Grim

Edie fell one floor and was saved by a combination of thick snow and a henhouse.

At least she imagined it was a henhouse, because it squawked alarmingly when she hit it and rolled off into the alleyway.

It was still clucking in outrage as Edie ignored the fact that she was winded and her shoulder felt dislocated, as she ran off into the snow. Somewhere in the distance a barrel organ was playing and a church bell was cheerily tolling the hour as Edie thudded through the snow, the arms of her straitjacket flapping wildly behind her as she tried to put as much distance as she could between her and the House of Pain.

The street was dimly lit by occasional oil lamps, and Edie ran from pool of light to pool of light, checking behind her as she did so. The houses hunched over the street with drooping eaves and second and third floors that overhung a narrow thoroughfare, as if ready to pounce.

She was very conscious that her footsteps were the only ones in the virgin snow. She wasn't going to be hard to find. She ran out into a wider street, where the surface had been churned up by the passage of carts and cabs, hoping her footprints would be hidden in the general confusion.

She didn't, however, want to run in the middle of any street for long, because she was too visible. She also had a strong sense that she was being watched; but when she whirled to look behind her, she saw no one in the road, and only blackness stippled with falling snow above her. The sense of being seen became an unbearable itch that needed to be scratched, so when she saw a chance, she leaped across the strip of virgin snow and into a narrow alley, leaving, she hoped, no clues as to where she'd left the general melee in the middle of the street.

She looked back and noted with satisfaction that she'd left no trace at all. She ran along the side of the alley, keeping in the shadows, then turned a sharp corner, only to come to an even sharper halt.

Straight across the street was a church, and beside it a small churchyard. The high wall surrounding it was topped with ornate multibarbed spikes that poked through the soft topping of snow like a thornbush. There was an arched stone gateway, also topped with spikes, above a black iron gate that stood ajar.

Edie normally stayed well clear of churchyards, but there were two reasons that she started across the street, heading for the gate. First, there was a mash of footprints and wheel tracks leading into it, so her footprints would be lost among them. And secondly, she heard the chilling noise of dogs baying, coming closer. Her plan was to get through those metal gates, close them, and wait behind their safety for her pursuers to pass. She knew without a doubt that the barking came from the mastiffs from the House of Pain.

As she approached the gate she looked up and saw that it was decorated with stone skulls. There were two on each side, buried to their eye sockets in snow, impaled on savage barbs. There were three in the center of the arch, resting on bones. The central skull wore a laurel wreath like an ancient Roman, which made it look even more ominous, like the Emperor of Death.

It was too late for her to stop now, because the baying was closing in, and there was nowhere else to hide. She ducked through the gate and pushed it shut. The latch clunked, but there was, she noted, no way to lock it. She griped the obsidian blade and listened, ready to fight.

The dogs were suddenly silent. Edie hoped this was because they had taken a wrong turn and run on. She crouched in the shadows of the wall and looked at the graveyard behind her. It was a cramped space, hemmed in by the blind-eyed backs of houses on two sides, and by the square tower and side of the church on the other. It was a mad jumble of snowcapped gravestones, as if the bodies beneath were stacked four or five deep. The spaces between the stones were far too small to leave room for the full length of a coffin between them.

There were no lights in the houses, but there was a dim flicker from within the church. She saw a narrow door in the base of the tower. Without thinking, she slipped through the closely stacked ranks of gravestones.

She heard a voice and froze.

"What a busy night."

"A busy night indeed, Majesty."

The voices had a hollow, doomy quality to them. They sounded dry and were accompanied by a bony clacking.

"One goes out, one goes in."

"No rest for the wicked, Majesty."

"No rest for the good either. Not with the resurrection men abroad in the night."

Edie realized with a chilling certainty that she was hearing skulls talking to each other on the other side of the arch. The three central ones on the outside face of the stonework were, of course, invisible to her, but the two skulls on top of the wall were outlined against the night sky. And she knew what resurrection men were. She'd always listened in school, even when making it look as if she weren't. Resurrection men dug up dead bodies and sold them to surgeons to cut up.

She looked down and realized that the muddy footsteps and wheel tracks in the snow were just the kind to have been made by people digging and wheeling something away in a barrow. That explained why there was such a churn of markings leading into a graveyard at night.

One of the end skulls swiveled on its impaling barb and looked at Edie.

"She's listening, Majesty."

"Impossible. Unless . . ."

"Exactly."

"Ask her."

"Are you a glint, girl?" said the skull that Edie could see.

She nodded.

"She says yes, Majesty."

"I didn't hear her."

"She nodded. She's hiding."

"Tell her there is much hidden in the boneyard of Ghastly Grim, but that none of it is alive. Tell her to go."

"You must go," said the skull.

"Please stop talking!" Edie said urgently, ears straining for the sound of hounds or footsteps beyond the prattling chatter of the skulls.

"What does she say?"

"She's arguing, Majesty."

"She can't argue with me."

"You can't argue with the Majesty."

"I'm not arguing. I'm asking."

This was the noisiest deserted churchyard Edie had

ever been in. She backed up to the narrow door and tried it. It was locked.

"She's trying to get in the church."

"Will you please be quiet," Edie hissed again, stepping around a newly opened grave. She hunkered down behind a gravestone. She noted the name carved across it. It read: Aemilia Bowles. "Please stop talking."

"No. We always have the last word."

She was really regretting her decision to seek refuge in this "quiet" graveyard.

"Okay," she said urgently. "Have it. Just be quiet."

"She says have it, Majesty."

"Tell her we don't need her permission to have it. We have it by right, for we are Death!"

Edie boiled over. "You're not Death," she said. "You're a bunch of chattering stone skulls that can't keep their mouths shut."

"She says . . ."

"SHUT UP. You are not Death—"

There was silence. Then another voice said quietly.

"No. But I am."

It was the Walker. Edie could see the two dogs silently pawing the other side of the gate.

Only now did she remember to look down at her hand holding the heart stone. She had been gripping it so tightly that she hadn't seen the warning light blazing from it.

Something large leaped to the top of the wall and

crouched there, and where the dogs were panting, this thing was breathing in short, choppy shrieks of hunger. In excitement, it clapped its stubby wings together over the hunched mass of its torturously enclosed body.

It was the Icarus.

All the energy seemed to drain from Edie as she slid down behind a grave marker, realizing that now the Walker had her and would have George, and the Gunner was probably dead, and it was all over. And even though she knew she was done for, she used the last piece of her energy to scrabble away the snow and mud at the foot of the gravestone she was hiding behind and stuff her heart stone deep into the earth.

And then she stood up and kicked the earth in on top of it and stamped it down, hoping her legs were hidden as she did so.

And she saw the Walker come through the gate, knife in one hand, the other covering one of his eyes.

And she dropped her head and closed hers.

CHAPTER FORTY-FIVE

How to Fall Out of a River

As the Gunner crawled his way against the flow, he felt life returning to his body in more ways than just the renewed strength. His hands felt like his hands again, not clumsy obstacles at the end of his arms. He could think straighter, too, as if layers of thick cloth had been lifted from his brain.

He wondered if this miraculous increase in well-being extended to a lifting of the Walker's power over his ability to dig his way to the upper air. He flexed his muscles and reached for the roof of the pipe. Somehow the instructions were blocked between his head and his arms, which just stayed where they were and didn't attack the roof as he had told them to do.

He ignored his disappointment and pushed on.

The dark water-filled pipe seemed to go on forever, and the absence of any visual clues made it even harder to bear. At times he hallucinated that he had become weightless and was crawling on the ceiling of the pipe; other times it seemed that the pipe was moving past him and he was keeping still.

He realized he could fight these disorienting feelings if he concentrated on what his hands were touching on the wall of the tunnel as he went forward, because the texture beneath his fingertips was the one thing that did change. Some of the time it was bricks, some of the time it was long curves of stone or concrete piping. At one stage it appeared to be just clay, and he felt his fingertips leaving a groove as he squirmed forward. He imagined the cloudy trail his hand must be leaving in the clear water, invisible in the darkness.

He had been feeling a brick side to the tunnel for quite a long time, and had just wondered if he could work out how far he was going by counting them as his fingers moved from gap to gap. Then he felt a new texture. It was unbroken by any mortar cracks, so his first thought was that it was more concrete piping; but he quickly realized that it was different. It was metal.

He rapped his knuckles against it, and the answering vibration confirmed his first impression. He moved on for a few paces, and then the implication of that answering vibration hit him: a metal pipe, bedded in the clay of London, would be deadened and sound damped by the surrounding earth. There would be no answering vibration.

The implication was that he was in a metal pipe, and

that there was air, not clay on the other side of it. His first instinct was to hit the roof of the pipe, but his hands wouldn't obey his commands. He kicked the floor of the pipe in frustration.

His boots set off a bigger vibration. He did it again, harder. And then he smiled.

"Didn't say anything about digging *down*, did he?"

He turned on his back and hacked the metal-shod heels of his ammo boots onto the floor of the pipe. He sledgehammered them down again and again, and every time, he felt the answering vibration in the wall through his braced fingertips. Every kick of his boots got the same result, and then suddenly the vibration wasn't there, but a sharp single shock shuddered through the pipe. He had no idea what it meant, but he stomped down one last time with all the power in his body. Instead of the jarring impact of his boots, there was a slight resistance, and then his feet continued downward, through the bottom of the pipe, and he was suddenly falling—

The Tyburn is one of London's lost, hidden rivers. But it does show itself in one place, and that's where the Gunner was: it crosses over the Regent's Canal in an aqueduct disguised as a footbridge, close to the London Zoo, and it was out of the bottom of that aqueduct that the Gunner tumbled, in his own personal waterfall.

He had a moment of elation as he felt the air, and then a jolt of surprise as he depth-charged into the water of the canal. The surprise was, under these circumstances, understandable. Not many people fall out of a river, and even fewer fall out of one river into another.

He pushed off the muddy bottom of the canal and breathed in the night air. He looked back at the bridge out of which he had just fallen, and the liberated Tyburn pouring out of it into the water below. He realized what must have happened, and grinned. Then he lofted the bundle of heart stones onto a footpath and pulled himself out after it. He paused only to put his helmet on, and then he picked up the bundle, vaulted a fence into Regent's Park, and started running southeast.

He knew it was after turn o'day and that he should be dead. If he wasn't, it meant someone had stood his watch, and he wasn't going to waste a minute getting back to Hyde Park Corner to see who it was.

He smiled as he ran.

Because of course his gut told him exactly who it must have been; and where George was would also be his best chance of finding Edie before the Walker got to her.

The glasses chinking in the bundle as he ran were all the evidence he needed to know that once a glint was in the Walker's grasp, there was no escape.

CHAPTER FORTY-SIX

In the Walker's Grasp

The Icarus stood in the middle of the dusty library, his cropped wings brushing the roof as he loomed over Edie, panting short angry screams.

Edie turned her face away.

"If you find him worrying, you shouldn't have broken the window," said the Walker. "He would never have been able to get in here without an opening that size."

Edie looked at the Walker's face. There was no blood where she had slashed him, but an impossibly healed white scar cut across his face, just below one eye, taking a nick out of the bridge of his nose and ending in the other eye. That eye was now dead, clouded a pinky white, with no iris or pupil to be seen.

"And if you didn't want him angry with you, you should never have killed his brother."

"I didn't kill his brother," said Edie quietly.

"The Minotaur was his brother. Not an actual brother,

but a brother in that they were the creations of the same maker, the same sculptor. They had much in common as a result."

Edie didn't need to look to confirm the truth of that. The Icarus had the same powerful legs and body, the same sense of dark energy bunched up and ready to erupt.

The Walker stood up and looked down at her. One of her arms was again tied to the chair.

Far off in another part of the house, Edie could hear the despairing sobs of the Blind Woman. The Walker noticed her listening. He smiled and snapped his fingers. The Raven flew in the window and settled on his shoulder.

"You're wondering why she is crying so heartbreakingly."

Edie didn't say anything. The Walker's hand traced the scar across his face.

"You're wondering what I am going to do to you. For what you have done to me."

He was right, but she wasn't going to give him the satisfaction of letting him know. She was unnerved by how calm he had been ever since finding her at the churchyard. He had almost been polite as the Icarus had trapped her and they had led her away.

He smiled without a shred of humor, and started writing on a sheet of paper. His voice was quiet, conversational, almost warm.

"I am doomed to walk the city until the Stone releases me. And so I cannot die. I heal, as you can see, prodigiously well. But in four hundred years, no one has done what you have done. . . ."

And here he looked up from the writing and pointed to the blind, pinky-white eyeball next to it.

"Now, because of you, I must walk the world one-eyed. Be sure that that is a wound and an affront that requires a magnificently well-thought-out punishment. I shall not deny myself the pleasure of planning the gradual stages of your end by rashly killing you now in anger. For despite what foolish men say, revenge is not a dish best served cold: to my taste, it is a dish best served after exquisitely detailed preparation and execution, and enjoyed at blood temperature."

He finished off his note. Edie found that the more he tried to frighten her, the angrier she got. And the angrier she got, the stronger she felt. Unfortunately, it was also true that the more he tried to frighten her, the more frightened she became.

She tried to suppress the mind-killing fear and watch what he was doing as he folded the note and produced the two interlocked circular mirrors from his pocket. She watched as he unsnapped them, and then unsnapped them again, revealing a second set of mirrors clipped inside. He took one set of mirrors and carefully adjusted a tiny bezel running around the edge.

"That will bring them straight back to where I shall

be," he said to himself, then noticed her listening.

"We shall meet in an open space. That way, if George brings help, I shall see them and you will suffer the consequences."

He reached over to the table. Edie saw that he had sandwiched the black mirror between the two wax disks and tied them in place. He had also knotted a leather thong through the hole in the mirror's handle. He put the thong around his neck so that the heavy package hung on his front like a giant medallion. Then he pushed it inside his sweatshirt and buttoned his coat.

He pulled his dagger out from behind him and turned back to her. As he moved, he revealed a woman's cloak and a bonnet on the desk. She had seen them before. She had seen the bonnet tangled around her own face as the Walker drowned her. In the open spaces of the ice-covered Thames. At the Frost Fair.

Despite herself, she shrank back in the chair. He waved the knife, imagining that it was causing her to flinch.

"Now. Do scream if you like. The Icarus will enjoy it. I need just one thing from you before we go."

CHAPTER FORTY-SEVEN

The Challenge

"Here he comes," said the Officer's voice.

George swam slowly upward, out of a dark pool of sad dreams, as if he were made of lead. It was hard for him to leave unconsciousness; it was a huge effort just to open his eyes.

When he did, there were two pair of bronze boots in front of his nose. He was lying beneath a heavy greatcoat that was somehow as warm and supple as wool, even though it was made of the same bronze as the boots.

One pair of riding boots was the Officer's. The other pair was heavier and more workmanlike: laced boots topped off by mismatched leggings, one set of puttees, the other armored with a calf protector.

George knew those boots.

He scrambled to a sitting position and looked up.

The Gunner smiled down at him.

"Hey," he said.

"Hey," said George.

"You okay?"

George thought about it for a moment.

"Not really."

"Good enough," grunted the Gunner, and he squatted down in front of George, eye to eye. "There'd be something really wrong with you if you done what you done and felt all tickety-boo about it."

George suddenly had to get the great thing rising in his throat out before it choked him.

"I saw my dad."

"Yeah." The Gunner nodded. "You would."

After a beat the Gunner pointed over his shoulder at the body lying at the north end of the monument. "It's him, isn't it? The Unknown Soldier. That's why his face was made covered, so he could be everyone's lost one. So, you just made him your dad. . . ."

George nodded and put on a tight smile. He didn't want anyone to know that somewhere inside, there was a well of sadness that he had been drowning in. He didn't trust himself to speak.

"Must have been rough," said the Gunner.

He put his hand on George's shoulder and looked away.

George took a series of long deep breaths, getting himself back together.

"You want to let it out, son, no one here's gonna think any the worse of you."

"Absolutely not," said the Officer, busy looking with great interest anywhere but at George. "Couldn't think more highly of you, as it happens."

He coughed in embarrassment and lowered his voice a little. "And for what it's worth, I blubbed like a baby all the way through my first bombardment. . . ."

Maybe because they gave him permission, maybe because they understood, but George didn't need to let it out. He swallowed and found that it went back inside and didn't seem so terrible.

"I'm okay."

The Gunner turned back and looked at him with a raised eyebrow.

". . . in a not entirely okay way," finished George.

"Look at your arm," said the Officer.

George had forgotten about the marble groove jagging its way toward his armpit and the heart beyond. He tore at his shirt and looked.

The entire flaw had disappeared, leaving only a faint red mark like a scar, well on the way to healing.

"It's gone!" he said.

"A duel is a duel, I'd say." The Officer smiled. "Whether it's fought with dueling pistols, rapiers, or great big hulking artillery pieces like that one. . . ." He nodded up at the huge stone gun topping the monument. "And you certainly stood your ground. I'd say that's one down, two to go."

George smiled and felt the other two grooves still

twining below his forearm, the gritty stone one and the smooth brass one.

"I'd say." The Gunner grinned and gripped his shoulder. "And by the by: thank you."

He held his big hand out. George took it. The Gunner gripped it firmly.

"Saved my bacon, no mistake. And if you don't mind me saying, I reckon your dad would have been proud of you."

"Yes," said George.

The truth of it was suddenly there inside him. It was as if it had always been there, but he hadn't noticed because he'd always been looking the wrong way, staring at the pool of sadness. Maybe the soldier who had worn his dad's face had said it best: maybe it was like being on a stage that you thought you were the center of and then realizing you were on the edge of something much bigger behind you. Whatever it was, George realized that a very big pain in his heart had gone, simply because he had stopped concentrating on it and noticed that its cure had been right there all the time, waiting to be noticed.

"Yes. I reckon he would have been. I reckon he was."

It was as if by not crying on the outside, all the tears had fallen inside and left him feeling washed and clean. And clearheaded.

He got to his feet in one lithe move.

"Edie," he said decisively. "We need to find her."

"No question," said the Gunner. "The Walker's after her, and he's after you."

The Gunner repeated to George what the Walker had told him about the black mirror. George told the Gunner about everything that had happened to him; and just as he got to the bit about the Euston Mob, the Officer tapped the Gunner on the shoulder and pointed to a dark shape gliding in from the east.

The two soldiers unholstered their guns and aimed at the Raven as it coasted in toward them. George picked up his hammer.

"It's got something in its beak," said the Officer.

The Raven landed calmly on the white stone in front of them and gently laid the two mirrors on the ground. Then it stepped back. It wasn't going to make any fast moves with two revolvers trained on it, but it also had too much self-respect to look interested in what might or might not happen.

"There's a note tied on it," said the Officer.

"Last pair of mirrors I saw like that was in the Walker's hands," said the Gunner.

George darted forward and slid the note out. It was a simple message:

> Come to me. Beneath the main banner
> at the Frost Fair. Step into the
> mirrors and they will bring you.
> Come now, or the girl dies.

The Gunner and the Officer read it over his shoulder.

"He could be bluffing," said the Gunner.

"He lies like the rest of us breathe," said the Officer.

"No," said George. "He's not lying."

He gently lifted the "string" that had been used to attach the note to the mirrors. It was not quite black. It was a dark, almost eggplant color.

"It's her hair."

The Gunner swore under his breath. Then he aimed his gun at the Raven.

The Raven wasn't surprised. It knew what was going to happen next. In his experience, people always shot the messengers when they brought bad news.

What did surprise him was that it wasn't a bullet in the chest bone that sent him to Hell again. It was a spear, thrown with great force and accuracy from the opposite direction.

George, the Gunner, and the Officer looked at the sudden explosion of shocked black feathers, and then across the grass to where the spear had come from.

There was a parked chariot, and a very businesslike queen was striding over the grass toward them, to retrieve her weapon.

"What are you men all staring at?" she said. "It sounds like we have a girl to rescue."

"I think we can manage, thank you, ma'am," the Officer said stiffly.

"No we can't," said George sharply. "We'll take all the help we can get."

He picked the spear out of the pile of feathers that was already being winnowed into the night air and handed it to the Queen.

"Thank you, boy. Now, what I suggest is—"

"You don't suggest anything. If you want to help, you listen, because Edie told me about this. She glinted it, and it ended badly. . . ." The unmistakable crack of authority in George's voice made the spits look at him in surprise.

The Queen swelled in indignation. "Why, I will not—"

"Yeah, you will," the Gunner interrupted. "If you want to help the girl, listen in. The boy knows what he's talking about."

The Queen bit her lip and kept quiet as George quickly told them about how Edie had glinted the Frost Fair and seen herself chased by the Walker and drowned in an ice hole. He told them every detail he could remember.

"I don't know if it really was herself that she saw being drowned; and if it was, I don't know if you can change the past. All I know is she saw it, and I'm going into those mirrors and do everything I can to stop it from happening."

There was a beat of silence.

"I could do with a hand, but either way I'm going."

He turned and retrieved the hammer from where it was leaning. The weight felt right as he hefted it in his hand.

The spits looked at each other.

The Queen turned and snapped her fingers at her daughters. "Girls," she said, "come and hold the mirrors. It's going to take very careful riding to get the chariot through in one piece."

CHAPTER FORTY-EIGHT

Frost Fair

You can't change the past. Even if it hasn't happened yet.

This was the thought going around and around in Edie's head as the Walker led her from the House of Pain toward the frozen Thames. She scarcely noticed anything except the snow in front of her and the strap binding her wrists together. Her vision was restricted by the bonnet the Walker had tied around her head. It jutted forward on either side like blinders. Her bound hands were hidden in a muff: a roll of padded rabbit fur that hung from the front of what she assumed was the Blind Woman's cloak.

She knew what the Frost Fair would look like when they escaped the narrow warren of snow-deadened streets leading down to the river's edge. She'd seen it all before when she'd glinted her own death.

You can't change the past. Even if it hasn't happened yet.

348

The thought kept whirring 'round and 'round. If she was going to be able to escape, then she wouldn't have seen herself in the ice hole. If she wasn't going to be able to stop this from happening, why try to escape? But if she didn't try to escape, how could she stop this from happening?

Edie was a fighter. She knew one of the reasons she was beginning to spin loose in her mind was that she didn't have her heart stone anymore. But neither did the Walker. That was something. It probably wasn't enough to keep her alive by itself, but it was enough of a spark to keep her trying to figure out how to.

"Cheer up, girl. This is a sight rarely seen."

If she hadn't already glinted it, the sight that met her eyes as the Walker led her on a plank over a narrow open channel of icy water onto the frozen surface of the river would certainly have amazed her. Having previously seen it as a background for her own murder took the edge off, somehow. But it was an extraordinary sight.

Below the looming span of Blackfriars Bridge, the entire width of the Thames was iced over and covered in snow. The night was banished with the light of hundreds of lanterns and flaming torches that illuminated the ramshackle street of makeshift tents and shelters, which had been set up on the center of the river. There was music and laughter and the sounds of a holiday crowd enjoying itself, mingling with the smell of roasting meat and wood smoke. London's tavern owners and cooks had taken to the ice, selling their wares and hospitality out of hurriedly built temporary premises decorated with garish signs and billboards. And it wasn't only food and drink that were for sale.

There were souvenir shops and portrait painters, there were jugglers and acrobats, there were fairground games and a huge swinging boat full of shrieking men and women of all ages. There was even a printing press being cranked by hand next to a man with a monkey and a barrel organ. A huge painted banner straddled the street, reading FROST FAIR—COME ONE, COME ALL!, and from the numbers thronging the icy street, it would seem all of London had responded to the invitation.

Again, if Edie hadn't already seen all this before, she would have been captivated by the magic of the sight. As it was, seeing it all, especially the monkey and the barrel organ, just terrified her. She remembered all of this, but the monkey and the organ were a very specific part of what she had glinted. She had seen and heard them and then noticed how their music had been drowned out by an approaching sound of bagpipes as a parade moved down the street, led by a white elephant, which had stolen everybody's attention.

On cue, Edie heard the warning rattle of snare drums as a bagpipe band skirled into life in the distance.

The Walker was pushing her ahead of him, one hand firmly on her shoulder.

She needed to stop her mind from unraveling. She

knew she needed to think fast and move before everything closed in on her and her diminishing series of options disappeared altogether, leaving her with nothing. She needed to choose something, and she needed to do it now. Even if it didn't work, she would go down fighting.

The flash of the knife blade caught her attention and gave her the something to focus on. A cook was serving slices of beef from a joint turning on a spit in the entrance of a booth just ahead. He had stabbed his blade into a wooden carving block as he took a customer's money.

The sharp steel blade was her way out. In the absence of any other options, this was the one she was going to choose.

She pushed the muff awkwardly up one arm, shoving it against her stomach, disguising the wriggle with a cough. The Walker just shoved her forward, not noticing that she had exposed her wrists to the cold night air and the cruel blade beckoning just a few short steps away.

She held her breath, and then, once the blade was in reach, she threw herself forward. Her hands chopped through the air on either side of the blade, slamming onto the red juices covering the carving surface. The blade was not as sharp as the obsidian razor she had used to slash the Walker, but it was sharp enough to give her the escape she wanted.

It cut through the strap that was binding her wrists

together, and as soon as she felt the constraint part, she pulled her hands back up and grabbed the handle of the knife, yanking it out of the wooden block.

And as the Walker grabbed for her, she ducked and spun. His arm swung over her head, just missing, knocking the bonnet awry. She kept spinning and slashed the carving knife into his leg, catching him behind the knee.

She heard a yell of pain and fury, and left the knife in his leg. As he buckled forward clutching at his knee, Edie saw the bright blaze of the Blind Woman's heart stone in the chest pocket of his coat. Without thinking, she plunged her hand in, grabbed it, and just ran, cannoning off people, heading for the open ice.

As she ran, she remembered that when she had glinted this scene before, she had seen the bonnet fall in front of her face as she'd tried to escape. That had been the thing that had done her in, because she had run blindly into an ice hole, where the Walker had caught up with her. So as she ran, her first thought was to get rid of the stupid bonnet before it killed her.

Her fingers fumbled at the ribbons, which was a good idea but a bad mistake: because fumbling at full tilt, trying to get the bonnet off, turned out to be the very thing that made it fall in front of her face and blind her in the first place.

You can't change the past.

Even if it hasn't happened yet.

CHAPTER FORTY-NINE

Last Ditch

"How's this going to work?" asked George.

Its working didn't seem likely from where he was standing. Mind you, he was standing in a pretty unlikely place, in a chariot being driven by a queen of the ancient Britons, next to a World War I gunner, cantering toward two small mirrors being held parallel to each other by the Queen's daughters.

"I touch the mirrors as we pass, and we will go through," said the Queen, lowering her spear.

The mirrors seemed impossibly tiny, and then they were right on them, and the Queen jabbed with her spear point and missed.

"Okay," said George, looking across at the Gunner. "We don't have time for target practice."

The Queen circled the chariot so tightly that it turned on one wheel, and for a moment George and the Gunner could do nothing except hold on to avoid being spun out onto the grass. Then the wheel landed with a thump, and the Queen raced back at the mirrors.

"Just getting her eye in," said the Gunner.

The mirrors approached again, and the daughters didn't flinch as the whirring blades on the wheels whipped past, inches from their knees. The Queen jabbed her spear—and missed again.

"Third time's the charm," she said, reining the horses into another tight turn.

"There's no time for this!" said George, and he leaped clear of the chariot. He heard the Gunner shout after him, but he ignored him and ran toward the Queen's daughters.

They looked at him in shock.

"How does it work?" he said, hand grasping the hammer tightly.

"Just step in," said the daughter to his left. "Either mirror. The Walker has set them to bring you right to him."

It didn't seem likely to George that this was going to work either, but he remembered how he'd seen the Walker step into the mirrors and pull the Gunner with him; and he thought of Edie, and the urgency of that thought made him reach into the mirror and step impossibly into it.

He felt the surface tension give, and then he was falling through layers of blackness that strobed at him, making him feel suddenly nauseated with plunging vertigo—and then the fall ended abruptly and he was facedown on the ice with a mouthful of snow.

He looked up and saw the lowering black wall of a barge in front of him, a boat that had been frozen in the ice. He turned around and saw, a hundred feet away, the lantern-lit carnival of the Frost Fair, and a parade with a white elephant wending through the tented street.

He had dropped the hammer as he'd landed, and he scrabbled in the snow for it. He had just found it when there was a popping noise from behind him, and the Gunner tumbled out of nowhere. He looked at George with a short grin.

"She's going to take forever getting through."

"We don't have forever," said George, getting to his feet and pointing. "The elephant's already here."

He started to move forward. The Gunner's hand stopped him.

"George. Thought just hit me. I broke my oath. The Walker's got some power over me. He used it. Couldn't control my arms."

"What?" said George, eyes raking the distant crowd for signs of Edie.

"I'm thinking if he saw me, he could make me do something bad."

The Gunner looked shamefaced. "Shoulda let the Officer come instead."

"No," said George decisively. "Someone had to stay behind and watch for us coming back in case the

Walker's on our tails when we do. Someone's got to be ready to shoot him down."

"Yeah, but—"

"No buts," said George, kicking into a sprint.

He'd seen Edie.

"Just don't let him see you first."

He tore across the expanse of snow toward Edie, who was running away from the crowd at an angle. He yelled as he ran, trying to cut her off.

"Edie! Over here!"

She didn't seem to hear him. Maybe because she was fumbling with her bonnet.

The Gunner started running too. He saw the Walker break out of the crowd at a fast hobble. The Gunner saw him turn and shout at something in the darkness on the other side of the river. Heard the words:

"Get the girl! Icarus! Where's the Bull? Get the bloody girl!"

The Gunner saw what was going to happen before George did. He stopped going for Edie and ran toward the side of the river, where the Thames boatmen had cut a wide channel between the shore and the ice so that they could charge people for crossing over on planks they had erected. He saw a portly father quibbling about the fee, while his beribboned daughter jumped excitedly up and down at his side and pointed to the ice beyond. Her voice was sharp enough to cut straight through the sound of bagpipes and drums and into the Gunner's ears.

"Oh, Daddy. No, Daddy, please, pay the little man! It's there and we're missing it! The elephant—"

George heard the voice and remembered Edie saying she'd missed seeing something because of the elephant, and he raised his hands like a megaphone and yelled at Edie, who hadn't seen him yet.

"Edie—don't look at the elephant!"

And then he hit an ice hummock and tripped.

But not before Edie saw him. As she was about to shout back, the Walker hit her from behind, and they fell to the ice. Edie kicked and hit and bit like a wildcat, without thought, as furiously brutal as any animal fighting for its life. She smashed the Blind Woman's blazing heart stone into the Walker's good eye. He managed to close his eyes and duck his head away just in time, but the searing light temporarily blinded him.

"Now you die, girl!" he screamed.

She booted him in the chin and tumbled backward onto her feet and ran, while he swiped at her through his stone-dazzled vision.

He pulled the long burnished dagger from inside his coat and ran after her.

Edie was struggling with the bonnet that had been mashed forward over her face in the struggle.

Her heart was pumping so hard from the adrenaline of the fight, she forgot to look out in front of her.

Her foot hit water instead of hard ice, and she plunged forward, straight into the hole. The shock of the cold and the water in her mouth hit her simultaneously, and she scrambled up through the icy Thames. Her fingers clawed onto the edge of the ice, and she tried to pull herself out of the hole. As her face broke into the air, covered in hair like a thick flap of seaweed, she remembered that she must be watching this happening as she glinted this past death in a future and faraway London. She screamed a warning to herself as she tried to scramble out of the water's icy grasp:

"Edie. The Friar's okay! Don't trust Little Tragedy! He's not what he seems! Tell George! Walker's trying to open evil—"

And then a rescuing hand reached over and grabbed her hair; only it wasn't rescuing at all. It was pushing her back under, and there were bubbles and splashing and black water, and then she broke free for an instant and fishmouthed for air and used her last words to try to complete her warning:

"—gates in the mirrors—"

The Walker's hand grabbed the bonnet and plunged her spluttering face under the water for the last time. She carried on shouting as her lungs filled with water, and the last thing she saw as she sank into the inky blackness was the Walker's face, lit red by the distant lanterns, grinning down at her through the floating tangle of her own hair.

In that terrible last moment, Edie wanted everything. As she started to fade, the years of her life peeled away, and she became younger and younger. All the layers of toughness she'd had to put on to survive dropped off and left her feeling helpless and young and tiny. As she hurtled toward the full stop of her life, she felt outrage that this should be so, and she just wanted to start everything again. She wanted her mother before she had changed, before she'd gone strange, before she'd become mad, before she'd just gone away and never come back. . . .

—And more than anything, she wanted that child's first and best sanctuary, the heart's last ditch—the warm embrace of her mother telling her it would be all right, that today's pain would fade and tomorrow the sun would shine.

But her final thought was the desperate despair of knowing it wouldn't be all right, as her eyes dimmed and the freezing blackness took her, alone and in the dark.

And then Edie died.

CHAPTER FIFTY

Ironhand

George hit the Walker at full speed, every ounce of power and rage in his body powering him into the larger man like a runaway train.

He knew he was too late. He knew Edie was dead. He knew it was his fault.

The impact cartwheeled the two of them into a cloud of snow.

George swung the heavy hammer in his fist right at the Walker's body, as if he could stop the black heart in one massive blow.

The hammer slammed into something the Walker was wearing under his sweatshirt, something thick that gave way and cracked at the same time.

The Walker gasped as the air was pile-driven out of him, but his left hand clawed out and gripped George by the hair and ear. The two of them staggered to their feet, eye to eye. The Walker got a breath and snarled at George, his good eye blazing.

"Are you going to try and fight me, boy?"

"No," gritted George. "I'm going to kill you."

As he accepted the challenge, George felt a searing pain in his arm jagging toward his armpit, and he knew without being able or needing to look that the twisting channel of bronze in his arm had ripped forward, heading for his heart.

He knew this was the second contest; this brutal tussle in the snow was his next duel, the moment he would live or die by.

And he didn't care.

Because there was no way on earth that he wasn't going to make good on his word.

The Walker was a dead man.

"It's a waste, boy. But I have all the time in the world."

Time slowed. George saw the flash of the knife as the Walker pulled it back and slashed it up toward his belly in a cruel, gutting blow.

George's hand was moving before conscious thought kicked in, and this time it didn't flinch. It closed around the sharp blade and held it tight, stopping it an inch from his belly.

The Walker's eye widened in shock at the strength of the boy. And what the Walker saw made him step back a half pace. The boy's eyes were as hard and unforgiving as stone.

"I don't think so," said George.

He jerked his hand sharply and snapped the blade clean.

Then he pulled his hand back behind his shoulder, and when the Walker let go of his hair and tried to get away, George gripped the Walker's hand and held him as he stabbed the blade down into the Walker's heart.

The blade hit something hard and skittered sideways; but with all the cold rage George had put into the blow, it still buried itself in the Walker's shoulder, so deep that George couldn't pull it out.

He let go and took a microsecond to notice that his hand wasn't cut at all, despite the fact that he had gripped the double-edged blade like a vise.

The Walker stared at the broken blade in his shoulder and howled in fury.

George had time to look down at the black hole in the ice. Edie was long gone. He quickly stooped and picked up the blazing piece of sea-glass she'd dropped in her struggle. He could see it wasn't hers; it was the wrong shape and color, but he knew it for what it was, and without thinking, he dropped it into the water. If she was alone and dead in the inky blackness, somehow, the least he could do was leave the light on.

He turned back to the howling Walker, stepped across the gap between them, and punched him in the face. The Walker went silent in shock at the force of the blow.

In the distance, there was the approaching sound of something screaming in short, excited bursts. But George ignored it and kept on coming. He hit the Walker with a straight punch that knocked him flat on his back. Only then did George step back, in order to pick up his hammer and stand over him.

There was a thunder of hooves, and the Walker's eyes flicked left. He sneered up at George through a bloody mouth.

"Now you die, boy."

George turned his head and saw the Bull thundering across the ice.

"Maybe," said George, "but you die first." He raised the hammer. "I'll deal with your bull after that."

"It's not the bull." The Walker smiled, his eyes flicking upward.

The Icarus hit him like an airborne sledgehammer.

Chapter Fifty-one

Under the Ice

The Gunner hit the narrow channel of water between the ice and the riverbank like a depth charge.

He'd seen Edie go under, and that neither he nor George would get there in time to save her. So he made the only choice that remained, which was to go under the ice.

Tons of bronze don't swim too well, so he hit the bed of the Thames and did the best he could to plow through the blackness toward the spot where he estimated the hole in the ice was. The human part of him went through the searing drowning pain of oxygen starvation, but he was so driven that he didn't bother trying to hold his breath—he just sucked in water and got on with it.

He couldn't see a thing, and surged forward by instinct alone. The snow-covered ice made a perfect roof over the river, blocking out all light. And as he moved ahead, he realized he wasn't going to be able to see Edie's ice hole either, since looking straight up was only going to bring a dark view of the night sky, which would be indistinguishable from the impenetrable murk surrounding him.

He flailed around with his arms as he went, hoping that if he couldn't see Edie's body, he might at least touch it by chance. But as he stared blindly, he realized it was a forlorn hope.

The girl was gone.

Then an orange light dropped out of the ice roof overhead, and he looked up and caught a brief glimpse of the world above, with George staring sightlessly downward, his face momentarily lit up by the falling heart stone before he jerked away from the hole.

The Gunner reached out his hand and caught the stone on its chain and held it high, like a lantern in a storm. The orange light shone so brightly that the turbid river water became somehow less opaque—and that's when the Gunner saw the body, its foot caught in a broken cart wheel half buried in the ooze, its hair lifelessly going with the flow, pointing toward the sea.

He freed Edie's foot and grabbed her, surging toward the riverbank. As he powered forward, he looked down at her pale dead face and looped the heart stone around her neck so he could get a better grip. He hugged her tightly to his body, as if he could force some of his life into her.

And of course you can't cry under water, so the sting-
ing in his eyes must just have been the Thames resisting
his attempt to run through it.

He scrambled up the slope toward the torch-lit strip
of light, and pulled himself out of the water. He felt
Edie's body flop against him as he coughed his way to his
feet. He was about to start pumping water out of her,
when he heard the ice scrabble and the angry snorting
that heralded the approaching bull. He scooped her up
and ran.

Out of the corner of his eye, George saw the Gunner
emerge from the ice. The Icarus flew George away from
the Walker, who was lying on his back and tugging at his
clothes, trying urgently to get something out of his
sweatshirt.

The Icarus screamed at George, and he looked into
the blind curve of the creature's breastplate. Somewhere
inside the intricate structure, a mouth was shrieking
angrily at him.

The Icarus was a worse flier than Spout. George was
only about twenty feet off the ice, but he was heading
away from the Gunner and what he had pulled from the
water. He was unable to see what the Walker was doing.
The only good thing was that he saw something pop into
existence and gallop across the ice, heading for the Gunner,
the whirling blades on its chariot wheels twisting ice
devils out of the snow as it thundered beneath him.

George still had the hammer in his hand.

"One chance," he said to whatever was behind the jutting hull masking the face in front of him. "Put me down."

The Icarus howled and shook him angrily. When George looked down, he realized that the thing was gripping him with its human feet, which crushed him with toes like sinewy talons.

"Fine," he said.

He smashed the hammer into the hull. He hit it again and again, and as he did so, the Icarus shrieked and lurched in the sky. There was a crack, and the breastwork gave way, and George was staring into the mad eyes of the Icarus.

The Icarus was a man cramped and jammed into the narrow confining space of a basketwork hull. His arms and hands were folded in on themselves, and his mouth and lower face were bound with some kind of webbing— but not so obscured that George couldn't see the hostile insanity snarling out of the face.

"Last chance. Put me down," said George.

The feet tore at him angrily and the eyes burned brighter. The head shook violently back and forth in an unmistakable "No."

"Then I'm sorry," he said, and whacked the hammer dead center on the straining forehead. The mad eyes rolled back, and the Icarus plummeted, unconscious and, for the first time, silent.

George had time to see that they were going to land

in open water, just beyond the point where the ice began. He booted himself free of the Icarus's limp feet in the instant before they hit the water.

The Icarus hit the river and kept going down. George kicked for the surface and gasped for air, then turned in time to see the edge of the ice approaching as the river pulled him toward it. The edge was a confusion of trapped driftwood and branches, and he had a horror-struck premonition that he was about to be sucked beneath the ice. He grabbed at the edge as he reached it, but the ice bobbled away beneath his fingers, and he was pulled under.

On the surface of the ice, the Gunner had seen the Bull just in time. He grabbed Edie's body and leaped clear as the sharp horns thundered in. The Bull tried to hook him, but its momentum made it overshoot, and it crashed into the snow piled on the riverbank.

The Gunner heard his name being called, and whirled to see the Queen approaching across the flat ice field, her horses straining against their harness, their feet kicking up great divots of impacted snow as they raced to the rescue. There was another figure on the chariot, and because the man was hatless, it took the Gunner an instant to realize it was the Officer.

He sped toward the incoming chariot, cradling the dead body as he ran. He heard a snort and the drumming of hooves behind him and knew that the Bull had turned and was now running after him.

As the chariot approached without slowing, the gap behind him closed almost as fast.

He saw the Officer point urgently straight down and shout something.

"Mind the wheels!"

The Officer snapped his arm out, leaning so wide over the spinning blades that the Queen had to lean far in the opposite side to stop the chariot from tipping. Then time went very quickly as they closed in on the Gunner at breathtaking speed. He felt the Bull's breath on his back and a light tug as it tried to hook him again, but he had no time to think about how close the creature must be, because he had to concentrate on the spinning blades whirling in toward his knees. He stuck his arm out as if he were signaling a turn and hurdled the blades as they swept in under him. This open hand slapped onto the Officer's reaching forearm and gripped it at the same time the Officer grabbed his arm.

The momentum swung him up and around as the Officer anchored himself on the chariot rail, and the Gunner was on board.

The Bull had no time to slow his headlong pursuit, and the spinning blades opened him up like a giant can opener, splashing twisting curls of bright bronze in its wake. The Bull pitched forward, its horns digging into the ice and throwing it into a slamming somersault, where it lay still, upended and wreathed in its bronze entrails.

The Queen looked back. "He won't be killing any more women."

The Gunner dropped Edie to the bucking floor of the chariot and started to pump water out of her. It was like trying to work on the pitching deck of a ship.

"Help me," he said.

The Officer grabbed him and held him steady.

The Queen was turning the chariot. "Hold on," she shouted.

The Officer looked up and saw she was racing toward her two daughters, who were holding the mirrors up.

"George," shouted the Gunner as he futilely pumped water from the dead girl.

"*You* hold on," shouted the Officer. As the Queen hit the mirrors the first time with the tip of her spear, the Officer let go of the Gunner and leaped off the back of the chariot. There was a pop, and the chariot disappeared. The Officer scrambled to his feet.

"Stay there," he said to the girls, and ran away from the lights of the Frost Fair, toward the dark end of the ice.

CHAPTER FIFTY-TWO

Heart Stone

"She's dead," said the Gunner as the Queen reined her horses in and brought the chariot to a sliding halt in front of the Artillery Memorial. The Queen dropped to her knees next to where the Gunner was pumping at Edie's chest with the heel of his hand.

"Then why are you still doing that?" she asked as she moved around to Edie's head.

"Because I don't know what else to bloody do," he said.

The Queen looked up and saw big tears rolling out of his eyes.

She bent over Edie's open mouth, tilted her head back, and pinched her nose. She took a breath and blew it into the waterlogged lungs. She did it again. She listened. And when there was no answering breath, she did it again. For a while, the two of them tried to revive the small dead body, refusing to accept the truth that she had gone.

Eventually the Gunner looked at the Queen. His eyes

had emptied and were now deserts of dry despair.

"Why are *you* doing this?"

She wiped her eyes, and the Gunner saw an echo of the dead girl in the way her jaw came stubbornly forward.

"Because I don't know what else to do either. Except keep fighting."

"Fair enough." He pumped Edie's chest. "Neither did Edie."

He thumped his fist into Edie's breastbone in frustration and grief, just as the Queen had blown in, and suddenly Edie threw up a great lungful of river water and then convulsed in a terrible coughing spasm.

Her eyes flickered open, then closed again as she passed out. The Gunner felt her heart. It was beating faintly. He stared at her in disbelief. He looked at the Queen. He'd never seen her smile before, but now her face shone back at him.

"Neither *had* she, I think you mean," the Queen said.

He beamed back at her. "If you weren't a bloody queen I'd kiss you."

"If I weren't a bloody queen I might well let you."

Then her face snapped back its normal businesslike demeanor.

"She's not out of the woods yet. She could still die of cold. We need a fire."

"We haven't got a fire."

The Queen was unfastening her cloak. "Well, get a coat or something. We need to warm her up."

The Gunner held Edie's wrist. "Her pulse is hardly there at all."

"Get a move on, then," she snapped, and started stripping the cloak from Edie's body.

The Gunner ran over to the monument, where he saw the Officer's coat and hat sitting next to the wet bundle of heart stones he had brought from the underground tank. As he picked up the Officer's coat, he noticed that the bundle was steaming.

"Hurry up," shouted the Queen. "We've got to get her into something warm. She's slipping away again."

"Hold up," he said as he threw the coat over his shoulder and untied the bundle. Light blazed at him. He quickly looked around to see if there was a taint or the Walker creeping up on them. But then he noticed something about the light. The glass stones had been of all different colors, but now they were glowing with the same warm hue, like the orange at the heart of a well-banked-up fire.

"Gunner!" shouted the Queen. "We're losing her."

The Gunner dumped the heart stones next to her.

"Heart stones. The bloody Walker kept them as trophies of all the glints he'd culled."

Like him, the Queen looked around searching for danger.

"No," he said, as he started placing the stones around Edie. "They're not warning us. I think they feel her. I think it's the spark of all them troubled girls kindling one last time. I think it's them having a last laugh at the Walker."

The Queen watched him carefully place a stone over Edie's heart, and then she dug her hands into the blazing stone pile and helped him surround Edie with the warmth, and wrapped her with her own cloak and the Officer's coat.

And in the end, it wasn't just the fact that the Gunner and the Queen wouldn't let her die that saved Edie. It was as the Gunner thought: it was all the lost girls and the lonely girls, all the odd women who thought they might be a bit mad because they didn't quite fit in—because they didn't understand that their glinting could be a gift and not a curse—it was all of *them* who surrounded this last lost lonely girl and gave her the final warm sparks that their lives had stored in their stones, so that she could go on and live for them.

Because the Queen knew this was so, she wept as she watched the color return to Edie's face and her eyes flicker open again.

Edie's small hand twitched where it lay in the Gunner's big bronze palm. He closed his hand gently on it. Her eyes focused, and as she recognized him, she gripped his hand fiercely, and he again saw the rare small miracle of her smile break across her face like sunshine.

"It's all right," he said gruffly. "I've got you. You were too tough for the Walker to kill. And you were too bloody tough for the river to kill. You're safe."

Edie nodded and coughed harshly.

"Where's George?"

CHAPTER FIFTY-THREE

Ice Devil

The Officer didn't find George at the ice edge. He found his hammer, caught in a branch. When he pulled at it he found George's hand still attached to it through the thong. He pulled on the hand, and that's when he found George, and pulled him spluttering and shivering out of the river and onto the ice.

"W—where's Edie?" was the first thing he said. As he had flown over the river with the Icarus, he'd seen the Gunner dragging something out of the river, and he hoped, with an intensity that hurt worse than the cold, that it had been her.

"I'm afraid she's dead, old man," said the Officer. "They took her through the mirrors already. Can you run?"

George looked terrible as he stood there trembling, teeth chattering, fist clenched on the hammer.

"Yeah," he said, staring across the ice.

In fact, he looked like murder. Because he was

staring at the hunched figure of the Walker, who was bent over something in the snow, scratching marks all around himself.

"Good," said the Officer, taking his shoulder. "Because the real trick's going to be to get to those girls over there, the ones with the mirrors, without him seeing us."

George shook the Officer's hand off his shoulder.

"No," he said, hefting the hammer, "that's not the bloody trick at all." He began to walk determinedly toward the Walker.

The Walker was oblivious. He was so excited he could barely breathe, and the reason for that was in two pieces in the snow in front of him.

When George had hit him in the chest, the blow hadn't stopped his heart. He had been protected by the two wax disks surrounding the mirror. The disks had been there to protect him from unintended contact with the mirror, but they had failed to protect the mirror itself.

George had broken the black mirror in two.

The one solution to not having two mirrors, which had never occurred to the Walker, came to him now: take the one mirror and split it.

The marks he was scratching in the snow were a pentacle of protection.

George had just broken into a trot, the Officer on his heels, when there was a pop from behind him, and the chariot appeared.

"Boy!" yelled the Queen. "Get over here!"

George kept going.

"I'm going to finish him," he shouted.

"No, George," she shouted. "The girl is alive!"

George stopped dead in his tracks.

"What?"

She reined in next to him. "Jump on. She's badly shaken and very miserable, but she's going to be fine, and she's asking for you. Come quickly, we should hurry and get out of here."

The Officer grabbed George and dumped him into the chariot and jumped in after him. "Home, James, and don't spare the horses." He grinned.

George and the Queen were both looking at the Walker and the intensity of his activity in the snow. They looked at each other.

"What?" said the Officer.

"On the other hand, why not?" said the Queen. George grinned through his shivering teeth as the Queen clicked her tongue and urged the horses forward into a gallop.

"Oh hell," said the Officer, unbuttoning his holster. "But he doesn't stay dead long, you know. . . ."

"Every little helps," said the Queen, snapping the reins and smiling fiercely, her hair flying out behind her in the wind. "Every little helps."

The Walker was so intent on lining up the two broken halves of the stone mirror to face each other in the snow that he didn't look up until the first shot kicked ice into his face.

What he saw were horses careering toward him at full gallop, with the Queen hefting her spear, the Officer firing at him, and George—leaning out the side of the chariot with a hammer held ready, above whirling scimitars attached to the wheels.

"Fools!" he screamed.

They were going to run him down. There was nowhere for him to run. So instead of standing up, he crouched down with his nose to the snow, making sure that the two stone mirror surfaces were facing each other exactly.

He knew he had it set up right, because there was a burst of heat and steam as snow began to melt under each mirror edge.

Without a microsecond to spare, he muttered something under his breath and reached into the stone mirrors.

As the whirring blades tore through the space where he had just been, the mirrors pulled him in and out of the way.

As they rushed toward the Walker, the Queen leaned over the back of the chariot and stabbed her spear through the ice in the very spot where he should have been. George looked down and saw that the Walker had disappeared and that they were riding through the pentagram of protection, obliterating the boundaries the

Walker had scratched in the snow. As the Queen wheeled the chariot in a fast U-turn, they saw something else.

The stone mirror halves melted their way straight down through the ice and disappeared, but not before something almost invisible, like a living ripple in the air, came out of the mirror through the door the Walker had opened.

And because that something was made of nothing, it needed substance to survive in this world, and the first things it encountered in the empty air were the ice devils kicked up by the spinning blades of the chariot. The Queen's chariot raced over the pentagram, and she leaned out and retrieved her spear, and then they were hurtling back to her daughters and the safety beckoning in the mirrors they were holding.

As George looked back, he saw the invisible ripple take the ice crystals in the air and whirl them into a body shape that suddenly grew and rushed after them.

"Faster," he shouted. "Go faster!"

The ice devil grew bigger. It gained on them impossibly fast. The Queen twitched the reins, and the lead horse hit the mirror. There was a pop, and for a beat they all fell through layers of black. As they did so, they had the sense of something flying past them, something very cold and alien indeed, like a blast of otherworldly frost. . . .

CHAPTER FIFTY-FOUR

Crackstone

The London Stone sat behind a protective grille, in its usual niche on Cannon Street.

Nobody noticed it, nobody stopped as they passed. Nobody detected the dark hum of power that throbbed through the city, connecting its streets and buildings and the stone creatures that peopled the landscape.

But something noticed. Something noticed the stone the moment it arrived, and went to it faster than thought.

There was no movement in the stone, but suddenly it was covered with an intense white frost that was so cold it cracked.

It was only a small fissure.

But it was enough.

CHAPTER FIFTY-FIVE

Last Stop Is Nowhere

The chariot bumped onto the grass, and the Queen pulled the horses to a halt. She turned in time to make sure her daughters had reappeared behind them. They nodded at her, and all three shared the same fierce grin.

"Did you feel it?" said the Officer.

"Feel what?" said the Gunner, looking up from where he sat next to Edie, a red-faced, warm-looking Edie swaddled in the Queen's cloak and the Officer's coat.

"Something followed us back," said George, jumping out of the chariot and racing toward Edie. She grinned at him but threw up a warning hand—

"Mind the stones!"

The warning stones were spread out on the ground around them, and all were now dull. Except for a small blue one clasped in Edie's hands, a blue the exact same color of the bonnet a duck had worn in a story that had been read to her as a child. A small blue warning stone that had been made into an earring.

George stepped carefully over to her, and not knowing what to do, punched her on the shoulder. She smiled up at him and punched him on the leg. And that seemed to be okay for both of them.

In the distance, George heard the strangely comforting sound of Big Ben sounding the hour.

"Get the boy that blanket," said the Queen, pointing to the Unknown Soldier's draped body.

"But . . ." said the Gunner.

"No buts," said the Queen. "Boy's catching his death; he's already half dead."

George put down his hammer and started to unbutton his soaking coat with fingers like frozen sausages.

"Nice hammer," said Edie, a small hint of mockery at the back of her voice.

"Nice earring," he replied, equally unimpressed.

"Yeah," she said. "It's my mum's."

"What was it doing in there with the rest of—Oh," said the Gunner.

"She went mad," said Edie. "That's what they said. That's why she got taken away."

She looked at the earring.

"No question about why she thought she was mad, and I guess—"

"She was a glint too," said George.

"Yup," Edie replied. "Only, nobody told her."

"The question," said the Queen, "is why all the other stones have faded, but it keeps blazing."

The Gunner cleared his throat. "Those stones belonged to glints the Walker killed or sent off to die, mad in loony bins. . . ." He looked at the Queen. She nodded. He went on. "Maybe it's still alight because she is too."

"Alight?" said George.

"Alive," said the Queen.

Edie looked down at the ground. She couldn't speak. George looked at his arm. The second flaw that he had felt jagging up his arm when he'd accepted the Walker's challenge had gone, as he knew it would.

He caught the Officer looking at it too. The Officer smiled. Held up three fingers, then folded two down.

In the background, George could see a police motorcycle flashing its blue lights as it roared down Piccadilly and leaned into the curve that would take it around Hyde Park Corner.

"One to go, boy. Good man."

George wrapped himself in the blanket the Officer handed him. He decided he'd worry about the final duel with the Last Knight later.

"My mum could be anywhere," Edie said in a very small, flat voice.

"Budge up," said George, and sat down next to her. "The Gunner could have been anywhere too. And so could you. But we got ourselves back together, didn't we?"

She nodded.

"There may be a bigger problem," said the Officer.

They all looked at him.

"Can't you hear it?"

They listened; there was only silence. And silence in London doesn't happen, even at night.

"The city's gone very still, and the clock just struck thirteen."

They all stood up slowly and looked around.

The city *was* still. Unnaturally still. The city was so still that nothing moved.

There was no breeze.

No noise.

No people.

The few cars on the street had stopped dead.

George walked to the edge of the road.

The police motorcycle was frozen leaning into the curve. There was no rider.

George looked up at the familiar red mass of a night bus. There were no passengers, and no driver.

The others slowly walked out into the street, seeing what George was seeing.

Edie peered into an empty taxi and looked at George. "Where have all the people gone?"

He shrugged, turning in a slow circle, looking for signs of life.

"And why has everything just stopped?"

The only thing moving in the whole city was the thick snow that had begun to fall silently around them.

The five spits and the two children stood in the rapidly whitening road and stared about them as the shock of what they were seeing slowly dawned on them.

"Whatever we brought back with us," said the Officer slowly, "I don't think it's good."

Unconsciously, they moved a little closer to one another, each feeling strangely alone in the silence as they peered down the unmoving streets, too caught up in what was happening around them to notice what was happening above them.

Which was a shame. Because what was above was definitely noticing them.

The stone gargoyle was perched on the very tip of the giant stone field gun on the top of the Artillery Memorial.

The Gunner saw it first.

He stepped in front of Edie and George, fumbling for his pistol.

"Look out, here we go!"

Everyone turned suddenly.

George's hand shot out, and he pulled the Gunner's hand down hard.

"Wha—" began the Gunner.

"It's okay!" said George. "It's okay."

"*Gack?*" said the gargoyle.

George grinned. "He's one of us."

They looked at Spout. Then at George. Then back at Spout.

The Gunner put his revolver away. The Officer gave

him a cigarette, which he lit, and they all stood there looking at the grinning gargoyle through cigarette smoke and heavily falling snow.

"Blimey," said the Gunner. "If he's one of us . . . we're *really* in trouble."

ACKNOWLEDGMENTS

It's hard to write in a vacuum, and talking to other writers seems to ease things along on the tough days—especially when you have to raise your game to keep up with them. Thanks to the game-raisers for the help, provocation, and support over the years and across the disciplines—Alex "Nander" Cary, Fergus Fleming, Jonatan Darby, Al Whiting, Katie Pearson, Patrick Harbinson, Robert Harris, Amanda Silver, Rick Jaffa, Kate Bucknell, Rose Baring, Mary Miers, Barnaby Rogerson, and Mary and Philip Contini. Special thanks to my family, *consiglieri,* and other secret readers for all the help and support in getting *Ironhand* on the page—Kate Jones, Ron Bernstein at ICM, Michael McCoy at ITG, Jack, Ariadne, Zillah More Gordon, Finn Younger, and Charlie Harris. Much belated gratitude to the photographer Andrew Errington for taking a fantastic portfolio of images of London statues to get me going, and apologies to my dad for the bits where the Gunner was trapped underground—I forgot about the claustrophobia. Honest . . .

Don't miss the thrilling conclusion of

THE STONEHEART TRILOGY

SILVERTONGUE

PROLOGUE

The Ice Devil

The Ice Devil swirled in over the City, reveling in this new otherworld it had found. It sensed the lines of power and the old places of magic buried beneath the thin skin of the modern streets and buildings, and as it rose higher it tried to make sense of what it was experiencing.

The first thing it noticed as it crashed into this unfamiliar dimension was the dark pulse just barely contained in the London Stone. The Stone, set behind a wrought-iron screen in the side of an undistinguished building on Cannon Street, looked like nothing important. Only the tiniest percentage of the thousands of normal people who walked past it every day actually noticed it, and of those who did, none sensed the malevolence imprisoned within the rough block, or realized that the flaking iron cage was there to protect them from the Stone, rather than the other way around. But the Ice Devil was not "normal people"; it was "other." It had come through the black mirror from a dimension wholly and implacably different to ours, and was attuned to a very different register of forces. To the Ice Devil the darkness in the Stone blazed out like a flaming beacon on a starless night, and that was why it had made straight there to get its bearings.

What it hadn't expected was the effect of its sudden arrival: the ice that it had made its shape out of was in fact only half as cold as the otherworldly chill that was its normal state, and when the Stone met the shocking subzero blast that attended it, it cracked. And when it cracked, the true power and depth of the darkness within made itself apparent. If the darkness had been light, then it would have been a blinding flare of whiteness. The darkness revealed through the crack in the Stone was the purest most malevolent gloom, a sinister dark pitched far beyond black. It was not a darkness made from the mere absence of light and hope, it was the darkness that actively sucked light, hope, and life into it and obliterated them.

The Ice Devil recoiled from the darkness, surprised at the power it had released by cracking the Stone. It soared up and away into the night, and came to rest on the highest perch it could find: the black blockhouse structure on top of Tower 42, a tall triangular skyscraper on Old Broad Street. It was on this bunker in the sky that the Ice Devil waited as it surveyed the City beneath and got its bearings, never forgetting to keep part of its consciousness on the darkness below. And the darkness also waited, looking back out of the crack in the Stone, waiting to take shape, in no hurry now that the doors to its long prison stood open.

And then their looks met.

What passed between them was nothing more cataclysmic than a nod and a tiny flicker of kinship. And something as delicate as laughter dropped cold and soft from the Ice Devil and joined the heavy snow starting to fall on the city below.

One command, pitched below sound but audible to every Stone Servant and taint in the city boomed out through the night: "COME!"

CHAPTER ONE

Chinstrapped

"Where have the people gone?" said Edie, voicing the question in George's head. "Why's everything frozen?"

George tried to ignore the insistent twinge of pain in his arm, where he knew the vein of stone was inexorably twisting toward his shoulder, and looked at the unmoving traffic curving around the uphill bend of Hyde Park Corner. The cars and buses were empty of drivers or passengers, and a riderless police motorbike was stuck leaning forty-five degrees into the turn behind them, as if kept upright by invisible strings.

"And why's it snowing?" asked George, looking around at the Gunner.

The Gunner shrugged snow off his shoulders and looked at the Officer. The Officer cleared his throat and looked up into the sky at the fall of thick, fluffy flakes tumbling straight down on them out of the sodium glare that ceilinged the city.

"Well. Ahem. I should say it's, ah . . ."

"*Gack,*" said Spout, hopping down off the stone howitzer above them, landing in the snow already stacking up at their feet.

"Exactly," finished the Officer. "I don't know."

"How can you not know?" asked George. "You must know!"

He followed the Officer's gaze into the night sky and then turned slowly, scouring what he could see of the city for anything reassuring, like someone hurrying home along a pavement, or people moving in the lighted windows of the hotel opposite. There was nothing.

"We don't," said the Red Queen.

"You don't?" said Edie shakily.

"No," replied the Gunner. "This hasn't happened before."

George stopped turning and looked at the statues standing around him in the increasingly white cityscape. The two World War I soldiers had snow massing on their tin helmets, and the Red Queen and her two daughters looked entirely underdressed for the eerily sudden winter tumbling down around them. The horses attached to her chariot nickered in the background and tossed white flakes from their manes, eyeing Spout, the winged gargoyle, with suspicion. Even without the snow, it was a strange sight.

"Great," George sighed. He knew three things with equal conviction and clarity:

He knew they were in deep trouble.

He knew that whatever that trouble was, they had somehow brought it with them through the mirrors from the Frost Fair.

And he knew he was in no shape to begin to figure it out. The white stone vein twining up his arm was not just counting off the time he had left to face the unavoidable doom of his third and final duel, but it was also remorselessly draining his remaining energy, drip by tiny drip.

"I'm knackered," he said.

"Knackered?" shot back the Queen in surprise. "What is knackered?"

"Chinstrapped," said the Gunner.

"Exhausted," explained the Officer. "As in the only thing holding him up on his feet is the chinstrap on his helmet. It's not surprising."

Edie looked around at them, and then down at her mother's sea-glass earring clenched in her hand. She felt a deep and private pain, one that she'd never allowed herself. It was the pain of hoping against hope, a confusing ache of elation and fear spreading through her so fiercely that she almost couldn't breathe. It felt like she was drowning in "maybes," because the light in that little fragment of glass shouted that maybe things were not as she had thought them to be, that maybe she had been lied to, maybe the great hole in her heart would again be filled with the thing she thought had abandoned it, and maybe, just maybe, she would not have to carry the pain alone and forever.

"We can't just go to sleep," she said. "We've got things to do. . . ."

"The thing about having things to do," declared the Gunner, "is that before you start, it's a good thing to have some idea about what they are and how you're going to do 'em."

"I'm going to find my mother," retorted Edie, jutting her chin as if daring him to say no.

A look ricocheted from the Gunner to the Queen to the Officer.

"Er," said the Officer.

"Fair enough," cut in the Gunner. "But how?" He thumbed over his shoulder at the empty streets. "Right now I'd say, bar you and George, there ain't any other bugger in this whole city, let alone your mum."

Edie shivered and gripped the earring tighter. She caught another look flying between George and the Gunner.

"She *is* alive," she exclaimed.

No one said anything.

"Edie?" began George.

"She IS," she said, eyes burning as fiercely as the heart stone in her hand. "She is. Otherwise why would her heart stone still be alight when all the others have gone out?"

She pointed at the loose scrabble of sea-glass pebbles at her feet quickly being covered by the falling snow. They were dull and sparkless now.

"I thought she was dead. He told me she was. My

stepfather. The people, the official people, they told me she was. But she *isn't*. The bastard lied about that like he lied about everything. And I never, I never . . ."

George—horribly—realized she was on the brink of crying, and suddenly he knew he didn't want her to cry, not because he minded her crying, but because *she* would mind, mind terribly if anyone else saw her with tears running down her face.

"Edie," he cut in sharply. "Look. I'm cold. You're cold. I'm exhausted. You're exhausted. I can't think straight. And nor can you."

"Don't tell me what I can't do," she said, her spirits kindling.

"You can't do anything until you're properly dry and rested. . . ."

"And fed," said the Queen. "Children need to be—"

"I'm not a child," rasped Edie. "I can look after myself."

The Queen knelt in front of her and gripped her shoulders, bringing her eye to eye. Edie tried to shrug out of the grasp of the bronze hands, but they just gripped tighter.

"Let go," she gritted through her teeth into the calm face of the Queen.

"No."

"I mean it," said Edie, squirming harder, to equally little effect. "Let go or I'll glint you."

The shadow of a smile passed across the Queen's

face, so fast that if you'd blinked, you'd have missed it. She fixed Edie with her eyes until she stopped trying to wriggle free.

"The fire inside you has brought you a long way, child."

"I'm not a ch—"

"You are. I don't call you child to belittle you. I call you child to honor you. What you have survived, what your heart and courage have enabled you to endure would have beggared the strength of a grown man long since. Indeed, some grown women might have been able to outface the pain and hurt you have sustained, but precious few. You have a wild and rugged heart, child. And its fire has brought you a long way. But right now the fire you need is not of the heart, but one to banish the cold in your bones, a warmth that will let you sleep and ravel up the tattered threads of your energy so that we can face whatever tomorrow brings."

"If the people have all disappeared, there's a perfectly good hotel opposite, with deep beds and thick blankets," interjected the Officer. "Be a snug place to rest for the night, until this snow stops."

"It's ridiculous," said George, shaking the flakes out of his hair. "It's like being stuck inside a snow globe."

"*Gack,*" said Spout, shuffling forward and flexing a wing above them. The stone membrane stretched and umbrellaed overhead with a sharp snapping noise. Edie flinched, but George held her arm.

"It's okay," he said. "He's sheltering you."

"What's he called?" she sniffed, looking up at the wing arching over her head.

"Spout."

"That's a stupid name."

"I know." George smiled. "I gave it to him."

"You named him?" said the Queen, raising an eyebrow. "You. A maker. Named him. Named a taint?"

"Yes," he replied.

The Gunner whistled in surprise.

"No wonder he's following you," he said. "He's your pet."

"*Gack!*" said Spout, eyeballing the Gunner frostily.

"No," said George. "He's not a pet. He's a friend. He saved my life."

"Did he, now?" said the Gunner. And he grinned into the gargoyle's snarling face. "Then I reckon he's my friend too."

And he punched him on the wing.

"Good job, Uglynuts."

"*Gack,*" replied Spout, losing the snarl and looking confused.

Edie's teeth were chattering. The Queen stood and pointed across the road.

"Inside, warm bed, now."

"Come on, little 'un," said the Gunner. And before she could protest, he'd hoisted her into his arms and was striding across the street, between the cars.

The hotel had a portico over a driveway that looped in and out, and the ragged group stood for a beat looking into the warm, softly lit interior.

"Nothing but five star for you, my girl." The Gunner grinned and took a step up into the doorway—just as a high-pitched whistle pierced the night above them. He froze.

"What's that?" asked Edie.

"The Quadriga," said George before the Gunner could answer. "It's a warning sign, right?"

"Right," said the Gunner. "Well remembered."

His eyes scanned the sky above them. The Officer cleared his throat.

"Quadriga's a statue. Up on the arch. Boy in it, driving a runaway chariot. He can see stuff coming."

"What kind of stuff?" said Edie.

There was a sudden flapping noise as Spout looped in under the portico, flexing back on the pillared columns so that he was hidden under the roof along with them. He knuckled George with a talon and then pointed it urgently into the sky to the west of them, where there was a low but insistent rumble.

"*Gaings, Eigengang, genny gaings!*"

"What kind of . . . ?" began Edie.

"Taints," translated George. "Many taints!"

"Don't move a muscle!" hissed the Gunner urgently as he and the Officer instinctively stepped in front of George and Edie.

And then the rolling thunder in the sky hurled through the snow in front of them and revealed itself to be a phalanx of stone pterodactyls, just like the one that had chased George at the beginning of his adventure. The great stone dinosaurs flapped past, long toothy beaks pointing east, their unblinking saucerlike eyes looking neither right nor left.

George found that his hand had somehow picked up his hammer on the way here, and he squeezed the handle, ready to fight for his life if one of them broke formation and noticed them. He felt the flat metallic tang of fear in his mouth, and tried to ignore it. And then the pterodactyls were followed, somewhat higher and more indistinctly by a flight of stubby-bodied creatures with batlike wings, also heading east.

"What are they?" whispered Edie.

"Gargoyles. Born ugly an' built to last. No offense," said the Gunner with a nod to Spout.

"Taints. Gathering and flying together," murmured the Queen. "Heading east."

The spits looked at one another. Edie looked at George.

"What's east?"

"The City."

"And . . . oh." She stopped and looked at the Queen. The Queen nodded slowly.

"The City is in the center of London. The Stone is in the City. And if the taints are gathering at the Stone . . ."

"It's war then," finished the Officer. "A bloody meat-grinding war. And we're going to be in the middle, damn it."

"War's damned without you needing to curse it, my friend," sighed the Queen, eyes fixed on the now-empty sky to the east. George looked over the road at the dark tree-shrouded park. The snow was now deep enough to reach the bottom of the hubcaps on the cars frozen in the middle of the street.

"Nothing worse than war," replied the Officer.

The Queen turned and looked at him. The smile at the edge of her mouth was entirely without humor.

"You couldn't be more wrong, sir. There are many things worse than war. Some of them live in the outer dark that lies beyond the stone mirrors the Walker escaped through. One of them followed us back here, and now things long feared, things that have never happened, will happen, and there will be hell to pay."